THE HATEFUL HUNGER

Strikingly beautiful Destiny Regan loathed one man more than any other in the world—Conal Carmichael, owner of the great Irish estate on which Destiny and her family lived, and master of all their fates in the Great Famine sweeping Ireland.

It was this ruthless, magnificent animal of a man who brutally possessed Destiny on a chance encounter. It was he who woke her to the mingled agony and ecstasy of unfettered desire. It was he who inextricably linked her life with his, in a searing drama of fierce passion and fearful vengeance that pitted the hate in Destiny's heart against her hungering flesh. . . .

HARVEST OF DESTINY

Big Bestsellers from SIGNET

- ☐ **BELLADONNA** by Erica Lindley. (#J8387—$1.95)
- ☐ **DEVIL IN CRYSTAL** by Erica Lindley. (#E7643—$1.75)
- ☐ **SUNSET** by Christopher Nicole. (#E8948—$2.25)*
- ☐ **BLACK DAWN** by Christopher Nicole. (#E8342—$2.25)*
- ☐ **CARIBEE** by Christopher Nicole. (#J7945—$1.95)
- ☐ **THE DEVIL'S OWN** by Christopher Nicole. (#J7256—$1.95)
- ☐ **MISTRESS OF DARKNESS** by Christopher Nicole. (#J7782—$1.95)
- ☐ **MADAM TUDOR** by Constance Gluyas. (#J8953—$1.95)*
- ☐ **THE HOUSE ON TWYFORD STREET** by Constance Gluyas. (#E8924—$2.25)*
- ☐ **FLAME OF THE SOUTH** by Constance Gluyas. (#E8648—$2.50)
- ☐ **ROGUE'S MISTRESS** by Constance Gluyas. (#E8339—$2.25)
- ☐ **SAVAGE EDEN** by Constance Gluyas. (#E8338—$2.25)
- ☐ **WOMAN OF FURY** by Constance Gluyas. (#E8075—$2.25)*
- ☐ **THE HOUSE OF KINGSLEY MERRICK** by Deborah Hill. (#E8918—$2.50)*
- ☐ **THIS IS THE HOUSE** by Deborah Hill. (#E8877—$2.50)

* Price slightly higher in Canada

Buy them at your local bookstore or use this convenient coupon for ordering.

THE NEW AMERICAN LIBRARY, INC.,
P.O. Box 999, Bergenfield, New Jersey 07621

Please send me the SIGNET BOOKS I have checked above. I am enclosing
$_____ (please add 50¢ to this order to cover postage and handling).
Send check or money order—no cash or C.O.D.'s. Prices and numbers are
subject to change without notice.

Name _____

Address _____

City_____ State_____ Zip Code_____

Allow 4-6 weeks for delivery.
This offer is subject to withdrawal without notice.

HARVEST OF DESTINY
ERICA LINDLEY

A SIGNET BOOK
NEW AMERICAN LIBRARY
TIMES MIRROR

NAL BOOKS ARE ALSO AVAILABLE AT DISCOUNTS IN BULK
QUANTITY FOR INDUSTRIAL OR SALES-PROMOTIONAL USE.
FOR DETAILS, WRITE TO PREMIUM MARKETING DIVISION,
NEW AMERICAN LIBRARY, INC., 1301 AVENUE OF THE
AMERICAS, NEW YORK, NEW YORK 10019.

Copyright © 1979 by Erica Lindley

All rights reserved

SIGNET TRADEMARK REG. U.S. PAT. OFF. AND FOREIGN COUNTRIES
· REGISTERED TRADEMARK—MARCA REGISTRADA
HECHO EN CHICAGO, U.S.A.

SIGNET, SIGNET CLASSICS, MENTOR, PLUME AND MERIDIAN BOOKS
are published by The New American Library, Inc.,
1301 Avenue of the Americas, New York, New York 10019

First Printing, December, 1979

1 2 3 4 5 6 7 8 9

PRINTED IN THE UNITED STATES OF AMERICA

One

1845

Destiny Regan stretched out in the low truckle bed, yawned, and rolled over. Her husband lay still sleeping, his dark curls fanned out on the blanket like the feathers of the black hen, she thought with amusement. A fine man he was, James Regan, big and strong and gentle, a husband for any girl to be proud of. Slow-thinking and slow-spoken he might be, but Jim Regan was as honest and loving and hardworking as any man in Ballymachree.

Destiny was content. It was strange how twelve short months could change a girl's life. Only a year ago she had been a fickle wench, laughing and teasing all the village boys, and then big Jim had taken her in his arms and made her his wife. Now she was happy working beside him, and the mother of his child. She ran her fingers down over her body, slim and flat as a maid's once more but for the full breasts, hard as stone to the touch. As if by some kind of primitive understanding, the babe in the wicker basket on the floor began to wail, and Destiny threw aside the blanket and lifted the tiny mite in her arms.

"Whisht now, macushla. Mammy is here," she crooned softly as she unlaced the front of her cotton bodice and put the child to her breast. Jim stirred and rolled over, but he did not waken. Time enough to rouse him when the babe's greedy sucking was satisfied, she thought contentedly. It was peaceful to sit in close companionship with her baby daughter while the air was still cool and the relentless heat of the coming day was still only a thin shaft of early sunlight through the shutters.

She gazed fondly at the baby's downy head nuzzled against her breast and felt only the slightest twinge of disappointment. So proud she would have been to bear Jim a son, a Jimmy Two, to follow in his father's footsteps. It was a fine life, to be a tenant of the master of Ballymachree, Mr. Carmichael himself. Destiny felt proud of her husband and his strong wooden cottage with its thatched roof, far grander than the mud hut where her mother lived and she herself had been reared. So long as the potato crops flourished, Jim would have no problem paying his rent to Mr. Carmichael. Already he had built himself a byre alongside the cottage to house the cow, and soon he would build more, for the potatoes bloomed high and yellow in the field and this year promised a handsome harvest. Jim would have been so proud to have a fine boy to train to follow after him. But he had said nothing. He loved his daughter, Destiny knew, and made no word of reproach, patient man that he was. Next year, God willing, Destiny vowed to herself, she would give him his son.

The baby fed at last, Destiny put on a faded blue cotton skirt and moved quietly out into the cottage's only other room. Her bare feet padded softly across the mud floor as she shooed the hens down off the smoke-blackened rafters and unlatched the door to let them out into the yard.

She poked the banked turf in the hearth until it reddened. Hot as hell it was in the room, she thought, but the water must be boiled. She filled the iron kettle from an earthenware jug and set it on the fire to boil. After she'd fed the chickens and fetched more water from the well, she'd make the gruel for Jim's breakfast. He would have preferred potatoes, but there was not one left in the pit from last year's crop. He'd have to wait for the digging of the new ones. Soon now, only a few weeks away.

Straightening up from the hearth, Destiny reached for the wooden comb and cracked mirror on the mantelshelf, combing back her mane of long black hair and surveying herself in the mirror. She smiled as she recalled Jim's murmured words.

"Destiny, my black Destiny, dark as a raven," he had said.

"Don't say a raven," she had quipped. "It's an evil-omened bird." She did not know why she had said it, but she had shivered and then felt angry with herself for casting a chill over the moment of love. Jim had looked at her with puzzled eyes.

"Why do you say that, mavourneen?"

"Oh, I don't know. Ravens steal corn, don't they? And they're always in the graveyard at the church. Ravens seem to spell death somehow."

Jim had crushed her close to him, as though in wordless apology, and in the sweet hours of love that followed, their child had been conceived. Destiny pushed the stupid thought of evil omens from her mind in a surge of protective love for her husband and her child. Putting down the comb and mirror, she filled a bowl with corn and went outside.

As she unlatched the cottage door, the morning sunlight dazzled her momentarily after the contrasting gloom of the living room. She decided not to take down the shutters yet, for the room would grow hotter still with the heat of the sun added to that of the fire. She fed the chattering chickens and milked the cow in the barn, then carried the pail of creamy, still-warm milk back into the cottage.

Jim was already up, humming to himself as he pulled on his rough working shirt.

"Is my breakfast ready, Desty?"

"Ready now, Jim." She measured a handful of meal into a wooden bowl and added hot water from the kettle, topping the thin mixture with a spoonful of cream off the milk. She watched while Jim ate hungrily.

"Are you to slaughter the pig today, Jim?" she asked. He nodded. "Then I'll be off up to the wood to look for mushrooms. I'll be back soon."

Taking up a basket and her kerchief, Destiny left. If there was anything she hated, it was to hear the squeals of a dying pig, and with luck Jim would have the job over and done by the time she returned.

The sun's rays were growing hotter as Destiny walked

across the cobbled yard and out through the gate into the dusty lane beyond. Setting down the basket on the low stone wall, she tied the bright red kerchief about her head. As far as the eye could see, down the lane winding to the village and up across the sweep of fields to where the big house stood, nothing was visible but field upon field of yellow, waving blooms. Undoubtedly the potato crops would yield well this year, Destiny thought contentedly. Everyone in the village of Ballymachree would be able to pay his rent without difficulty.

If only it would rain, just a little. For weeks now there had been not a drop, only scorching sunshine, day after day. She looked down at the clouds of dust rising under her bare feet. It was difficult to remember that at times this lane was rutted with runnels of deep mud. So long it had been since she had last felt the cool blessing of rain on her skin.

Destiny turned off the lane and away up over the grassy bank. As she neared the edge of the wood, she saw the swarthy, unkempt figure of Paddy Feeney coming toward her, a bundle of rushes under his arm.

"Top of the morning to you, Mrs. Regan," he said cheerily. Destiny smiled in reply to his greeting. "I'm after fetching rushes from up the glen to make more baskets," Paddy told her brightly, then, glancing down at the shabby basket she carried, added, "You'll be one of my first customers, I'm thinking."

Destiny laughed, "Not I, Paddy Feeney, for I've not a penny piece to my name. This one will have to last me for a long time yet."

Laughing still, she left him and went on up toward the wood. Its cool dimness was a welcome relief after the glare of the sun, and for the next half-hour Destiny busied herself gathering the mushrooms that grew in profusion under the trees.

The sun was high now, glinting through the interlaced branches of the trees and casting a latticework pattern on the grass of the clearing. Destiny pulled off her kerchief and sprawled on the grass to rest. She lay back, closing her eyes and breathing a deep sigh of contentment. It was so peaceful to lie here listening to the song of the birds and smelling the scent of crushed wild garlic. Soon, she told herself firmly, she must go back down to the cottage and carry on with her chores, but for the moment the lure of the peaceful wood was too great for her. She lay there dreaming.

Suddenly the morning peace was shattered by a piercing whistle, and Destiny sat upright. Someone was coming. Then another piercing whistle echoed through the woodland glade, followed by a man's voice, loud and commanding.

"To heel, Dusty, you brute! Where are you? Heel, boy!"

Over the clump of bushes bordering the clearing, Destiny caught sight of him. He was a stranger to Ballymachree, of that there was no doubt, a tall man, broad-shouldered, and black hair rippling about his face in the morning breeze. A frown marred his handsome face as he called again angrily for his dog.

"Where the devil are you, Dusty? To heel, boy!"

Destiny crouched low behind the bushes, anxious not to be seen. Whoever the stranger was, it was evident that he was a gentleman, judging by his fine white silk shirt and his velveteen breeches. Through the undergrowth Destiny could just see him, standing still now and tapping a riding crop against his thigh in an angry gesture. Then, to her dismay, the dog he was seeking came bounding into the clearing, sniffing around at the tree stumps, and then it caught sight of her. It was a great silver-gray animal, a wolfhound. It bared its teeth and began to growl.

Destiny shrank farther back, alarmed both at the dog's hostility and that its master could discover her. After all, the wood was private property belonging to the Carmichael family, and the gentleman there beyond the trees might well be a guest at Ballymachree House. Although old Mr. Carmichael himself rarely came over from England these days to stay on his Irish estates, his fine English friends often came to spend the summer there.

The dog sniffed closer, a growl still rumbling in its throat, and Destiny held out a timid hand.

"There, boy, there," she whispered. The dog sniffed

curiously at her outstretched fingertips, then, losing interest, turned away. The man's voice bellowed again.

"Dusty, you brute, come here this instant or I'll flay the hide off you!" he cried. Obediently now the dog gamboled off through the undergrowth to join him. "So there you are, you evil creature." The man smiled. Destiny caught a glimpse of his even white teeth. He was a beautiful man, this stranger, whoever he was, Destiny thought, but thank God he had not caught sight of her, for although Mr. Carmichael was a lenient landlord, absent so often though he was, his visitors might take a different view of the situation if they found a trespasser in the woods.

With a sigh of relief she brushed back her tumbled hair and tied on her kerchief again; then, picking up her basket, she made her way up to the glen toward the stream.

On the bank of the stream that tumbled sparkling to the village below, Destiny sat down and bathed her hot feet in its cooling waters. Far below she could hear the laughter and chatter of the women as they washed their clothes in the lower reaches of the stream before it flowed on to join the river down by the city.

Summer drowsed heavily over the land, hot and relentless. Destiny stared down over the valley and the miles upon miles of yellow potato flowers and felt a chill come over her despite the heat of the day. It was too hot, too languid, too still for comfort, like the ominous silence that comes over the land before a storm. Destiny glanced up toward the west. Sure enough, there on the horizon the blueness of the summer sky dipped into a bank of heavy gray. Before long, much-needed rain would come to Ballymachree, but even the prospect of rain did not lighten Destiny's spirits. The chill that lay over her heart was one that she recognized too well, a feeling she had had many times before, and each time had heralded tragedy.

It was a feeling she knew well, a presentiment of danger to come. It had been there on the morning her little brother had disappeared unaccountably and been lost in the peat bogs. It had been there again the night she heard the banshee howl and none but she had heard it, and in the morning they had found her mother dead by the fireside, cold and stiff. It was the same chill, oppressive feeling that lay upon Destiny now. She shivered and tried to brush the feeling away.

Rain was coming, she reminded herself, the rain all the villagers had prayed for in the church on Sundays for many a week. True, they had pleaded for gentle showers, many and often, but now it looked as if they were in for a real downpour. Even as Destiny dried her feet on the grass and picked up her basket, she felt heavy spots of rain on her bare arms. She would have to hurry if she were to get down the valley and back to the cottage before the rain came down in earnest.

Clambering up the grassy bank of the stream, she began to run across the field toward the woods. Even as she did so, she heard the distant sound of thunder and hesitated. If this was to be a summer storm, the woods were no place to shelter, for lightning could strike the trees. She turned instead upstream toward the caves. The caves that pitted the limestone cliff would be a safer place to shelter, for a summer storm would surely end just as suddenly as it had begun.

Heavy rain sliced down incisively, turning to great gray solid curtains of water before she reached the cave. Her feet stumbled and slipped on the stones as she ran, and her gown became molded to her body and her hair plastered around her face and neck. Stumbling at last into the shelter of the cave, she stood there panting and trembling. She was soaked to the skin. Leaning on her forearm against the arched entrance to the cave, Destiny stood still until her panting subsided. Then she could hear the hiss of the rain outside and see the mist rising from the hot, parched land. She watched in wonder, sensing the earth's gratitude. Greedily the dry land sucked up the rain's refreshing coolness. She looked anxiously across the fields. God knew the potato crops needed rain, but would the blooms be able to withstand this sudden onslaught?

Her sodden clothes forgotten, Destiny stood in wonder, savoring the new scents, the almost-forgotten smell of wet earth and soaked grass. The aroma was a sheer delight to the nostrils, refreshing and intoxicating.

Thunder crashed again, only this time closer and far more deafening. Destiny retreated farther into the cave, out of reach of the intrusive torrent of water cascading over the cave mouth and filling the rocky ledge outside with pools. So tumultuous was the roar of rain and thunder that she could hear no other sound, and the sudden eruption of another figure into the cave alarmed her. It was the Englishman she had seen in the woods, water dripping from his clothes, but this time he had no dog with him.

He was scowling angrily. "Damnable weather," he muttered, "and they told me Ireland was always mild and sunny. That blasted dog has led me a merry dance, and the stupid horse was no better."

Destiny watched him curiously. He was speaking to himself rather than to her, and he was certainly in a furious mood. He shook his head fiercely, droplets of rain flying in all directions and spattering her. Freed from the water, his hair sprang back into curls again. Through the silk shirt clinging wetly to his broad chest Destiny could see the outline of his muscles and the black hairs on his chest. He was a fine-built man even if his ferocious scowl lined his handsome face.

"Who are you?" he demanded fiercely, as if he had just become aware of her. "Have you seen my wolfhound?"

"My name is Destiny Regan, sir," she answered politely. The villagers always said it was wise to be polite to the gentry if one should ever chance to meet any of them. "And no, I have not seen your dog."

He grunted and looked at her more closely. Destiny was aware of his gaze traveling over her face and down her body, and she felt embarrassed. Her soaked bodice and skirt clung tightly to her breast and thighs, and she felt naked before him.

"You're soaking," he said. His voice was low and vibrant, with that slightly affected accent the English always seemed to have.

"I know," Destiny replied.

"Why don't you take your things off and let them dry out. I could light a fire," he suggested.

Destiny did not care for the eager, persuasive tone in his voice. "No," she replied shortly.

"And I could dry out too," he continued. "The rain is set in for hours yet."

It was true. The sky outside was leaden gray, with a promise of hours of rain to come.

"No," she repeated firmly. "My husband will be looking for me."

"Your husband?" he echoed. "Why, you're only a child."

"I'm eighteen," Destiny told him proudly. He was older than that, about in his mid-twenties, Destiny reckoned, roughly Jim's age.

He lifted a hand and touched her bare shoulder lightly, then ran his fingertips down over the outline of her breast.

"Eighteen, and married," he remarked musingly. "You surprise me."

Angrily Destiny broke away from his intrusive touch and walked to stand by the mouth of the cave. He was right. The grayness of the sky and the incessant hiss of the rain indicated that this was no brief summer storm. She began to shiver, not only because her wet clothes clung coldly to her body but also because she could feel the electrifying presence of the man behind her.

"I pray to God the potatoes are not all destroyed in this rain," she said, her back still toward him.

He laughed shortly. "What matter if a few potatoes are lost?" he said.

She spun around sharply. "It may not matter to you, but to us it's our living. If the crops fail and we cannot pay our rent to Mr. Carmichael, where would we be then? It doesn't matter to you, but to us it's our livelihood."

"So you're a tenant of Mr. Carmichael, are you?" he asked.

"Yes, or at least my husband is. He farms a piece of Mr. Carmichael's land."

The man's dark eyes narrowed. "Do you know Mr. Carmichael?" he asked.

"Well, no," Destiny admitted. "I've never seen him, only the fine carriages coming up the road from the city with lots of fine ladies and gentlemen inside, but I've never met Mr. Carmichael himself. He doesn't come here very often."

He smiled. "Then did you see me come in a fine carriage yesterday?"

"No, but I guessed you were a visitor at the house. Another Englishman who does not understand us," she added with a touch of asperity. It was obvious he was ignorant of their lives, if he did not know the value of the potato crops.

"I'm only half English," he told her, as though in apology. "My father is Irish and gave me an Irish name."

"And have you been in Ireland before?" Destiny demanded.

"Not since I was a child. But I plan to come more often, especially since I find the Irish girls are so pretty," he murmured, moving closer. "You are very pretty, Destiny, your skin honeyed by the sun and not all white and waxen like the English misses I know. And you smell so fresh, like rain on a summer rose."

Destiny saw his hand rise again, and felt his touch. His fingers were soft and white, not callused like Jim's. She shivered at his touch. He lifted a tendril of her hair where it clung about her neck and kissed the spot where it had lain.

"No," Destiny gasped. "Leave me. I'm a respectable married woman. I'll be going home now."

But before she could reach down for the basket of mushrooms, he had seized her. There was no gentleness now in his touch, only a burning, savage fierceness. Wildly, clumsily, he tore at her bodice.

"You can't go, you can't leave me," he moaned hoarsely.

"I must! I don't care about the rain!" Angrily she tried to stay the clawing hands, scratching and fighting, but the man's determination gave him added strength, and she found herself flattened on the floor of the rocky cave, pebbles biting into her back.

"Let me go, you beast, let me go!" she cried, but the thunder drowned her cries. "I'll report you! My husband will kill you!"

For one brief second he paused, looking at her with evil amusement in his eyes. "I have the right to claim my

Destiny, woman, the *droit de seigneur*, and have you I will."

Bruised and incapable of movement, Destiny realized he was not to be deterred. Her cry of despair was cut short by his mouth imprisoning hers, and she felt his swift, sudden onslaught. In moments her despair melted to a startling, terrifying ecstasy, the sweet savagery of it consuming her soul. It was an eddying torment of delight and terror mingled in a soul-confusing whirlpool where she recognized no time or space. It was as if one had melted from this world into a bewildering eternity that was neither heaven nor hell, but a terrifying confusion of both.

Suddenly it was over. As Destiny's senses began to clear, she felt his inert weight lying limply on her, and her eyes focused on his neck, for his head was averted. There, below his right ear, she could see a mark, a mole or a birthmark, dark and clear against his pale skin. It was shaped for all the world like a perched black bird. A raven. Great shudders ran through her frame at the thought of what had just occurred. It was evil, a sin, a huge and mortal sin that would blacken both their souls forever and condemn them both to the fires of hell.

Stricken at the enormity of it, Destiny pushed frantically at his weight, and he rolled over. Leaping to her feet, she straightened out her sodden clothes, and looked down at the prostrate figure in hatred.

"You swine," she cried loudly. "I hate you." He put one arm lazily behind his head and regarded her with amusement. "I'll get even with you for this, I swear I will! My husband will avenge me!"

His dark eyes laughed at her. "I should think twice about that, Mistress Destiny, if I were you. He risks losing his tenancy if he lifts a hand against me, and where would you be then? Let your reason rule your heart, is my advice to you."

As he spoke, he rose slowly. Destiny glared at him. "Justice is on my side, for you forced me against my will. I shall seek justice, whoever you are, for you had no right to touch me, a married woman and all."

"I had every right, by a law so ancient you would not

have heard of it. And Conal will have what he wants. But I do not want you now, so hasten home to your husband if you will. I have lost interest in you, Destiny Regan."

His careless words were even more hurtful than he had been, and in a blind fury Destiny turned and ran from the cave, out into the cold rain. Her basket, now only half-filled after the scuffling in the cave, spilled a trail of sodden mushrooms behind her as she fled, tears scalding her eyes, down the slippery grass toward home.

Jim was waiting, anxious-eyed, in the doorway of the cottage as she unlatched the yard gate. "Macushla, where have you been? You're soaked to the skin," he said in concern.

"I was up the glen when the rain came."

"But that was an hour ago! You never stayed out in all that?"

"I sheltered in the caves for a while," she replied truthfully, longing to tell him all as he helped her take off her clothes and fetched a blanket off the bed. Then he looked at the basket.

"You've precious few mushrooms, Destiny. Were there not many in the woods?"

"I lost them running home." She spoke no words other than the truth, but less than the truth, and her heart bled that she could not tell him all, for what the man—what did he say he was named, Conal?—had warned still rang in her ears. She knew her Jim, gentle till the anger roused him, and then he was wild as a bull, and if he learned of the incident, no one would hold him. And if he broke the Englishman's head in his wrath, Mr. Carmichael would surely evict a tenant who behaved so toward his visitor. That unpleasant bailiff of his, Mr. McPherson, would take malicious pleasure in carrying out the order.

"You're very quiet, mavourneen," Jim commented, stroking back her wet hair.

"I had that strange feeling again today, Jim, you know, that feeling I sometimes get, and it's always been true before." No need to tell him the presentiment had already been verified by the stranger.

"Have no fear, my lovely. I am here with you," Jim said, opening his arms to her. Destiny crept into their reassuring warmth with gratitude and raised her head for his kiss.

"Love me, Jim, love me. I feel so cold and afraid."

And in the gentleness of his love Destiny began to feel purified from the evil of the cave. It was only later, when she saw the brown stains on Jim's forearms. The blood of the pig. She felt sick. Blood and a raven—two evil omens this day that surely prophesied more evil yet to come.

Two

In the gray days that followed the onset of the rain, Destiny's heart remained heavy. Perhaps it was the weather, she reassured herself as she tended her child and did the chores around the cottage and watched Jim come in soaked from the field. Perhaps it was only the persistent leaden menace of the August skies that made her feel so depressed.

But secretly she feared it was due to more than just the filthy weather. That strange premonition had come over on the hill above Ballymachree while the sun still shone, and moments later she had encountered the rapacious Conal. It was he who had cast a blight on her contented life, assailing her virtue without even the provocation of a beckoning glance. He had defiled her purity wantonly, and as she recalled with secret shame the wild and wonderful passion he had aroused in her, she felt glad the weather had kept her home. If she had been to church with Jim, she would have had to confess her shameful joy in that encounter, for no one would dare to receive communion with such a sin on one's soul.

Gradually the rain slackened, yielding to a September

drizzle, but Destiny's melancholy did not lessen. God forgive me, she prayed inwardly, but I have no right to feel so bad when I have all a girl could wish. She looked fondly at her child and her tall husband, droplets of rain in his hair as he came in from the field, and felt her heart swell with love for the both of them. But the ache persisted, and Destiny felt the need to confide in someone. Shuna always had a willing ear to listen.

Wrapping a thick black shawl tightly about herself and the child, Destiny made her way down to Shuna's cottage. Her older sister was a woman to admire, as darkly attractive as herself, and capable and loving, her two children playing contentedly on the mud floor as she worked. Shuna's dark eyes searched Destiny's face.

"You in one of your moods again?" she teased. "Not been fighting with Jim already, have you, and the babe not two months old yet?"

"Not I," Destiny said as she seated herself on a stool and laid the child on a blanket. Shuna's little boy peered at the baby, then lost interest and went back to chipping a piece of wood with a sharp stone. "Jim is fine. 'Tis myself, Shuna. I cannot understand the darkness in me. I'm afraid of myself at times."

"You were always so, even as a child," Shuna replied. "Mammy used to say you were bewitched by the little people, the way you used to dream and were deaf to everyone. I used to think it was just your way to get out of doing the chores so I had them all to do. I thought you'd grown out of it."

"So I had. I'm not dreaming now, Shuna, only this heaviness lies in my heart and I don't know why. I feel sick in my soul."

Shuna eyed her sharply. "You've not fallen again already, have you? 'Tis common enough then."

Destiny shook her dark head. "I think not. I feed the child still."

"There's no certainty in that, as Mammy would tell you. And if it's not that, then just shake yourself, mavourneen, and get about your work. There's no time for slacking, with the potatoes soon to be lifted. No time for childish moods now, my girl."

Shuna was right, Destiny reflected as she prepared the meal for Jim's coming home that evening. Some carrots, a half cabbage, and a few scraps from the pig's carcass thrown into the pot filled the cottage with a savory scent. There had been no potatoes left for months now. It would be grand to have the new ones soon, and eat a fine, filling meal again. Shuna was right. There was no time for useless brooding, but her words had raised a new and terrifying misgiving. What if Destiny were pregnant again?

There would be no terror in the prospect if she knew it was Jim's child, the son she longed to give him, but what if the child was that evil Conal's child? Destiny felt sick at the possibility, and then terrified. Her sin would become evident to the world, and there would be no hiding it. Unless, of course, it was taken for Jim's child. After all, she had lain with him the same night, the first time since the baby had been born. Even Destiny herself would never know for sure who had fathered her child—if a child were to be born, that was. It was too early yet to know.

One thing was for sure. She would never tell Jim about Conal. Not that he would be angry with her, but he could be furious enough to attack Conal, kill him even. Destiny herself he would not harm, for he would not touch a hair of her head, loving her as he did. He would forgive her and let the world believe the child was his rather than hurt her. But she would never tell him. Those terrifyingly strange moments alone with Conal in the cave would remain her secret forever.

Dear God, she prayed, let me not be with child, not yet. Let it be in a month or two, when I shall know that it is Jim's child I bear.

At last the rains receded from Ballymachree and the sun shone again. When the time came for harvesting the potatoes, the valley was bathed in sunlight, and the fields were dotted with men and women and children everywhere, hard at work digging and lifting the new potatoes, letting them dry in the sun before packing them into the pits prepared by the men beforehand. Jim had dug a deep pit not far from the cottage and lined it with fresh turf, ready to receive the new crop. Destiny felt proud as she carried the great basket to and from the pit. They were beautiful potatoes, large and white and firm, and within days it became clear that there was a plentiful enough crop to see them safely through the winter. The rent would be paid again this year. There was no longer cause to worry.

If only the other secret worry nagging at the back of her mind would disappear, then Destiny could be content indeed, and she felt shame for the blackness that still lay across her heart. And shame too because she could not rid her mind of Conal's handsome face. She had no business to be thinking of the man who had been so cruel to her, the man who had robbed her husband of his rights. And why should she think of him often, like some lovesick young girl yearning for her lover? Conal held no attraction for her. She did not love him, but hated him, rather, for the wrong he had done her.

But time and time again as she bent over her work in the field, following along behind Jim as he dug, the image of Conal's face rose before her, handsome and taunting. The shame in Destiny's heart gave way to a feeling of sick revulsion.

The nauseous sensation was still there the morning Destiny rose early to shoo the chickens out into the yard and feed the baby so as to be ready to go out with Jim to the field to start work again. But as she stood at the cottage door, a sweet and sickly scent came to her nostrils, pungent enough to turn the stomach queasy. Destiny looked about her. There was no pig dung on the cottage floor, nor in the yard, no reason she could see for the foul smell. Jim came out to join her, rubbing the sleep from his eyes.

"What is it, Desty, that stink?"

"I don't know, Jim, but it's enough to turn the stomach of an elephant."

Jim strode away across the yard, his great shaggy head uplifted and sniffing like a dog on the scent. Destiny shrugged and went back to fetch the baby from its basket. The little one nuzzled close to her breast, her tiny mouth agape and searching. Destiny smiled as she opened her bodice, but the pleasure did not reach her heart as it once did. The child was sucking noisily when Jim suddenly burst in.

"Desty, the taties—they're all bad!"

Destiny looked up, uncomprehending. Jim was standing before her, his face bewildered.

"What's that you say? 'Tis a fine crop we have," she rebuked him.

"It was, but it isn't," he repeated in baffled tones. "They've all gone bad in the pit. Come and see. They looked so fine, but now they're all black!"

With the baby still clinging to her breast, Destiny followed him out across the yard and past the byre to the pit. The stench was appalling, and now she could see why. Where yesterday had lain a heap of fine potatoes, there was now only a putrefying, blackened mass. Destiny could only stare in disbelief.

"What's happened, Desty? They looked so fine," Jim whispered. "Something must have befouled them."

She laid the child on the grass and picked up a potato, still half-white and half-black. It exuded a sticky black mess on her fingers. She tossed it back.

"Like you say, Jim, something must have befouled them. But no harm, there is still half the crop to be lifted. Dig a fresh pit and we'll put the good ones in there. We'll still have enough to pay the rent."

Pay the rent, maybe, but not enough to feed us all through the next winter, she thought as she watched Jim start to dig. He knew it too, but he would not say it. Still, she could try to save what was still edible from the rotted crop. Patches of white were still visible in the rapidly moldering heap, and if she were quick about it, perhaps she could cut away the good bits and save them. Something had to be done if they were to avoid starvation. After all, it had happened before. She could still remember the winters in her childhood when the crop had been bad and her mother had kept them alive on what she had managed to salvage from the pit.

Jim's face was set and unsmiling that night. Destiny did her best to reassure him.

"We'll have to forget our pride, Jim, and borrow from

our friends. If Shuna and Mick have a good crop, I'm sure they'll help us out."

He made no answer, but she could see it hurt his pride to think of begging. No doubt he would come to it in the end rather than see his family starve, but it would be at enormous cost to his self-esteem.

Without warning, Shuna threw open the cottage door and hurried in, her pretty face ashen and her hair awry. Destiny started up to greet her sister, but Shuna ignored her.

"Jim, are your potatoes bad too?"

"They are. And yours?"

Shuna's face crumpled. "Every one of them, and we're not alone. Not a soul in the village has sound ones. Oh, God! What are we going to do?"

She turned an agonized look on Destiny, who could only hang her head. What hope was there now of help, if everyone in Ballymachree had suffered the same fate with their crops?

"Perhaps Mr. Carmichael will have pity on us and help in some way," she ventured to suggest. Jim laughed shortly.

"There's little hope of that. Every landlord expects his dues," he snapped.

Shuna brushed away a tear. "Well, at least Mick has some money put away, enough to pay the rent, I'm thinking, so at least we should have the roof over our heads this winter. It's how to feed the little ones that troubles me. How will you manage, Desty, with one little mite already and perhaps another on the way?"

Destiny saw Jim's quick look of surprise, but he held his peace. He was too proud a man to reveal that he did not know.

"Ah, sure, it's too early to know. We'll manage, same as we always have," she said with a false brightness that belied the heaviness inside her.

"Is it true, Desty?" Jim asked when they were alone together that night. "Are we to have another child?"

"I don't know," she replied miserably. "I feel so strange, just as I did last time."

She heard Jim's slow sigh. "Never fear, macushla. We'll

manage." he said quietly. But she knew his fear—that there would be little enough food for three, let alone four in the coming year. The new child she would feed herself, and perhaps next autumn the crops would yield well and they could hope again. But the optimistic thought was hard to believe in.

For weeks Ballymachree reeked of the foul smell of blighted potatoes and everyone wore the same expression of dejection. Some borrowed from more provident relatives and friends, and Jim set aside his seed potatoes for the next year's crop. The sensation of sickness and misery lingered in Destiny despite the fine autumn days soaked in golden sunshine. By November she was sure.

She was with child, undeniably, for she felt the first flutterings of its movement, too frequent and persistent to be attacks of wind. She had to face the truth. But whose child was it? Jim's, or the Englishman's? The son she longed to give her husband, or the fruit of a willful, wildfire encounter with a stranger in a cave?

Her dreams by night left Destiny in no doubt, for the face of the handsome Englishman haunted her, strong and possessive, fascinating as the devil himself. There was no shadow of doubt in Destiny's mind that he had fathered the child she was to bear, and she felt racked with guilt and misery. There was no chance now of consulting old Widow Dwyer for one of her potions renowned for bringing about a miscarriage, for Destiny was too far gone for them to work. And Father Clancy would never forgive the mortal sin, for he had threatened to excommunicate Widow Dwyer when she had helped an unfortunate girl down in the village last winter.

Jim's weary face expressed pleasure when she told him of the coming child. "We shall manage, macushla, have no fear," he promised, but she could see the doubt in his honest eyes. It was a lean winter for them, when Destiny's milk dried and Jim had to scrape food for three, with gleanings from the pig swill up at the house to eke out. As Destiny's body thickened, her heart grew even heavier. Her guilty secret was too great to be borne alone. She had to confide in someone.

* * *

Shuna's shocked expression rapidly reverted to its normal calm capability. "There's no help for it, Desty, but you must hold your tongue and let Jim believe the child is his—you'd break his heart else. For the sake of you both, hold your peace."

"But I feel so bad, Shuna. I'm a wicked woman, betraying a good husband so."

" 'Tis the Englishman who is wicked, not you. That has always been the way of the English, since time began, to ravage the Irish and plunder what they wanted, with no care for what became of us. 'Tis his shame, the devil, not yours. But if it preys on your conscience, why not go to confession? Father Clancy may scold you, but he'll not tell. With absolution you'll feel much better."

As always, Shuna was right, Destiny thought. Shuna could always be relied upon for sound advice. Difficult as it might be to keep the truth from Jim, she would do it for his sake, and confess the truth to Father Clancy.

The village church was crowded with penitents that evening when Destiny went in, tying her red kerchief over her head. Saturday, of course, the villagers were anxious to be shriven of their sins for Mass in the morning. Patiently she sat in an old oak pew until the last of them had made their penitential prayers and left. She wanted no eavesdroppers near the curtained confessional box to hear her sin.

Father Clancy's cheerful face peered through the wire grille as she knelt to whisper, "Father, forgive me."

"Mrs. Regan, to be sure, it's a pleasure to see you here again." He beamed. "How long is it now since you were last at confession?"

"Six months, Father."

"Too long, but I'm glad you're back. Now, tell me, what have you been up to in that time?"

Destiny hung her head in shame. He expected no worse confession from her than that she had snapped thoughtlessly at her husband or gossiped about a neighbor, and she dreaded the effect her words would have on him.

"Father, I have sinned grievously."

"Then tell me of it, and all will be forgiven."

" 'Tis a terrible sin, Father, and it fills me with shame to speak of it."

"Remember, child, that so long as you are genuinely contrite, no sin is too great to be forgiven. Our Lord is merciful."

Destiny closed her eyes and screwed up her courage. "Father, I have lain with another man, not my husband."

"For shame, Destiny Regan, and it not eighteen months since I married you to Jim Regan! Now, tell me, who is your lover?"

"I cannot tell you, Father." Destiny's whisper seemed to her ears to re-echo through the deserted church, and she was glad no one else was near.

"Come now, child. You cannot help your lover by concealing his name from me."

"Is it not enough that I confess and repent, Father? Surely it is up to him to confess his own sin?"

"True enough, but it is my job to reprimand him if he does not. I cannot have loose living in my parish. Now, tell me, how often did you commit the sin of adultery?"

"Only the once, Father."

"I see. Some misguided frolic after the fair, perhaps?"

"No, Father. He took me against my will."

Father Clancy leaped from his stool. "What's that? Violating a married woman? Does your husband know?"

"No, Father, nor dare I tell him."

"For fear he should break the other fellow's skull, I've no doubt?"

"Because I am to have a child, Father, and because I think it is not Jim's."

For long moments there was silence in the little church, a silence so intense Destiny could hear her heart thudding in her ears. At last Father Clancy leaned forward, his wooden rosary clattering against the partition.

"This is bad, Destiny. Are you at least repentant of what happened?"

"I am."

"Can you truly tell me you did not want it to happen?"

Destiny hesitated, remembering the wild abandonment of those moments in the cave. Father Clancy seized at the hesitation.

"You found pleasure in it, confess it. You enjoyed your sin."

"No, well . . . yes . . . no, I did not," Destiny stuttered, tears of shame starting to her eyes.

"So I insist on knowing who he was. I command you to tell me," the priest said sternly. "I must do all I can to put matters right, and you must tell me all you can so that I know you are contrite before I give you absolution. Who was he?"

Destiny looked up through tear-filled eyes. "I don't know, Father, truly. He was a stranger. An Englishman."

"An Englishman?" Father Clancy repeated in surprise. "And you know no more than that?"

"Only his first name."

The priest rubbed his chin thoughtfully. "Then he must have been a visitor to Ballymachree House. No doubt Mr. Carmichael could trace him from his first name. What was it?"

"Conal. That's all I know." Destiny wept.

Through her tears Destiny saw the thunderstruck expression that leaped to the priest's face. His heavy jaw sagged.

"Conal? Are you sure?"

She nodded dumbly, watching the priest as he raised his eyes ceilingward.

"When was this, you say? Last summer?"

"July, Father."

"Then that fits. He was here then. Destiny, my girl, you must speak no word of this to anyone, not to Jim or anyone else. There could be great trouble for us all."

"Trouble?" she echoed. How could there be trouble for anyone but herself?

"If it had been any other man, I could have brought him to task and made him help you financially or some other way, but to accuse this man would be more than our lives are worth. You and Jim could lose your living, and I mine too. Go, say three Hail Marys, and I grant you absolution, child, so long as you tell no one else what you have told me. Do you understand?"

Destiny stared at him, bewildered. "Yes. But . . . no, why? Who is he, do you know him, Father?"

"I do. The man you speak of is Conal Carmichael, only son of the master of Ballymachree. Spoiled and willful as they come. It would go hard with us to point a finger at him. His father lies ill in England, and any day now young Conal could be the master in his place. So you see why I say, child, go home to your husband and let him have joy in his new child, for it must not be the child of Conal Carmichael if we are to live in peace."

Three

The winter was a cold and cruel one, but Destiny toiled on, mindful of the warnings of Shuna and kindly Father Clancy, keeping her silence and struggling to look after her husband and child and to feed them through the bitter winter months. It was a difficult task, with not a single potato to eke out their frugal meals, but Destiny managed. Like everyone else in Ballymachree, one had to manage somehow.

Melancholy still lay heavy over her heart, but when spring came and the buds began to burgeon on the trees, she felt the hope of new life lifting her spirits. It would not be long now before the child was born, and with the promise of new life within her, Destiny began to feel peace.

One April morning when the air was balmy enough to walk into the village without a cloak, Destiny took her daughter and went down to the village to fetch fresh water from the pump. Even before she reached the bottom of the lane, she began to feel tired. It was no easy matter, toting a heavy child who danced about restlessly on her hip, when her stomach welled so protuberantly before her. It would be a difficult matter climbing back up the hill with a heavy pail of water added to the weight.

She could hear the laughter of the women before she reached the pump. They were all there, a great gaggle of women laughing and joking in the sunlight while their children splashed the water. Destiny smiled. It was as if they too had been brought to life by spring's sunshine. She hurried to join them eagerly. After so long an enforced solitude in their own homes in the winter, there was much gossip to be exchanged.

The air was full of comment about who was betrothed to whom, and who expecting another child. But no one, Destiny noticed, made any reference to their hunger, despite the gauntness of their faces, which betrayed the emptiness of their stomachs. Not one of the women complained about her lot. They were a proud race, these villagers of Ballymachree.

Only Moira Feeney, the pretty flaxen-haired daughter of Paddy, the basketmaker, made an indirect reference to the hardship of the winter.

"I think young Liam Mulcahy fancies me," she said pertly, fluttering her long dark eyelashes.

"Come, now," said old Biddy Murphy, "and you not sixteen yet."

"I am so," retorted Moira hotly. "I was sixteen at Christmas. Twice young Liam came round of an evening, and both times he brought a rabbit for the family pot. I think he was concerned that I should not go hungry."

Old Biddy Murphy snorted. "Don't you go giving yourself the airs and graces of a fine lady, Miss Moira, and you only a child yet. And Liam himself can be no more than seventeen."

"Old enough to be married," Moira snapped.

"You're far too young to be thinking of marrying yet, the two of you."

Moira colored up. "Who said I would marry him, Mrs. Murphy? I only said I think he fancies me."

"Well, don't you be leading him on, now, my girl. Don't let him take you in the barn, or you'll regret it."

"That I'll not. Though it seems a good way to keep warm of a winter night." Moira laughed.

"There's turf enough to be had from the bog to keep you warm by your own fireside," the older woman rebuked her.

Destiny was too intent on watching her little daughter's antics with the water to pay too much attention to the other woman teasing Moira. It was only when the sound of wheels clattering over the cobblestones interrupted the conversation that she looked up. A fine carriage was drawing to a halt outside Murphy's bar. It was dark green and instantly recognizable as the Carmichael coach by the family crest emblazoned in gold on the door.

Destiny drew in her breath sharply. Even before the coachman had leaped down and rushed to lower the step and open the door, she knew as if by some sixth sense who was about to emerge. A tall figure bent almost double to pass his top-hatted head under the door frame, and as he reached the bottom step, he straightened.

Destiny stared at him with a mixture of hate and admiration. Conal Carmichael stood there, every inch a handsome English gentleman in his elegant topcoat of finest broadcloth with its gleaming silver buttons reflecting the spring sunlight. All the women stared in silent fascination. Only Biddy Murphy moved. Dropping her empty pail, she rushed forward to greet so distinguished a customer, bobbing him a curtsy.

"Top of the morning to you, Mr. Carmichael, sir, and a fine morning it is too," she greeted him enthusiastically. "What can I get for your worship, sir? A jug of our fine ale?" She was beaming at him with a wide, toothless smile.

Destiny saw Conal Carmichael's gaze flick past the old woman to the group of women gathered around the pump. She averted her gaze, gathering up her child instead. She had no care to be recognized and be obliged to talk to him, especially now, thick and unattractive as she was.

"Indeed, I'd be glad of some refreshing ale," she heard his deep voice behind her. "I've just this morning landed at Cobh after the filthiest crossing ever from Liverpool."

Biddy Murphy bustled away into the bar, and Destiny busied herself cradling her daughter close, so as to avoid meeting Conal's gaze. She was aware that he was still surveying the group of women speculatively.

"Don't I know you? Haven't I seen you before somewhere?" she suddenly heard him say. She started in alarm and looked up. He was looking, not at her, but at young Moira.

"To be sure, sir"—Moira dimpled and blushed—"but how strange that you should remember after all this time. I took some eggs up to the big house last summer while you were there."

"That's it, and I saw you from the window with the stableboy. I knew I'd seen you somewhere," he rejoined with a smile. "I never forget a pretty maid."

He was smiling broadly at the whole group now. Destiny blushed and turned away on a pretext of scolding her little girl, who was pinching her arm and squealing to be put down again to play with the tantalizing water. Destiny set her down and straightened, to find she was looking directly into Conal's handsome face. He glanced incuriously at her and looked away again. Destiny was horrified. There had been no glimmer of recognition in his expression. He had seen both her and Moira last summer, and it was only Moira he remembered. Yet it had been Destiny he had taken by force, up there in the cave. The event must have been of little importance to him, for he was turning away now, and it was painfully obvious he had found her too plain to warrant a second glance.

Destiny felt full of shame and alarm, for it could be this man's child she was carrying, now so near its time. Agitation and fury made her heart pound against her ribs. Dear God, she murmured inwardly, I had hoped he would not recognize me, but to see me and not know me is more than I can bear.

Biddy Murphy hastened back with a foaming jug of ale in her hand. "There you are, sir," she said. "I'll warrant you've never tasted finer ale this side of Dublin."

His teeth gleamed in the sunlight, and Destiny could not resist a surge of admiration for this handsome man. He threw back his head and tossed off the ale like a man who had not slaked his thirst in a week.

"God, but I was thirsty," he said, handing back the jug

to Biddy and running the back of his hand across his mouth. He turned toward the carriage. His foot on the bottom step, he paused, and as if in afterthought, unbuttoned his topcoat and slid two fingers into his waistcoat pocket. Withdrawing a coin, he tossed it toward Biddy, who pounced on it eagerly.

"The Lord's blessing on you, sir," she crooned. Climbing into the carriage, he was gone. As the carriage vanished over the hill in the direction of Ballymachree House, Destiny did not know whether to feel relieved or chagrined that he had not recognized her. How could a man make love to a woman, however violently, and a few short months later not even recall her? But thank heaven he had not acknowledged her, or the village women might have come to know of their encounter in the cave.

Moira Feeney was pink with pleasure. "He remembered me." She preened. "Mr. Conal remembered me. I would not be surprised if the big house does not send down for eggs again while he's there. He's a beautiful man, Mr. Conal. He's the handsomest gentleman I've ever seen in all my life."

"Handsome is as handsome does," snorted Biddy Murphy. "He never once asked how we fared during the winter, and we his father's tenants. Mr. Carmichael had his rent from every one of us, even though it meant we had no money left for food in the winter. And a fat lot Mr. Conal knew or cared about that. He doesn't concern himself with the likes of us, Moira Feeney, so don't you be after having fancy notions about him. He's forgotten you already, you can be sure of that. And if he does send for you, it will be for his own pleasure and not for your benefit."

That was true, thought Destiny as she trudged back up the lane carrying her child and a heavy pail of water. Conal Carmichael was a willful, selfish man who cared not a jot for others. She had proof of that.

By the time the cottage came in sight, Destiny's back was aching fiercely with the effort of carrying the child and the heavy pail. It was with relief that she saw Jim come hurrying out of the yard gate and down the hill to meet her. He took the little girl and pail from her.

"You should have let me fetch the water," he reproached her gently.

"No harm, Jim. I'm not sick, you know."

"But you're near your time, macushla. No time to carry heavy weights like these. How long should it be now?"

"Oh, a week or two more yet, I'm thinking. Come on home and let's see what I can find to cook for your dinner."

But as the afternoon wore on, the ache in Destiny's back persisted. No wonder Conal Carmichael had not recognized her, she thought as she looked in the cracked piece of mirror. I'm haggard and old-looking, no longer fresh-cheeked and rosy. Giving up her share of food during the winter to Jim and the baby had left her gaunt and gray.

Time and again she had to pause in her chores to rub her back until the pain eased, but by evening it became clear that the pain was not going to leave her. A sudden fierce spasm caught her unawares, and she leaned on her hands over the stool, arching her back to ease the pain. Jim came in through the cottage door, and as he caught sight of her, his forehead furrowed.

"Are you all right, Desty? It's not time yet, is it?"

As the pain passed, she straightened and smiled at him. "It could be, Jim. I'm not sure."

When, only a few moments later, the next pain seized her body, Destiny could not help wincing. Jim looked up in alarm.

"I'll go fetch Shuna," he said.

Before she could protest, he was gone. No sooner had his footsteps faded than Destiny heard the fierce patter of raindrops on the cobblestones. By the time Jim returned, the rain was falling hard and his hair was spangled with raindrops. Shuna threw off her shawl and came to Destiny with concern in her eyes.

"How is it, Desty? Are the pains bad?"

Before Destiny could reply, the next spasm seized her. Her face contorted in pain. Shuna took her arm and led her toward the bedroom.

"Jim, put the caldron on to boil," she said over her

shoulder. "Put the child to bed and find the clean linen Desty has prepared. Leave me to see to her."

As the pain subsided, Destiny felt reassured by her sister's presence. Shuna—always so calm, so capable, and in control. It was a blessing to have her close by at a time like this. It seemed no time at all since Shuna had last ministered to her, delivering her first baby. Ten months ago it was now. It seemed only yesterday.

As the night wore on and the rain crashed down on the cottage roof, Destiny struggled on. Hour after hour she was assailed by pain that seared her body like a thousand knives, and it seemed at last that she was in a sea of relentless pain. Her body felt to be torn apart by the struggle inside her. Time and space lost all meaning for her as she moaned and writhed in this paroxysm of agony. Dimly she was aware of Shuna's murmurs of encouragement and the crash of thunder overhead. To her the wild severity of the weather seemed but an extension of the tumultuous torment within her. At last, when she felt she could bear the agony no longer, she squatted on the blanket and strained.

"It's coming! At last, it's coming!"

"Then lie back and let me help you," Shuna commanded. Obediently Destiny rolled over, continuing to heave and strain. Within moments, on the edge of oblivion, she felt the blissful relief of the child slithering from her. At the same moment, there was a deafening crash of thunder immediately overhead. Destiny lay back, panting, filled with a glorious sense of relief. Thank God, the excruciating pain was over.

"A thunderstorm," she murmured. "A thunderstorm for the child's birth, just as there was at the time of his conception."

Shuna was busying herself wiping the child with rags. Then she wrapped the baby in a length of clean white sheeting and offered the bundle to Destiny.

"Here she is, your second daughter."

A girl, thought Destiny in surprise. Somehow she had always visualized a son. Jim deserved a son. If it were a girl after all, then it must be Conal's child.

"I don't want to see her." Destiny turned her head away.

"Nonsense," said Shuna. "Take her."

"I don't want her. I can't love her. She's that devil's child."

"Don't talk soft, girl. Look at her. She's as beautiful as an angel. Look at her." . .

Reluctantly Destiny took the child. True, she was pink and rounded, not wizened and ugly as most newborn babies were. Diffidently she cradled the little one. The child stared up with wide blue eyes.

"Shall I fetch Jim in now to see his new daughter?" Shuna asked.

"No, no, not yet. Give me a moment." She had to get used to the idea of this being Jim's child. She would to God it had been a son, for his sake.

"There," said Shuna reassuringly. "See how angelic she is, the little mite. How could you call her a devil's child? 'Tis profanity to utter such words. Now you'll have to get Father Clancy to baptize her soon. What shall you name her?"

"I don't know. I had planned 'James' for a son, after his father." Wonderingly Destiny laid a finger on the baby's tiny hand and felt its minute fingers grip her tightly. A warm glow suffused her. She could not deny the mother love within her. Whoever had fathered this child, it was her own flesh and blood. How could she deny it? She cradled the child closer and felt its searching mouth warm on her bodice. With a surge of love she unbuttoned her bodice, and then suddenly a cry of alarm escaped her.

"What on earth is the matter?" Shuna demanded.

"That mark, look, the mark!" Destiny whispered.

Shuna peered closer at the child. "Why, 'tis only a mole. What are you making such a fuss about? She has all her limbs and fingers and toes. There's nothing wrong in such a tiny blemish. A tiny mole, on her neck below her ear, where no one will ever notice."

"You don't understand," Destiny was whispering. "It's not the mark itself I mind, but what it signifies. Shuna, do you not see? It is in the shape of a bird, just such a mark as Conal Carmichael has under his ear. I saw it as he lay upon me in the cave. Don't you see? There is no doubt now—this child *is* the devil's child!"

Shuna's mouth sagged open, but only for a moment. Instantly she regained her self-control. "Now, look here, Desty. We agreed that you were to keep silent about this, did we not? Now, for your own sake and the child's, keep your peace still. It would not be safe for you or for Jim if Conal Carmichael came to hear of it. He might even take the babe away from you. You love her, do you not, your own flesh and blood? Hold your whisht, girl, and look after her as you would Jim's child."

The thunder was beginning to die away. The baby started to wail. Shuna regarded her sister questioningly. "Well?" she said.

Destiny looked down at the child, its mouth wide and searching still. As if in answer to Shuna's question, she continued to unbutton her bodice and put the baby to her breast. She knew what she must do.

"Go, fetch Jim in to see his new daughter."

Shuna nodded and rose to fetch him.

Four

If Jim Regan was disappointed that his wife had given birth to yet another daughter, he did not show it. On the contrary, his air of quiet self-respect as she accompanied his family down to the village indicated that he was proud of them. A look of love in his dark eyes for his wife and children filled Destiny with a warm glow.

Though she knew for a fact that the new baby was not Jim's, he at least believed the two little girls to be his. Not for the world would she break his heart by telling him the truth. She tried to quell the feeling of repugnance whenever she looked at the baby's neck, and gradually the feeling faded. How could one fail to love one's own baby? The only time the thought of that devil Carmichael was forced strongly into her mind again was when she and Jim took the child to church for Father Clancy to baptize her.

"A fine family you have now, James Regan," the priest commented with a smile. If he remembered Destiny's confession of months ago, he made no sign of it. "It's to be hoped that your crops fare better this year, with a growing family to support."

"Indeed, Father," Jim replied. "I have my seed potatoes in that I saved from last year and, God be willing, if the weather stays fine, we shall fare better this year."

"By the way," added the priest as he accompanied them out of the church door, "I hear old Mr. Carmichael is ailing fast. Young Mr. Conal has gone back to England to be by his side. The old gentleman is not expected to last long now. Soon Mr. Conal will be master of Ballymachree."

Jim nodded and made no comment. A few weeks later Father Clancy announced from the pulpit before he began to say the Mass that the old master was dead, and asked the congregation to pray for his soul. They did so willingly, for he had not been a bad master, and the hope must have been in many a mind, thought Destiny, that the young new master would be one-half so beneficent as his father.

If the potato crops, God forbid, were to fail again this year, would he, like his father, give them extra time to pay the rent? God help them if he did not, for to have no roof over their heads would be even more dreadful than the hunger.

Spring blossomed into a magnificent summer, and the lush, verdant countryside around Ballymachree had never looked more beautiful.

Destiny watched her children playing in the long grass of the glen, the older girl now running around joyfully and the little one stretching out her arms and rolling over in an attempt to join her. Down the hill Destiny could see the fields of bright yellow flowers. The potatoes were flourishing, God be praised.

The children looked fit and well, she thought with satisfaction, though her own stomach ached with hunger. She longed for the day soon when they could pick the fresh crop of potatoes and she could eat a filling meal again. It was only hunger, she assured herself, that gave rise to that strange feeling of unease in the pit of her stomach. Hunger, that's what it was, and no call to be thinking it was her silly sixth sense foretelling doom again.

"Here, alannah, leave the baby be. Don't be after teasing her so," she admonished the older girl, who was tickling the baby's face with a spray of wild barley. The baby sneezed, and the toddler laughed and ran away.

Jim said little, for he was a man who seldom revealed his feelings, but she could see his anxious gaze as he watched his potato plants grow and flourish. During August the weather changed with alarming suddenness. What had been lush, hot days lying sweetly over the land suddenly erupted into violent storms.

Lightning and thunder crashed over the silent land, and the sweet earth was deluged in rain. For weeks it persisted. No sooner had one storm subsided and a few hours of peace ensued before another began. For the whole month of August the southern part of Ireland was enveloped in raging storms.

Destiny saw Jim's expression grow even more anxious as he surveyed his crops forlornly from the cottage window.

"Mother of God," she heard him pray, "let the crops survive. Sweet Jesus, let us eat."

When the furor finally abated, he went out to the field. He came back with a broad smile.

"They're all right, Desty," he said quietly. "The plants are still blooming. They'll be all right."

And throughout September they kept their fingers crossed and prayed. The crop appeared to have survived. Still, the unease rumbled in Destiny's stomach.

One morning in October Destiny awoke to find the air filled with a strange scent. Dimly in the back of her mind the aroma awakened a memory. In alarm she clutched Jim's shoulder and shook it fiercely.

"Jim! Wake up! Can you smell that smell?"

Jim yawned and rolled over on the blanket.

"Jim! Smell!" she repeated.

He sat up slowly and twitched his nose. She saw his sleepy expression fade, and then the look of alarm that replaced it.

"Dear God!" he muttered, and leaping up off the blanket, he pulled on his trousers hastily. As he rushed out from the cottage, Destiny ran after him, still in her shift despite the chill in the air. The whole valley seemed to reek of that same abominable scent of last autumn. But it couldn't be, she raged inwardly. Then it had been after the potatoes had been lifted, after they had been stored in the pit. How could there be that same nauseous stink now, while the potatoes still lay in the ground?

"It can't be," Jim was moaning. "It can't be! So near lifting time, too."

He ran to the byre and fetched a fork, and Destiny watched fearfully as he plunged it into the ground and lifted the soil. The clutch of potatoes he brought up was barely visible amid the dark earth. Disbelievingly he moved on a few paces and dug again. Again the fork came up laden with black, rotting potatoes. A third time he tried, a fourth and fifth, and each time it was with the same result. The whole field was putrefying.

"It can't be," Destiny whispered, bewildered. "There was no smell yesterday."

"There is now," Jim replied grimly. "They're rotten, all of them."

He wandered all over the field, lifting here and there, and every time with the same foul forkful of decomposing vegetation. By now the babies were awake. The little one was crying, and her older sister came staggering out of the cottage door.

"Mammy! I'm hungry!"

Destiny felt the ache of unease in her stomach harden into an icy ball of despair. Casting a look back at Jim's bewildered face, she went back to the child.

"Come on, then, macushla. Let's see what we can find."

"What's that funny smell, Mammy?"

"Nothing. Come on, after we've eaten, we'll go down and see Aunt Shuna." Destiny tried to keep her voice level and calm, hiding the dismay she felt. Perhaps Jim would find yet that not all the potatoes were lost. Perhaps some survived, enough to pay the rent or feed them through the winter.

But when Jim returned an hour later, he sat on the one and only stool and slumped his head in his hands. Destiny knew the worst. Starvation faced them.

Shuna's news was no better. "Every last potato gone rotten, Desty," she said in a small voice. "Everyone in the village is in the same plight. God knows how they'll pay the rent this year. Mick says we'll manage—he has a bit put by. But then there'll be nothing left for food."

"We have nothing put by," Destiny replied miserably. She looked at the four children on the hearth, Shuna's two youngsters, Shaun and Deirdre, playing with her toddler, while the baby lay peacefully on a blanket, her little stomach filled at least, with mother's milk. But would those four little mites survive a winter of hunger and hardship? It was doubtful. One or all of them would not see next spring. Her heart ached with misery.

Although it was not her custom to frequent Murphy's saloon bar, she took the children there to find Jim. Destiny was struck by the subdued talk of the men in the bar. Though it was crowded, it was not filled with its usual gay banter and laughter. Jim was sitting gloomily talking with Mick in a corner.

"Some of the village men are talking of going down to the city in search of work," Mick told her as she joined them. Destiny made no comment. It was one hope of salvation, but not a solution a proud, independent man like her Jim would welcome. He had served no master but himself in all his life.

"I'll be going there meself in the morning." he announced suddenly. Destiny looked at him and felt a glimmer of hope. In the morning he packed a bundle and left.

The air of desolation and reeking decay lay heavy over

the valley, and Destiny tried hard to convince herself that the sensation of doom within her was only temporary. Things could look up soon now. The longer Jim was away, the more likely it was that he had found work. But the air of tragedy in the village and the look of stark fear in the women's eyes left her little room for hope.

A week lengthened into two, and then one drizzling gray morning she was just finished feeding the baby when she heard footsteps on the cobbled yard outside. A man's footsteps. Laying the child down, she leaped up eagerly. Before she could cross the room, a man's burly frame had filled the doorway, leaning nonchalantly against the doorjamb. Squinting against the light behind him, she saw his sandy hair and recognized him. It was McPherson, the surly bailiff. Disappointment filled her. Not Jim, but Carmichael's agent, no doubt after the rent. She began to rebutton her bodice hastily.

"Mr. McPherson," she said, trying to inject a note of welcome into her voice. "Come in."

He did not move, but stayed where he was. His speculative gaze shifted momentarily from her as he glanced around the room. The baby had fallen asleep by the fire. The older girl was down in the village with Shuna. Destiny bent over the baby, as though to ally herself with her family against the unpleasant bailiff.

Evidently the glimpse of her bared breast had awakened some feeling in the usually cold creature, for his close-set eyes gleamed and he sniffed and rubbed the back of his hand across his thin nose.

"Well," said Destiny brightly, "what brings you all the way up here on such a gloomy day? Not the rent already, surely?"

He was licking his thin lips slowly. Innate hospitality urged Destiny to offer him a drink, but what? She had no ale, no milk even, and water was too mean an offering. There was still a little of Jim's poteen hidden away, but the agent could cause trouble if he knew of its existence. She offered a smile instead. That was evidently a mistake, for he left the door and came close, standing over her till she could smell the stale sweat on him.

"The rent?" he muttered. "Oh, the rents will be due very soon now."

He raised a hand and laid it on her thin bodice. Destiny stared with revulsion at the red hairs on the back of his hand, then pushed it away.

"Then if it's not the rent, why are you here, Mr. McPherson?"

The hairy hand rose again. "A matter relating to your husband, Mrs. Regan."

Alarm seized Destiny. She did not stay the hand as it groped inside her bodice. "My husband? What of him? Oh, tell me! He's not come to harm, has he?"

McPherson uttered a hoarse laugh. "He's not, nor will he if you cooperate. Mr. Conal gives orders that we are not to harass those who cooperate."

"Where is he?" Destiny cried. The other hand was lifting her skirt. "Is Mr. Conal back in Ballymachree? What has he to do with Jim?"

"Nothing at all, Mrs. Regan, nothing at all."

He was pressing his weight against her now, pushing her down onto the mud floor. Destiny's eyes widened in terror. "For God's sake, Mr. McPherson, tell me Jim is safe!"

"Cooperate, and he will be." The words slid out of his mean mouth in a hoarse mutter. Resisting the urge to fight off this cold and heartless creature, Destiny fell back on the floor. Her nails sank into his shoulder.

"Cooperate, and all will be well," McPherson snarled. Terrified, Destiny submitted. It seemed better to yield than to endanger Jim in some unknown way, but the ignominy of lying there with her skirts about her neck, submitting to this man while her baby slept alongside her, was too shameful to believe. The enormity of what she was condoning appalled her. She felt dizzy, only half-conscious from shock and fear.

McPherson was oblivious of everything but the demands of the flesh. He was moaning and thrusting, droplets of sweat banding his forehead. Suddenly voices outside brought him back to reality. He leaped up, cursing and hitching up his trousers.

"Get up, woman!" he snapped. "Get up!"

With a sigh of relief Destiny rose and straightened her skirt. The cottage door opened, and Shuna stood there. Her wide eyes traveled from Destiny to the agent, and Destiny knew her shrewd sister had guessed something.

"Why, Mr. McPherson," she said, "I hardly expected to find you here, but I'm glad I did. I hear you've got Jim Regan up at the hall. What's it all about?"

"Keeping him safe, Mrs. Colgan, that's all." His shifty gaze tried to avoid meeting hers, inadvertently caught Destiny's, and looked away quickly. "I came here to tell Mrs. Regan, but you arrived before I had a chance."

"Safe?" repeated Destiny. "From what? I thought he was down in Cork."

"So he was, but on the way home he got roaring drunk. I took him in hand, and it's really my responsibility to hand him over to the magistrates."

"But why? He's done nothing, has he?" Destiny demanded.

"No," the agent agreed. "Not yet."

"Then you have no choice but to let him go," Shuna said with an air of finality. "After all, many a man gets drunk to forget his cares, and you don't arrest them all."

"I know," McPherson admitted begrudgingly. "But he could do harm. A man gets violent with the drink. I came only to get Mrs. Regan's assurance that she would see to it he practices sober ways in future."

"Jim Regan violent? You must be mad to think it," Shuna said stiffly. "There's no man more honest and industrious than Jim Regan in the valley."

McPherson looked slyly at Destiny. "Then I have your word for it, Mrs. Regan?"

Destiny understood his meaning. Jim's release depended upon her compliance, her willingness to let this vile creature have his way with her. If not today, then some other time he would come to exact his dues.

"Yes," she said quietly.

"Very well. Then I'll bid good-bye to the both of you, till I come to collect the rents," he said; then he was gone.

"What did he ask of you?" Shuna asked. "Did he want payment to let Jim go?"

"He asked nothing," Destiny replied. That was true, for McPherson had made no request, simply taken action. She could not for the life of her admit the shameful truth. "As he said, he'd told me nothing before you came."

"Then it's a good job I heard about Jim and came when I did. That man is not to be trusted. He has a mean and niggardly look about him."

"If Jim's back, then he evidently didn't find work in the city," Destiny remarked. "Now what's to become of us?"

"Wait and see what Jim says when he comes," Shuna advised.

It was nightfall before Destiny heard the sound of Jim's footsteps in the yard. She leaped to meet him, to throw her arms about him and hug his great body close to hers.

"Jim, macushla! You're safe!"

At this moment that was all that mattered. For the moment, all thoughts of rent, food, or starvation fled from her. Jim was alive and well, and she loved him. His great arms enfolded her, and for a few brief moments, loving and being together was all.

At last she stood back and looked at him. He stood, no longer tall and erect as a proud man should, but stoop-shouldered, bent like a broken reed. Pity flooded her. She did not need to ask if he had found work. The humiliation, added to that of being held like some drunken vagrant, had sapped Jim Regan's pride.

"There was no work in the city," he muttered in answer to her unspoken question. "There were hundreds of us tramping the streets in search. I did my best."

"I know you did," she said soothingly in a tone of reasurance she could not feel.

"I got drunk coming back. Mr. McPherson could have handed me over to the magistrates, but he let me off with a warning. I was lucky there, at least. Not a bad fellow, really, that Mr. McPherson, is he?"

Destiny turned away in silence. Filled with unconquerable foreboding, she began to undress for bed.

Five

The winter was unutterably cruel, miserable, and cold. Daily, Destiny watched her children grow thinner and more irritable, while Jim's gaunt look of helplessness tore at her heart. Now it was not only she who felt her stomach shrivel and cling to her ribs in hunger. All four of them were sinking fast.

Her face stared back at her from the cracked mirror like some haggard, wrinkled old crone. Where now was the smooth-skinned girl with flashing eyes that Jim had loved? She sighed. It mattered little now.

She piled more peat turf on the hearth. At least turf was free from the peat bogs and they could keep warm. The children were both whining miserably. Jim was staring out of the window.

"Here's Mick," he said abruptly. "He's running."

He opened the door as Mick came rushing in, tousle-haired and panting.

"Jim, come quick, there's food!" he gasped.

"Food? Where?"

Destiny stared, disbelieving. Mick grabbed Jim's arm.

"Come on, man! There's no time to lose! Father Clancy told me a wagon is due to arrive any minute, laden with food for all of us!"

"God be praised!" breathed Jim, grabbing up his muffler. "Has the master decided to help us after all?"

"Conal Carmichael? Not he. He's still in England. 'Tis the English government who's sending it."

"And well they might, after all this time."

"I'm coming too," Destiny said, snatching up the baby.

Two of us can carry more than one. I'll leave the babes with Shuna."

Jim caught up the older child, and they ran down the hill. Hastily depositing the children with Shuna, Destiny hurried after Jim and Mick toward the church. A large crowd was already gathered there, a mass of silent, gaunt-faced people all staring expectantly up the road that led from the city. Few spoke. Now and again Destiny could hear their hissing breath as they shivered and waited.

For two hours they waited, frozen but reluctant to move away, lest the longed-for food should arrive. Father Clancy appeared on the church steps, his kindly face marred by a puzzled frown.

"It can't be long now. Be patient, good people," he exhorted them. "The commander of the garrison where all the food is stored assured me he would send down the wagon today. It will be here soon, and then at last you can fill your children's stomachs. Only have patience, and thank God for His providence."

"Thanks be to God," some murmured, crossing themselves.

Dusk fell in the late afternoon, and hope began to fade. One by one the fainter-hearted villagers disappeared. His teeth chattering with cold, Jim suggested that Destiny should go home, or at least to the warmth of Shuna's cottage. As she was turning to go, Destiny stopped, listening. Far away the clop of horses' hooves could be heard. Every face in the small crowd brightened with expectancy. Father Clancy reappeared on the steps.

"Now, my children. Now your patience will be rewarded," he breathed.

The hoofbeats came closer, until in the dusk they could discern the shape of two riders on horseback. But no wagon. Destiny's heart thudded. After so long, were they to be disappointed?

The riders clattered into the square, two uniformed soldiers of the English army. One slid from his saddle, while the other remained mounted. Father Clancy went to meet him.

"About the food, sir, I'm sorry to have to disappoint you," the soldier said. The crowd swayed and moaned.

"Delayed, is it?" asked the priest. "Will it be here tomorrow, then?"

The soldier shook his head. "Afraid not. There was some trouble at the garrison. What wagons did set out were set upon by the crowd. Like demons they were, fighting and clawing like madmen. They spilled more flour and lentils all over the road than they took. Out of their minds, they were. So the commander regrets he will be unable to honor his promise. He sends his profound apologies."

He remounted and the two men rode out of the village again before anyone spoke. Moira Feeney began bawling like a baby, while others muttered and cursed.

"Whisht, now, good people," Father Clancy said, gathering his wits. "Try to understand and forgive."

"We're doomed to die of the hunger," Paddy Feeney pointed out. "And you ask us to forgive."

"The mob in the city were starving too," the priest reminded him. "Is there any wonder they went mad? Are you so sure you too would not have leaped on that food if it had come? Be patient, my friends. No doubt the commander will organize matters better when the next consignment arrives from England. We have only to wait."

"If we live that long," Jim muttered, grabbing Destiny's arm. "Come, girl, we're wasting our time here."

"I'm sorry you were disappointed," the priest called after them.

"Disappointed? Is that what he calls it?" Jim snarled. His voice was choked with emotion, and Destiny shared his bitter chagrin.

Cold winter days passed, until rent day came, and with it, the sound of the bailiff's horse clopping up the hill. Destiny deemed it wiser to stay out of McPherson's sight while Jim talked with him, but she listened behind the door of the inner room.

"Well?" demanded McPherson. "Have you your rent, Regan?"

"No. You know the crops failed again this year. I have nothing," she heard Jim say quietly.

"You too, like the others. Well, you can account to the master in person for your default. He's back, and he wants to see all of you up at the hall who won't pay."

"*Can't* pay," Jim corrected him. "Very well. When?"

"Tomorrow noon."

She heard the door close after him and came out.

"Conal Carmichael is back, then, come like a raven to glean every last drop from us," she remarked bitterly.

"It's only his right," Jim said. "I'll have to explain, and maybe he'll be lenient."

But Destiny knew that cold, hard man was in no way like his father. Old Mr. Carmichael may have been English, but he was kind to them. Perhaps because he had once had an Irish wife, long ago, before she died giving birth to Conal. But if he had had a soft spot for the Irish, his son had none, although he was half-Irish himself. She resolved to go with Jim up to the big house.

It seemed strange to be actually walking up the long drive toward the hall, far more impressive at close range than it was viewed from a distance. Destiny felt her heart thumping as she mounted the great steps to the colonnaded front of the hall and entered its huge portals. She gripped her baby close and held the other little girl's hand tightly. Jim, grim-faced, led the way into the large room where dozens of other villagers were gathered.

They stood silent, caps in hand, and the air was heavy with a sensation of fearful expectancy. All faces were turned toward the long trestle table with its papers and inkstand, and the great door behind it.

Some minutes after noon had struck on the church tower the door opened and Conal Carmichael strode in. Somehow he looked paler and plumper to Destiny, but it might only be in contrast to the thin faces she was now accustomed to seeing. As Conal seated himself at the table, the bailiff, McPherson, stood behind him, alongside a fair-haired young man Destiny had never seen before. He too was undoubtedly a gentleman, for his clothes were of the best quality. He remained standing until Conal signaled him to sit beside him.

"Right, McPherson, let's begin." Conal's voice was sharp. He picked up the papers. "Let's go down the list. Bannion, is he here?"

A small, squat man stepped forward. "Here, sir."

"Where's your rent, Bannion?"

"I have none, sir. My crops all died on me and I had not a potato to sell. Nor even to eat, sir. All my family is starving, and my little boy like to die even, if he doesn't eat a good meal soon."

"Spare me your wails," Conal snapped. "Colgan. Where's your rent?"

Destiny saw Mick step forward and lay some silver coins on the table. Shuna was not with him. "Here, sir."

Conal made a mark on the papers. "Well, one of you at least has had the good sense not to drink away all your money. You can go, Colgan. Cleary!"

A tall man with thinning gray hair stepped forward. "I have no rent, sir. All my crops failed too."

"Dennehy. Driscoll. Feeney. Horrigan."

One by one Conal called out names, and one by one, men explained their failure to pay. Only two besides Mick Colgan surrendered silver coins.

"Regan." Destiny let go of Jim's arm as he stepped forward through the crowd. "Can you pay, Regan?"

"I regret not, sir. I have tried to find work, but with no success. Give us time, though, and we'll try to pay our dues."

"Time?" roared Conal. "You've had a whole twelvemonth in which to put the money by, but you're a feckless, idle bunch of layabouts, the lot of you! You've drunk and gambled the money away, no doubt, and then have the gall to try to tell me your miserable potatoes failed!"

"That we've not, sir," Jim replied quietly, and Destiny was proud of the way he stood erect before the master's flashing anger. "We're every one of us decent, hardworking men. We're not to blame for our bad luck."

"Then how is it three men can pay if the rest of you cannot?" Conal remarked with a thin sneer. "The blight hit everyone's crops, did it not?"

"It did, sir, and they have sold all they had left to

pay." That was true. Mick had sold his cow months ago and hidden the money in a hole in the cottage floor, Destiny knew.

"Then do you the same," Conal snorted.

"We have already done so, to eat to keep body and soul together," Jim replied.

"Waste of time," Conal snapped, "for it seems to me your pitiful bodies are not worth keeping souls in. Stand down, man, I've had enough of your insolence. You're a harum-scarum ne'er-do-well."

As Jim turned, a child's treble voice began to sing. It was one of the village children, his memory jogged by Conal's words to recall the old song:

> Hello, Patsy Fagan,
> You'll hear the girls all cry.
> Hello, Patsy Fagan,
> You're the apple of my eye.
> You're a decent boy from Ireland,
> That no one will deny.
> You're a harum-scarum
> Devil-may-carem
> Decent Irish boy!

The crowd shifted uncomfortably. Conal looked up sharply.

"Who's that? Get that squawking child out of here!"

Jim grabbed his older daughter's hand and whispered to Destiny, "Let's get Kate and Rosanna out of here quick, girl. The master's in a foul enough temper as it is."

Destiny followed him with the baby. As Jim reached the door, Conal shouted out again.

"Get out of here, all of you! I'm giving you one month in which to pay, and any man who does not pay his dues then, God help him, for I swear I shall evict him and his family. You have been warned! Now, get out, the whole scabby lot of you!"

Destiny saw the fair young man lay a restraining hand on Conal's, but Conal snatched his away and thumped the table. McPherson was standing by with a thin-lipped smile of malice as the villagers trooped out. Jim had already gone out with the older child. Some instinct prodded Destiny to linger by the door, behind a tall palm tree in a copper bowl, while the other villagers silently passed her. Between the leaves she could just see the two young men at the table, and the thin figure of McPherson pulling on his cap and leaving by the far door.

Conal snapped the ledger shut and leaned back in his chair. The fair youth was sprawled back in a relaxed, nonchalant manner that seemed to irritate Conal.

"It's all very well for you to urge patience, Philip, but how am I to carry on my normal mode of life in London if these creatures don't pay up? I can't wine and dine and gamble with the rest of you without the revenue from my estates."

He was scowling blackly, a frown rutting his forehead and his dark eyes smoldering with annoyance. God, but he was a magnificent creature, Destiny breathed to herself. A villain, maybe, but a beautiful beast nonetheless.

"Patience, Conal. They'll pay when they can," the fair young man said reassuringly.

"But how, when they have nothing? I'm damned if I can see how I'm to get out of them what they have not got. It's easy for you to talk. Your father subsidizes your fine way of life."

"So did yours, Conal."

"But now he's dead and it's up to me to make sure of my income. Your turn will come when you inherit your estates over at Carrigaline, and see if you think it's so damned funny then."

He stood up and stretched himself. Destiny drew back, marveling at his fine body tensed like a cat rising from sleep. What broad shoulders he had! Tactile memory stirred in her, and she remembered the strong grip of those slim hands and the hard feel of these long, lean thighs against hers. God, she ought to hate this beast, but her stubborn body betrayed her mind, yearning for the feel of him again. He sauntered around the table.

"Well, of course, if you need cash soon, as well you might, to keep up your rate of drinking and wenching, you could always institute the public-works scheme the government ordains," the other man commented. "That way they could earn the money to pay your rent."

Conal laughed shortly. "Rob Peter to pay Paul, eh? No, very few landlords have taken that order to heart. Why should I incur so much expense just to pay myself? It doesn't make sense."

Though she understood not a word of what they were saying, Destiny found pleasure just in listening to the deep, vibrant sound of Conal's voice. Dear God, the very sound of him made her insides churn!

"If they enforce the order, you'll have no choice," the fair man remarked.

Conal snorted. "I'll face that if and when it happens. Come on, Philip, let's go and have a glass of port. My nostrils are sickened with the stench of peasants. This way."

He led his companion out by the far door. Destiny looked down at her sleeping baby.

"Psst!"

Jim was standing just down the corridor, clutching the older girl's hand and looking bewildered. Destiny went to join him.

"What kept you, girl? I was after thinking the master had caught you!" he said as he gripped her arm and hurried her outside. Cold sleet blew in their faces.

"Arrah, no. I was just curious, that's all. I wondered who the young gentleman was."

"That's young Philip O'Keeffe, son of the master of Carrigaline," Jim told her. "I saw him with his father at the horse fair last spring. There was a pretty fair-haired girl there too, Philip's sister, I think."

So that was it, thought Destiny jealously. A pretty sister Conal perhaps fancied for his bride. She felt sure she was right. After all, it made sense. The new master would want to be sure of sons to perpetuate the Carmichael line, and ladies of quality were few. His best friend's sister would be ideal. A whining, feeble creature who would not appreciate his fiery manliness, who could not thrill to his hot embrace. Tears burned Destiny's eyelids. This was ridiculous, she thought. The blond, simpering chit was welcome to him, evil, heartless brute that he was. Destiny had a fine, honorable husband. She looked up at Jim's earnest profile and felt warm tenderness for him. Not the fierce desire Conal aroused in her, but that was wanton, wicked feeling she must endeavor to forget. She must, and she would, God help her if she did not.

Jim's thoughts were evidently far away, for he spoke little on the homeward journey. In the evening he remarked, "Thank God for the month of grace. I must find work soon, though, Desty. I'd better go back down to the city in the morning."

But in a week he was back again, hollow-eyed and wretched. Thousands more like himself littered the streets of Cork, desperate for work, he told her. He told of the vagrant families he had seen sleeping in the hedgerows.

"Frozen, they were, and starving. I saw a sick mother still clutching her dead baby in her arms," he said. Destiny read his mind. In a few weeks more it could be his own wife and babies starving in the fields. She pressed his hand.

"Don't give up hope, Jim. Have faith, and pray."

But she wished she could believe her own words of advice, for the heavy feeling of doom lay once again like lead in her heart.

Conal Carmichael poured another glass of brandy for his guest and himself and then sat down, stretching out his legs toward the roaring log fire in the hearth. It was pleasant to sit here in the warmth of the fine oak-paneled drawing room, for Ireland could be damnably chilly and damp at this time of year.

"So you'll be away home soon, I take it, Philip?" he asked.

His companion nodded, swirling the brandy in the glass and surveying its color thoughtfully. "Tuesday, I think, if you agree. My father is anxious to open this new institution of his by the end of the month, and wants my help. I quite enjoy helping in his philanthropic ventures."

Conal grunted. "He must have more money than he knows what to do with. What is it this time? A hospital?"

"An orphanage, I understand, in Liverpool. So many travelers pass through the city, and many are so poor they find it necessary to abandon their children. Father was quite upset and made up his mind he had to do something to help."

Conal sneered. "He must be soft. Beats me how he's so successful."

A gentle smile played upon Philip O'Keeffe's handsome features. "Well, now it's your turn to play the benefactor, it seems. You can hardly ignore the letter from the government about the public works now. What do you plan to do?"

"I've no choice, it seems. I'll have to think of some scheme which will be to my advantage."

Philip drained the glass and set it down on the leather-tooled wine table. "You could build a new road up from the city to here. My coach sank up to the axles in the mud."

Conal considered for a moment. "You're right, we could do with a new road, but it's a hell of an expense for me just to enable my tenants to pay their rent."

"But take a long-term view over this, Conal. It's a way of keeping your tenants here in Ballymachree to farm the land next year when the blight's gone. Otherwise they'll drift away to find work elsewhere or immigrate to England or America, as so many have done already."

"That is true," Conal conceded.

"And the government says it is prepared to assist in financing any reasonable scheme."

"But they don't say what proportion they will grant."

"Well," replied Philip reflectively, "this new road of yours would pass at least two more estates on the way down to the city, would it not? You could approach those landowners to share the expense and provide some of the labor force. That, together with the grant from the government, would keep your outlay down to a more reasonable amount."

"I'll think about it," Conal replied, rubbing his chin thoughtfully. "Fancy a game of chess? I'll wager that black roan of mine you fancy against your bay mare."

"Done," said Philip.

* * *

A week later Destiny could hardly believe her ears. "What's that you say, Jim? Work? Where? When?"

"I told you," Jim cried, delight illuminating his haggard face. "McPherson was down in the village recruiting fifty men for the work force. I was one of the lucky ones, and so was Mick. We're to start building a new road at once. Desty, we'll be able to pay the rent!"

He snatched up the baby and danced around the cottage crooning, "Dada is going to work!"

"But who is it?" Destiny asked.

"The master, God bless him! He's taken pity on us at last! Go down on your knees, girl, and ask forgiveness for all our wicked thoughts about Conal Carmichael. He's a good man, and kind. The Lord's blessings on him."

"Bless him," echoed Destiny, but the strange, heavy feeling persisted.

Six

Conal Carmichael might have appeared at first to be an angel of mercy, providing much-needed work for some of the village men, but it soon became apparent that he intended to exact payment in full for his silver shillings. Destiny noted how Jim, shining-eyed on Monday morning as he set off to the site, was drooping, exhausted, and filthy by Tuesday night.

And the red weals on his back, standing out sharply in contrast to the pallor of his skin.

"Mother of God! How did you come by these marks?" she exclaimed.

Jim shrugged. "McPherson drives us hard. He says the master will tolerate no slackers."

"He takes a whip to you?" Jim nodded. "The beast! There's no call for that! You're no slacker, Jim Regan!"

"It's nothing. You should see Mick's back, raw it is, and bleeding. McPherson seems to have a down on him for some reason, but Mick says nothing. He says he wants the money."

So did they all, Destiny thought. The men of the village would put aside their pride for the moment in order to pay their rents and hold their heads high again. But Mick had paid his rent already. Why should he, of all men, submit to McPherson's cruelty?

The answer to Destiny's question became clear within a few days. Shuna sent word to Destiny that old Biddy Murphy was dying of the fever and had not long to live. As was usual in the circumstances, friends were being informed so as to enable them to be present for the final rites Father Clancy would perform for the dying woman. By the time Destiny had hastened down to the inn, she knew she was already too late. The wailing of the women's voices within told her that Biddy Murphy had gone to meet her Maker.

She found the group of women clustered about the low truckle bed in the back room, already washing and laying out the corpse. Shuna looked up and broke away from the group to join her sister, her face taut and white.

"She's the seventh this week, God rest her soul," she said, crossing herself as she spoke. "That's most of the old ones gone. It'll be the babies next."

Destiny shivered, knowing she was right. The years of suffering that had gone before had taught Irish peasant women the way it went—the blight, hunger, and then the fever. And after the children, it was the turn of the men and women. Few would be lucky enough to survive this second terrible winter, even if they escaped eviction, which would mean certain death.

"A grand woman she was," one of the women wailed. "As good a woman who ever breathed."

"Honest as the day," cried another.

"Except when she watered down the ale," muttered a third.

"That she did not! Don't be maligning the dead, Kitty Bannion!"

"She did so! I've seen her with my own eyes!" Kitty screeched. Shuna pulled Destiny to the outer room.

"Listen, Desty. There's no future for us and ours in Ballymachree. Do as Mick and I plan to do—use the money Jim will get to go to England. There's work there for all, and we can watch our children grow in peace. Forget the rent—use the money to pay for your passage to Liverpool instead. We're off just as soon as Mick has enough money."

Destiny stared at her sister. "England?" she said. It was a strange idea, to go to the land of those who had inflicted such misery upon them. But if there was work to be found, and food and shelter . . .

"Go home and talk to Jim about it," Shuna urged. "We've kept quiet, Mick and I, for it would not do for half the village to be up and away. The master would find a way to stop us."

Jim's reaction was in almost the same words. He heard Destiny out, listening in silence and then considering for a while before he spoke.

"The master would not allow it until the rent has been paid," he pointed out. "But it is an idea to consider. In a week or two, when I have paid off the rent, then I can start saving for the passages. How much will I need?"

"Deck passengers, ten shillings each from Cobh to Liverpool. The two children travel as one adult."

Jim reckoned slowly. "That's thirty shillings. Well, we'll see if I can earn that much after the rent is paid, if the job lasts long enough."

"Damn the rent, Jim! Let's go at the end of the month with Mick and Shuna. You'll have enough by then, won't you?" Destiny pleaded. "The fever is spreading. Soon it will be the children—our children—look at them, Jim."

She pointed at the two tiny figures lying asleep on the blanket, thin and pale and sucking their fingers in their sleep, from hunger. There was no way of telling which was the elder of the two, so small they both were. The only contrast was in their coloring, Kate as fair as a spring morning and Rosanna as dark as a raven's wing.

"Look at them, Jim. Can you bear to watch them die when you have the chance to take them away from all this? It's your duty, man, to God and to them, to save them!"

Destiny's voice was shrill with pleading urgency, but Jim shook his head resolutely.

"Not till the rent for the last year is paid. You cannot ask me to cheat on a debt, Desty, for that I will not do for any man."

Loud as Destiny railed, he would not be moved, and she realized at last that she could not sway him. It did occur to her to cry out, "You owe the master nothing, for he robbed your wife of her virtue," but with an effort she refrained. She knew Jim's wrath, slow to excite but wild once it was. Like that time at old Mr. Boyne's wake when the gathering had sung and drunk and made merry all night and one of the village lads had snatched a furtive kiss with her. Jim had said no word, just punched the lad's face so that his nose sprang with blood and gushed like the village pump; then he dragged her away. If he did that for a lighthearted kiss, what might he do to Conal Carmichael if he learned of the incident in the cave?

So Destiny kept her peace and prayed that her children would escape the fever until Jim had the passage money put by.

Of all the vague, swirling sensations of foreboding that had beset Destiny over the months, there was, strangely, no presentiment of the news that Mick flung at her. Her sister's husband, sweat-streaked and with blood on his lip, burst in the cottage door and grabbed Destiny by the shoulders.

"Bear up, girl, for the children's sake. Jim's gone, Desty. Killed in an accident."

She stared up into his filthy face, totally bewildered. Jim dead? What was he saying? Any moment now Jim would slouch in through that same door and slump on the stool, the same as every evening, wouldn't he?

Mick's fingers dug into her shoulders. "You understand me, Desty? He's dead. He won't be back."

She stared back at him, her eyes pleading to be told she misunderstood his words. "He can't be. He's working."

Mick's dark eyes filled with tears. "He was working when it happened, Desty. He was down a trench we'd dug, a long narrow one. He was the only one still down there when it happened."

"What happened?" Destiny whispered.

"There was this great wagon loaded with the earth we'd dug. It was across the road, see, turning to go back up the hill with the load. Somehow it backed on the trench and its load fell in on top of Jim. We couldn't save him, Desty. We all dug like demons, but it was a huge load of black mud and we couldn't get to him in time. By the time we did find him, it was too late."

Destiny caught Mick's wandering gaze and held it. "I understand you, Mick. My husband is dead, but I know also there is something else you don't want to tell me. What is it?"

"There is no more. I told you all, girl."

"It's how the wagon came to back on the trench, isn't it? I can see it in your eyes. Tell me, who was it, Mick? Who caused Jim's death. McPherson," she added on impulse. "Was it McPherson?"

"No," said Mick slowly, fingering his bloodied mouth. "Though he and I came to blows over it."

"Then who? For God's sake, tell me!"

"Himself, Conal Carmichael."

Destiny turned to stare blindly out of the window into the gathering dusk. Mick needed to say no more, for suddenly she could see it all clearly, out there in the gloom, as graphically as if it were happening at this very moment before her eyes.

A gang of men was maneuvering an overladen wagon that straddled the roadway, its tall burden of black, muddy earth tilting dangerously over the narrow trench that bordered the road. One lone man dug on in the pit. From far away uphill came the sound of approaching hoofbeats. She saw the overseer signal to the rider to slow and halt, and saw the rider's answering look of fury and his crop raised to spur his horse on. "Out of the way, dolts!" she heard him cry.

His mount leaped past the workhorses holding the wagon's weight, causing them to back in alarm. There was no saving their load. Inevitably and inescapably the great black tons of earth slid relentlessly down into the trench, burying from sight completely the lone man working there. Destiny moaned aloud.

"There was nothing we could do for him, macushla," Mick muttered, his voice broken in apology. "We dug like madmen. He was gone when we got to him."

"The swine, the evil bastard," Destiny whispered. "I would I could bring him one part of the misery he has caused me. I pray to God that the devil pursues Conal Carmichael and catches him at the end, killing his heart and hopes as the black devil has killed mine."

"Arrah, that's no way to talk of the master, Desty," Mick protested.

"Who are you to speak?" Destiny flung at him. "Aren't you yourself planning to run out on him soon? Aren't you saving every penny to get away from here?"

She saw the idea gleam in Mick's eyes. "I am, and why should not you and the little ones do the same and come with us now? I'll ask McPherson for the wages due to Jim, and then you'll have enough to buy the tickets, so you will."

He was right. Twenty shillings was all that would be needed now. But it seemed cheap and treacherous somehow, to run out on Jim now he was dead. Somehow his death still did not seem real, and hard as she tried, she could not visualize following his body to its resting place up there on Mount Ash, where a great communal grave had been dug for the famine victims once the graveyard was full. Daily she had watched the wagons with their sad burdens climbing the hill.

"Young Brian Murphy, and him only thirty-seven," Shuna had said yesterday. "Soon it will be his poor old man."

Strange, thought Destiny, that since so many families had lost at least one adult or child in the hunger, Shuna and she had both escaped. Until now. And now it had to be no unavoidable blow of fate which robbed her of her husband, but a willful and possibly drunken Conal Carmichael. Hatred for the man boiled up inside her. Reaching past Mick, she pulled wide the cottage door, letting in the chill night air and giving no mind to her two sleeping babies on the floor.

"Conal Carmichael!" she cried out of the open doorway. "Master of Ballymachree and murderer of my husband! May God forgive you, for I never shall!"

"Desty! Whisht your noise!" Mick cried in alarm, trying to close the door. "Even if the blackhearted devil himself doesn't hear, 'tis a certainty the bailiff will, and you know McPherson's wagging tongue."

"I hope he does hear me, devil servant of a devil master as he is! What did he do to save my Jim's life? I wish him to hell and beyond, him and Carmichael both!" She flung the words from the doorway out into the dark, no more out of a spirit of chagrin and helplessness than real hate.

The sound of clopping hoofbeats made Mick look out again. " 'Tis he, McPherson. He must have heard you," he mutttered. But the bailiff rode up to the door, dismounted, and came in without knocking.

"Your kinsman has no doubt told you the news," he said to Destiny in that crisp, cold voice she loathed.

"He did," she affirmed.

"I'll have the men bring his body back when we find a barn door," McPherson went on, as coolly as though they were discussing the transport of a dead pig. "In the meantime, I'm here to pay to you as his widow what was due to James Regan."

Mick nodded sourly. "But no question of compensation for the accident, I'll be bound. Just his wages, is it?" His teeth bared in a sneer.

The bailiff rounded on him swiftly. "Your concern for Widow Regan does you credit, but I'll tell you now she wouldn't have this but for me."

He held out six silver shillings. Destiny looked at it, unable to touch it. It seemed like blood money, Judas money, not hers to take.

"Mr. Carmichael has of course deducted the last quarter's rent," McPherson went on, "so there is no question now of your eviction at the end of the month. How you propose to pay the next quarter's rent, however, is your affair."

She saw the gleam of malice in his eye. God, how she despised his mean, narrow face and its close-set eyes!

There was a hint of satisfaction on Mick's face, and Destiny knew what he was thinking. Just a little more money and she and her babes could go to England too.

"I'll be back later," McPherson muttered, and left. Mick came closer to Destiny. "Shuna will tell you the same as me, girl. Get the little ones ready and come with us."

She glanced at the figures huddled on the blanket, fingers in mouths in their sleep, and a great ache engulfed her. Who was to know whether either child would see the morning?

"Get you home, Mick Colgan, to your wife and your own children," she said with quiet pride. "I can manage."

"I will go if y're sure," he replied, "for Shuna was worried about the little one this morn."

"Deirdre? Was she sick?"

He shrugged. "Aren't all the children? I'll be back with Jim later, Desty."

He was gone, leaving her to ache in a numb void which only changed to helpless fury when he and others returned with Jim later that night, the tall body she had loved so well looking strangely pathetic on its bed of a barn door. They left her alone then with him, and all night she sat beside his corpse, feeling only blind rage and useless, helpless grief.

There was no mark on Jim to show how he had died. The slurry of muddy earth must have suffocated him, she realized, and his mates had cleaned him well as a last mark of respect before bringing him home. She was almost glad that Rosanna and Kate were both too sick and weak to question their father's silent presence.

She looked at Jim's face, placid and at peace now, no longer marked by suffering pride. How remote he seemed, how divorced from the problem of survival she still had to face. It was the first time she had touched his hand and felt nothing pass between them. There was nothing left of love now, only bitterness and hate. All night she sat holding his hand, recognizing that with his death an end of an era in her life had come too. The two girls on the floor could be dead by morning, like their father. Despair and apathy in turn receded, leaving again only the backwash of hate, and all the hatred centered on Conal Carmichael.

It was a strange, hollow night of neither quite life nor death. All Destiny felt by the time dawn streaked the sky with gray was an unshakable determination that one day Conal must be made to pay. Master of Ballymachree or no, he must be forced to atone for his crimes.

"Mrs. Regan!" A voice outside roused her. It was the men come to draw Jim's body up the hill to Mount Ash. Mick was not among them.

"He'll be joining us along the way," one of the men said in answer to Destiny's query. "He's fetching his child to Mount Ash."

Deirdre. Destiny could feel no more sorrow. Just as Shuna and Mick were ready to escape at last to England, Deirdre's strength had failed. Poor Shuna. Destiny, her black shawl pulled close over her head, followed her husband's makeshift bier to the communal grave. No tear wet her eye, not even when Shuna and Mick joined the cortege with their little dead daughter. One sister could not console the other. No more sorrow can be wrung from a broken heart.

It was after the two bodies, man and child, had been tumbled into the grave that Shuna turned great dry, hollow eyes on her sister.

" 'Tis settled now. Mick do have the tickets and we leave for Cobh tomorrow. Will you come?"

Destiny shook her head. "I don't know what I plan to do yet, but it's not to run away. I'll stay, and may God speed you."

Shuna cocked her dark head. "We have the three tickets, one for two children. Now Deirdre's gone . . ."

Destiny saw her drift at once, and a jerk of emotion leaped in her dead heart. "You'll take one of my girls?"

Shuna nodded. "Mick agreed, but it's for you to say. Kate or Rosanna, Desty?"

The two sisters looked at each other, and Destiny felt an agony of indecision. The child who stayed here would probably die of hunger, but the child who traveled to England could have an equally uncertain future. How was she to choose which of her daughters to give the chance of life, which to condemn to almost certain death?

Shuna's dark eyes probed hers, asking yet another unspoken question. Which child would she choose, Jim's daughter or the child of the evil Carmichael?

"I'll think on it, Shuna. In the morning I'll bring the girl to you," she said quietly, and went home to sleep for the last time with her fatherless children.

Seven

All night long Destiny sat at the cottage window watching the dark clouds scudding across a pale silver moon. She could not sleep. The little ones lay huddled together asleep on the blanket, but for Destiny there was no restful oblivion. It seemed wrong to lie alone on the blanket without Jim's arms about her, reassuring in their strength.

Life would never be the same again now he was gone from her. With him by her side, silent but comforting, their troubles had never seemed insuperable, but now she was alone and she doubted if she had the strength to carry on alone. . .

Shuna had offered to take one child, but though that would lessen Destiny's problem of feeding three mouths, it still seemed wrong. Already the family was depleted, and to reduce it still further was unthinkable. By the time dawn was streaking the eastern sky, Destiny had decided. Somehow she must keep her beloved children with her, and cope. Maybe it was a wrong decision and she was robbing one child of a lifetime's chance, but mother instinct was not easily overcome. Despite her pain, love flooded her veins as she looked down at the two pinched little faces, and determination hardened. Kate and Rosanna both should stay with her.

A distant sound intruded on her thoughts, and Destiny cocked her head to listen. It was the sound of hoofbeats descending the lane. Peering out into the half-light, she could discern a tall figure on horseback coming down the hill toward her.

As the hoofbeats clopped closer, she could make out that it was McPherson, his gaunt figure cloaked against the chill of the early morning. As he neared the yard gate she drew back, but he had seen her. He reined in and dismounted.

"Mistress Regan!" he called out.

With a hasty glance at the sleeping children Destiny unlatched the door, drawing her shawl about her. McPherson was crossing the cobbled yard toward her.

"I saw you at the window," he said, his thin voice sounding mean and miserly after the deep resonance of Jim's voice. "It occurred to me that although you've paid the last quarter's rent you'll be hard put to it to pay the rent now you've lost your man. You've no way now of earning money."

"It's kind of you to be concerned for me," Destiny replied crisply, "but it seems to me rather late to worry yourself about us. Would you be after offering me work of some kind?"

She saw the thin fingers come out from under his cloak and rise to touch her, but she did not shrink. His bony hand on her bosom left her unmoved. There was no feeling left in her now.

"Well, I might, if you're willing."

She looked up at him warily. "What kind of work?" she demanded.

"Easier work than you trying to work your bit of land on your own," he countered quietly, and she could see the gleam in his pale eyes.

"What kind of work?" she repeated. Whatever it was, it might hold out the hope of keeping her precious family together.

"Widow Brogan, who keeps house for me, has fallen ill

of the sickness, and they tell me she is not likely to recover. I need another woman to keep house."

Destiny hesitated. Widow Brogan was in her sixties, a thin, morose woman who kept herself to herself. If she died, the position in McPherson's house would be an enviable one to secure, for his was a real house, built of stone and slate, with a real fireplace and an oven, they said. As bailiff to the Carmichael family, he lived in a superior style. There would be no shortage of food there. Destiny was tempted.

"And if Mistress Brogan does not die?"

"She is growing old. I need a younger woman who can scrub and polish with more vigor," McPherson replied. His hand probed further, cupping her bosom firmly. Destiny laid a restraining hand over his.

"Only to cook and clean for you? You are not suggesting I share your bed?" she inquired bluntly. McPherson's eyes narrowed.

"And if I am? It should not come amiss to you, accustomed as you are to lying with a man. A body such as yours should not lie unplowed, Destiny Regan."

"Mistress Regan," she corrected him.

"Widow Regan," he amended sharply. "You are a fine, handsome woman and only need a few good meals to put the flesh back on you. It's a good offer, one many a woman in Ballymachree would envy."

That was true, Destiny admitted privately, but she was not going to leap at the offer and sell herself cheap.

"Give me time to consider," she said at last, pulling away from his grasp. "With my husband but newly dead, I cannot think clearly."

"I'll give you until noon," he replied quickly. "I go now to the village to evict those who have defaulted on their rent—the soldiers are waiting there for me. By now the job should be complete, and I shall call again for your answer."

She watched him stride away across the yard, remount, and ride off down the hill. Rosanna stirred and whimpered. Destiny looked at her, helpless to feed and console her. It would be utter stupidity to decline the bailiff's offer, for whatever conditions he might attach to the job, it would at least mean she could see her children flourish again and grow straight and strong. Jim would surely approve, wouldn't he?

But the doubt lingered. Would any honest man agree to his wife's prostituting herself, however honorable her motives? She lifted the crying child and caressed her, trying to stem her tears. Kate awoke and began crying too. Destiny dressed both children in their little shawls and led them out of the cottage and up the hill toward the woods. Perhaps they would be lucky and manage to find a few nuts and berries not yet scavenged by the hungering villagers.

By midmorning they had gathered and eaten enough to allay the pain of hunger, though not enough to fill their stomachs. Only then, with the aching numbed, did Destiny's ears catch the unusual sounds from down the valley. It was voices, voices in distress crying out. Kate and Rosanna stood, fingers in mouths, as Destiny climbed a knoll to look down the valley.

She was alarmed, for even to speak these days was unusual for the villagers. They hid their suffering of hunger and of the loss of their loved ones behind a veil of silence, so why the cries? As she looked down, she began to understand.

It was the soldiers, enthusiastic in their task of evicting the defaulters. She could see the uniformed men dragging out weeping women and children, beating the stubborn ones with the butts of their guns, and driving them away into the fields. Terrified children clung screaming to their mothers' skirts, and on a rising piece of ground Destiny could make out the figure of McPherson, still on horseback, watching over the proceedings.

And as if that was not enough to terrify the villagers, the soldiers evidently had orders to ensure that the people did not creep back into their mud huts at nightfall when the frost began to numb their bones, for she could see them tearing the cottages apart, felling them into a chaotic tumble of ruins. And to make certain they were not hastily rebuilt, the soldiers flung torches into the ruins. Destiny could see the wreaths of smoke rising to eddy and mingle with the morning mist. No wonder the people wept. Robbed now of shelter and warmth, death was a certainty for many more.

Her numbed spirits sprang to life with anger. She glared at the mounted figure of McPherson with furious hatred, then remembered that he was only carrying out his orders, just as the soldiers did. It was Carmichael who perpetrated this evil deed, Conal Carmichael, of whom the very thought made the blood riot in her veins.

"You murderer! You shall suffer one day for this!" she muttered to herself; then, snatching the girls' hands, she hastened back to her own cottage, sitting with head in hands in frustrated fury. Was there no end to the wickedness of Conal Carmichael? How could any man, however avaricious, condemn others to starvation and death in the fields in the depth of winter? Surely one day heaven would punish him as mercilessly as he now treated his own people of Ballymachree.

And McPherson, though he had not instigated this vile deed, evidently felt no repugnance at carrying out his master's orders, possibly even enjoyed the task. Destiny felt fearful at the thought of living in the same house with such a man. He, who could lay forcible hands on the villagers, was hardly likely to treat her and her children with gentleness.

But if she did not accept his offer, chances were that next quarter it would be herself and Kate and Rosanna who would be forced to quit their home and watch it being destroyed, they who would in their turn be forced to roam the countryside until they perished. Life, she determined, however bitter with McPherson, was infinitely preferable to that.

It was not yet noon when she heard the horse clopping back up the hill toward the cottage. Leaving the two children in the back room, she sat silent, awaiting McPherson's knock at the door.

There was no knock. She heard his heavy step in the yard and then suddenly the door crashed open. He stood there, looking haggard and a little tired but with a gleam of satisfaction in his pale eyes. Destiny could not help wondering whether it was the sight of her or his recent successfully accomplished mission that gave rise to the gleam.

"Well, Widow Regan," he said harshly, "the job is done, and soon it will be your turn. Unless, that is, you have reconsidered my offer and feel ready to accept."

"I've been thinking all morning," Destiny replied slowly. For the life of her she could not yet be certain which way to jump for the best.

"And don't you agree it's a handsome offer? A fine prospect for you and the child, for I'm a generous man, no one can deny, and I'm prepared to take the brat too. You must admit that's fair, since it costs no mean penny these days to feed an extra mouth. But I'm willing to take you both on. I'm not saying as I'd be so willing if you had several brats, but one I'll accept. What do you say?"

Destiny stared at him, and her lips began to move and almost spilled out the truth before she collected her wits. So he believed she had only the one daughter? Her hope of salvation was lost if he learned of the other. She thought rapidly. If she played her cards carefully, she could still secure a place for herself and one child, and there was still Shuna's offer of a future for the other.

But she must not appear too eager, for McPherson was no fool. He would make the conditions tougher if he suspected. Picking her words with care, she spoke in a casual tone she did not really feel, her heart racing under her bodice.

"I might be interested in your offer, Mr. McPherson, but for one thing."

He moved closer. "What one thing?"

"Why, this, Mr. McPherson," she said firmly. "I am an honorable woman and will share a bed with no man, unless it be with the blessing of the church. If you are offering me marriage, then I'll think it over seriously, but a whore I am not and will not be."

She wished she could feel the determination in her voice. McPherson's eyes widened, and then his thin lips broke into a broad smile. Finally he threw back his head and laughed a full-throated, genuine laugh of surprise and disbelief.

"God, but I can't help admiring you, Destiny Regan,"

he said begrudgingly. "You've nothing but hunger and death staring you in the face, yet you barter as if you held the upper hand. You've got guts, woman, and I'll think none the less of you for that." He seized her about the waist and pulled her to him. Destiny could feel the hardness of his desire.

"So you will marry me," she persisted.

"I will, dammit," he muttered, and his hands began to move. Destiny stayed him, gently but firmly. She would not enrage him now by pulling angrily away.

"Then call the banns swiftly for I tell you I am an honorable woman," she whispered. "Call them soon, and then I shall be yours."

Whether he would have respected her wish, she was not to learn, for the sound of footsteps outside made him let go of her suddenly. He snatched up his fallen hat as Shuna came in the door. She eyed him with hate.

"Mr. McPherson, I saw a horse outside, but I little thought to find you here," she said sharply. "After your morning's work, you must be tired."

He ignored the malice in her tone. "Your sister's rent is paid now, Mrs. Colgan, so you and she are safe for the moment."

Destiny saw Shuna's dark eyes flash, but she saw her sister stifle the words she would have spoken, about her and her husband's decision to flee to England. But the thought lent her the courage to say more.

"I hope you are satisfied with your evil work, Mr. McPherson, knowing that you have robbed people of their home and sent them to a certain death. I hope your conscience can rest easy with that knowledge."

The bailiff's thin lips flattened into a hint of a smile. "I have no conscience, Mistress Colgan. I only obey my master's commands as a good servant should."

"Then may he rot in hell for his evil cruelty," Shuna snapped. "There is no humanity in such a man, nor any credit in being a servant to him."

"I hope he does not come to hear of your words, mistress, or you and yours could fare badly. But have no fear. Out of the close relationship I shall shortly bear to you, I shall keep silent."

Shuna's eyes widened, perplexed by his enigmatic words. She looked to Destiny for enlightenment. Destiny took a deep breath.

"Mr. McPherson and I are to marry," she said simply, and saw her sister's eyes widen yet further in shocked disbelief.

"What?" Shuna gasped. "And Jim not yet cold in the ground? I don't believe it!"

"Yet it is so," Destiny said quietly. Shuna's expression relapsed into one of resignation, and she shrugged. "What matter anymore? Life changes so fast these days, I can't keep up with it."

Destiny interrupted quickly, fearful that she might go on to speak of her dead child. To do so would give the game away. "You must see it is for my good, Shuna. As wife to the bailiff, I shall be well housed and fed. And Mr. McPherson is willing to take my child too."

"Your child?" Shuna repeated.

"Yes. He says it is fortunate I have no more than the one. And that reminds me, I take it you've come for your little one. She's safe in the other room."

She glared at Shuna, willing her to understand and act out the charade. Her sister's quick wits were evidently not impaired despite her recent tragedy, for Destiny saw the light leap into her eyes.

"To be sure, I'd almost forgotten. Will you walk down to the village with us, Desty?"

McPherson took his cue. "And I must be away. The master is entertaining friends from England, and I have work to do."

"You'll not forget about seeing the priest and calling the banns?" Destiny reminded him. He sighed.

"I'm a Presbyterian by faith, but since there's no church of mine about, I'll make do with your popish one. I'm a bighearted man, Mistress Regan."

"That will not suffice for Father Clancy," Destiny told him. "He'll expect you to turn Catholic before he'll marry you."

"Will he so?" McPherson said sharply. "That I'll never do—become one of you stupid pious papists. We'll see if a golden sovereign or two will stifle your priest's conscience."

Shuna waited until the sound of his horse's hooves clattered away and then turned to her sister. "If I'm right, you want me to take one of the girls to England after all. Which one, Desty? Which is it to be?"

Destiny shook her head miserably. "For the love of God, don't ask me. I only did what I thought was right. That brute means a chance of life for two of us, but he would not take three."

"I understand, but you must choose, Desty. I cannot make the choice for you."

"I'll think as I walk."

Taking the two little girls, Destiny walked in silence with her sister, but by the time Shuna's cottage came in sight, she still had not decided. The sight of tumbled cottages and the smell of burning wood only served to make the confusion in her brain all the greater. The world was turning topsy-turvy, the old values were gone, and even human life seemed of no importance anymore. Oh, God! How was she to choose between her cherished daughters?

Mick was already prepared for the journey down to Cobh, some fifteen miles away, the family's few possessions packed into a bundle and the stark-eyed Shaun clutching his father's hand.

"Well?" said Shuna.

"I don't know. I'll walk with you toward the harbor," Destiny replied, and with the tiny hand of a daughter in each of hers she set off along the road. No one took heed of the little group as they walked, for homeless peasants strewing the roads with all their worldly goods packed into one pathetic little bundle were a daily sight. Other peasants lay in the hedgerows and slept, exhausted after their fruitless struggle to protect their homes.

It was a grueling walk, slowed to a crawl to allow for little legs, and when night fell at last Destiny cuddled her little ones close to her inside her shawl. She slept little, agonizing still over the choice she had yet to make. In the morning the straggling group continued their journey until at last the islands in the great harbor came in sight. They crossed the bridge onto Great Island and soon reached the port of Cobh, from where the sailing ships left for England—even the amazing new steamship *Sirius,* which only a few years ago had made the first steamship crossing of the Atlantic. Destiny stared up at the masts and rigging, shrouded in clammy mist, and felt chill misery in her soul.

"Now," said Shuna, "you must choose. I know it is hard, but it must be done. Jim's child or the other man's," she added softly, so that Mick should not hear. "There is little to choose between them, both so much of a height they look the same age."

That was true, thought Destiny as she surveyed the little blond and the little black-haired girl fondly. The one barely two years old and the other nearing three, but both so undernourished and thin that they both looked babies still.

Mick left them, taking Shaun with him to the harbor master's office. In a moment all would be settled and the family would board the tall ship lying at anchor. Destiny raised her eyes heavenward, praying for a signal, but from on high came only the screech and whoop of seagulls.

"No matter who their father, each one is precious to me," she said with difficulty, choking on the tears in her throat. "I cannot choose. Let me close my eyes and you put the girls by me. Then you must take the one I touch."

Shuna nodded. Destiny closed her eyes and prayed. She heard movements. Shuna spoke.

"There is a daughter either side of you, Desty; raise one hand and touch one."

Destiny hovered, feeling her arms rooted to her sides. Which hand? The left—they say the left hand does the devil's work, and this was a wicked deed, to banish one's own child. Her left fingers twitched and fell still.

No, the right hand, the hand of God. This deed must be done with God's blessing or she could never face entering church and the confessional again. Her right hand moved, rose, and fell on a tangled head of hair. She opened her eyes.

"Kate it is," said Shuna, taking the little blond child's hand in her own. "Then make your good-byes quickly,

Desty, and be gone. It is not good to linger, and you know I will care for her as for my own."

"I know it," Destiny replied huskily. "God bless you both, and Godspeed."

Snatching up the child, she kissed her and then handed her back to Shuna, tears blinding her eyes. Then, grabbing Rosanna's hand, she turned to go, running and stumbling across the greasy cobblestones.

"I'll get word to you," she heard Shuna call, but she neither looked back nor waved. The deed was done. She had cast a child of her own blood out of her life, perhaps forever.

Eight

On the steep mountain road back on the mainland, Destiny did look back once, down over the harbor to the island. Through the mist she saw dimly a great ship, its sails billowing in the cold breeze, slipping down toward the open sea, and guessed it was the one which bore her trusting fair-haired child toward a new life. God grant it would be one of ease after the little one's early wretched start in life.

By turns she carried the fatigued Rosanna or set her to walk a little, and three full days elapsed between Destiny's leaving and her return to Ballymachree. It was nearing night when she entered the village, and its air of desolate misery made her shiver. It was like a village of the dead. Her own humble cottage offered a semblance of peace as she entered and laid Rosanna to sleep.

That night the air was filled with the sound of distant music. From her window Destiny could see the lights ablaze at the uncurtained windows of the hall. The master was entertaining his guests, his mind untroubled by the miseries his tenants suffered.

"God blast and damn you!" Destiny muttered to herself. "The likes of us can all work and fret and die so long as you have the money to eat, drink, and be merry. We can lose our husbands and our children so you can keep your horses and your servants. God damn your soul, Conal Carmichael!"

The ache in her heart kept sleep from her eyes that night. The path was clear now, be it for good or evil. She was to marry the mean-minded McPherson, if he did not change his mind.

She told none of the remaining villagers of her marriage, but by the Sunday they all knew. Destiny sat at the back of the church, her shawled head lowered, and heard Father Clancy announce the forthcoming nuptials of the bailiff and herself. Startled faces turned to look at her and then away quickly, and afterward in the porch she heard the muttered comments.

"She's a sly one, no sooner buries one husband than she sets her cap at a second, and he halfway to a gentleman at that," she heard an old gossip say.

"She'll not want for food nor clothes again," the gossip's companion replied, and then, the pair of them catching sight of her, they fell silent. Destiny felt no urge to scold them. After all, they were right. No other man in the village would she have taken to husband after Jim, but marriage to the Carmichael bailiff was different—it represented security, for herself and Rosanna. Holding her head high, she pulled her shawl off her head and led Rosanna toward the churchyard gate. Behind her she heard Father Clancy's voice call.

"Mistress Regan! A moment, if you please."

She waited as the plump-faced priest hurried down the path toward her. He stood until a knot of curious villagers had passed out of earshot.

"Destiny, my dear, I wanted to be sure. This marriage of yours to Mr. McPherson—is it really what you want? What I mean is, he's not forcing you to it against your will, is he? I would not consider performing the ceremony and bestowing the sacrament upon it if he was."

"No, Father. I have agreed to it."

"So soon after your husband's death?"

"These are wild days, and wicked, Father. I must do what is best."

The priest cocked his head to one side. "Are you certain it is best, my dear, for your little ones especially? McPherson is . . . well, a hard man. To be honest, I'm surprised that a bachelor of his age should consider taking on a woman with two children. He's a powerful man, set in his ways, and may be hard to live with. It's not for me to interfere if you've set your mind to it, but I had to be sure there was no coercion. And he a heathen and all."

"He is to turn Catholic, is he not, Father? He was to speak to you about it."

The priest's eyes slid away. "Ah, we have come to an agreement, Mr. McPherson and I. Just so long as you are agreeable to this wedding."

"I marry of my own free will, Father. And," she added, suddenly conscious that the priest might speak to McPherson of the two children, "I have but one child now. Rosanna here," she said, drawing the dark child closer to her.

"And Kate? What of Kate?" the priest asked. "Dear heaven, did you lose your poor child too? And your sister her little girl?"

"I lost her," Destiny agreed. It was as near as she could come to lying to the priest, and in a way it was true.

"God bless you and console you in your sorrow," murmured Father Clancy, making the sign of the cross in the air. "Such tragic times we live in. I hope your new union will bring you greater happiness, my dear."

"So do I, Father."

She was aware of his speculative gaze upon her back as she hurried away, his curiosity aroused as to her real motives in taking such an unprecedented step as to marry a man so well-known for his cold brutality. Let them think what they would, all of them. Surely McPherson would not ill-treat his own wife and stepchild.

It did not appear so, for over the next couple of weeks he called at the cottage occasionally, making no demand upon her and each time bringing a small gift of food. Once it was a hunk of cheese such as Destiny had not seen in years. As soon as he was gone, she and the child fell upon it hungrily, devouring every last crumb of it in minutes. An hour later they were both very sick, their stomachs retching violently from the unaccustomed rich food. Thereafter Destiny shared out McPherson's gifts more cautiously.

One morning, crisp and clear with the promise of spring, McPherson came with a loaf of fresh white bread. Destiny's eyes widened. Bread was the food of the rich, something she had never tasted. McPherson laid it down and surveyed her coolly.

"The last banns are on Sunday, Destiny. We can be married next week."

"Oh?" Her eyes lingered on the crusty bread, longing to savor it. Rosanna poked an inquiring finger into the strange object, and Destiny pulled her hand away.

"What day shall it be?" McPherson asked.

" 'Tis all one to me. Any day you choose will suit me fine."

"Monday, then," he said with decision. "No point in wasting time. Then you can move into my house."

"Monday?" Destiny repeated. "Oh, I must have time to pack my belongings."

"What belongings?" He spread his arms. "What have you got to pack, for heaven's sake, since you have only a stool, a blanket, an old iron kettle? You'll need none of these things in my house."

"Too poor for you they may be, but they're my dowry, Mr. McPherson. 'Twas my mother's stool and her kettle before they came to me, and I'm keeping them, however fine your house may be."

"Please yourself. Monday, then."

Abruptly he was gone. Destiny tore the bread apart, tasted a small piece, and gave another to the child. Rosanna ate it quickly, but Destiny savored its soft freshness and the feel of its crunchy crust on her tongue. It was delicious. The dullness inside her began to change to a hopeful yearning. Soon they would eat bread every day. Soon she would be the wife of a wealthy man. Well, not so wealthy as Mr. Carmichael perhaps, but a rich man compared to the villagers of Ballymachree. If McPherson continued to be undemandingly generous, life could become very pleasant indeed.

Rosanna was no longer in the room. Destiny saw her leaving the yard by the gate McPherson had left unlatched. She followed the child out into the lane.

"Come back inside, macushla. I don't want you straying."

Rosanna gave her an impish smile and scampered away up the lane. Picking up her skirts, Destiny ran after her, laughing. It was good to see an air of liveliness about the child again after so long—that was what a bit of food could do. The little one darted and turned to elude her, and Destiny played the game gladly. So engrossed was she in the game that she did not hear the sound of galloping hoofbeats until they were close on top of her.

It was Conal Carmichael, his black curls flying in the wind and his coattails flapping, his face dark and thunderous. He spurred on his horse as though unaware of the two figures in the lane ahead of him. Destiny stood riveted, staring at the grimly handsome face of the man she hated and yet who stirred her blood as no other man had ever done. He and she both became aware of the situation at the same moment.

"Out of my way, woman!" he yelled, crouching low in the saddle.

"Rosanna!" Destiny shrieked, realizing the lane was too narrow for the three of them. She flung herself on the child, rolling over in the mud toward the wall, the child in her arms, just as Conal crashed by. She felt the breath of air from the horse's hooves fan her face.

"You devil!" she shouted after him. His only reply was a coarse laugh and a crack of the whip as he spurred his horse on. Destiny sat upright slowly.

Rosanna was unharmed, but Destiny swore under her breath at Conal's merciless selfishness. In his haste, he could have killed the two of them, and he obviously cared not a jot. Peasants such as they were expendable, just as Jim and all the others had been.

A way downhill she could see his distant figure as he veered off the lane, leaped up the grass bank, and headed toward the woods. Would he there chance upon some other unwary maid as he had done once before? God, how she hated and despised Conal Carmichael! Shaking with shock and rage, she carried the child back to the cottage.

Two days later Destiny went to draw water at the village pump. The little square was lifeless, surrounded as it was by so many tumbled and burned cottages. Only a few souls were about, listless and lacking purpose. She was conscious of the way the other women regarded her with curious looks and yet refrained from questioning her. It was evident from their fragmented conversation with each other that they felt uncomfortable in her presence, as though she was no longer one of them. She made no effort to talk to them, to force them to talk to her. It was better so.

Heavy footsteps approached, and she looked up to see McPherson striding toward them. He joined the group and waited until the other women filled their pails and left.

"Destiny, I must put off the wedding day."

She looked at him in surprise, wondering if he had thought better of it. Disappointment filled her. "Put off? How long?"

A flicker of a smile lit his thin face, as though pleased at her evident dismay. "The master sends me to England to collect the rents from the bailiffs there. I shall return in a month, have no fear, and we shall be married then."

"I see." So it was no more than a delay, she thought, reassured. For a moment the tantalizing prospect of security had been snatched from her, and only then did she realize how much she counted on this wedding.

"I see no reason why you should not move into my house on Monday as we planned, or sooner if you wish," McPherson went on. "You can take the child and your possessions there and arrange things as you would wish. The maidservant, Tara, will give you a hand."

Destiny leaped at the offer. To live in a house, arrange it as she wished, and have a maid there to act as chaperon when McPherson returned, until she was safely wed—she could not refuse.

"Thank you. I will. When do you leave?"

"Today." He seized her hand, in public view though they were. "Oh, Destiny! I cannot wait to take you. I have waited so long. If only we could have tonight together, but the master makes up his mind so suddenly."

She withdrew her hand, grateful for once for Conal Carmichael's inpetuosity. "But, Mr. McPherson, you know I am a virtuous woman," she said demurely.

"Dammit, woman, you would try the patience of a saint!" he snapped testily. "I almost had you once, remember, and you made no protest then."

"That was different," she replied coldly. "Now you must wait until I have a ring upon my finger."

"Blast you!" he muttered. "Well, you may call the tune now, my lady, but just you wait and see who is the master once we are married."

His narrow face purple with fury, he strode away from the pump, Destiny watching his retreating figure with mixed feelings. Perhaps she had won her point for the moment, but she had the feeling that the bailiff meant what he had said. He would make her dance to his tune after the wedding.

Later that afternoon she saw him ride by down the lane on his way to Cobh and the ship for England. The next morning she could wait no longer.

"Come, Rosanna, we're going to live in a new house," she told the child. "Let's get our things together and go."

She took the iron kettle and the stool, the blankets, and her one and only knife. The child dutifully carried a few smaller objects, completely unaware of the significance of her mother's words. Reluctantly Destiny left Jim's spade and hoe and grass hook in the byre. She could collect them later. Without a backward glance she left the cottage behind and trudged uphill, Rosanna at her side.

McPherson's house took her breath away. It was a beautiful house, with real stone walls and a slate roof, a chimney with smoke wreathing up into the trees surrounding the house, and ivy climbing the walls and circling lovingly about the casement windows. The house stood high on the hill with an extensive view of the valley below, the village tucked into the hollow and the river winding down toward the city.

And across the fields, no more than two hundred yards away, she could see the big house between the trees. The hall lay tranquil now, no noisy festivities going on, but its quietness held an air of menace, like a cat lying immobile in the grass in the moments before it pounces on its unwary prey.

Destiny walked up the path to the front door and clanged the tarnished brass knocker. Moments later the big door creaked open and a pale-faced girl of about fifteen stood there blinking bemusedly.

"I'm Mistress Regan and this is my daughter, Rosanna," Destiny said proudly. "Mr. McPherson has probably told you to expect us."

"But he said Monday," the girl protested feebly, flapping her hands and then screwing them up in her dirty cotton apron. "I wasn't expecting you yet."

"No matter. He said I could come when I was ready," Destiny said, stepping over the threshold. The girl retreated before her, obviously ill-at-ease.

"Like I said, you weren't expected yet, Mistress Regan, and the house is not ready."

Destiny could see that. The stone-flagged floor of the hall and the kitchen beyond were thick with dust, the windows cloudy with grime. It would have been a pleasant, comfortable house but for its air of neglect, the copper pans tarnished and the jugs and bowls unwashed and covered in grease. The girl hovered, uncertain.

"I'm Tara, maid to Mr. McPherson, and my mother kept house for him until she took sick. I haven't had time to clean up yet."

"What were you doing when I came?"

"Feeding the cat." Tara jerked a thumb toward a doorway. Destiny went in. In a large parlor, comfortably furnished with a horsehair sofa and deep armchairs and a large mahogany table, she saw a half-grown kitten lapping a saucer of milk on the hearth rug. "I found him outside.

He was half-starved," Tara explained, her dark eyes wide with fear. It was evident she expected reproach from the new mistress.

"Well, never mind. Find bucket and mop and a broom and we'll set about cleaning the place up," said Destiny, setting down her possessions. Tara's eyes widened further.

"You'll help?" she said in surprise.

"Why not? I want a home fit to live in, and it's a shame to see such a fine place so filthy," her mistress replied. "Give the child some milk too, and then we'll set about it."

By evening Destiny and Tara sat at the big deal table in the kitchen to eat bread and cheese and cold pork, and Destiny felt a sense of achievement. Hours of scrubbing and polishing had brought a sparkle to the house so that now it looked cared for, a house fit for a king. It had given her untold pleasure to dust the beautiful china and polish back a radiance into the brass and copper ornaments. As mistress of the house she would cherish it and leave McPherson no room for reproach.

McPherson's bedroom with its huge feather bed covered with a chintz counterpane she declined to occupy. Not yet, she told herself. For the time being she would share the smaller upstairs room where Tara slept. Two truckle beds, one of them the recent housekeeper's, would suffice for now.

Tara washed hastily in the cold water on the washstand and then knelt by the bed.

"I'll just say my prayers," she muttered apologetically.

"And I," replied Destiny. Rosanna was already soundly asleep in the bed, her tiny face contented at last. Destiny knelt and closed her eyes. It was a long time now since she had prayed, for heaven had long ago seemed to close its ears to her entreaties. But she should offer thanks for her new fortune.

"Dear God, bless us now in our new life. Let us be happy at last. Let it be the right choice I have made."

Within minutes of climbing into bed she heard Tara's deep breathing change to snores, and minutes later she too was asleep.

The sun's radiance woke her, dancing through the

newly cleaned window and casting its rays across the bed. She opened the window and looked out. The air smelled fresh and alive, full of the promise of spring and new life. She felt her heart gladden, and experienced an unaccustomed sense of optimism and hope.

"Up, Tara! Come on, Rosanna! There's much to be done," she sang out to the sleeping pair. Tara grunted and rolled over, and Destiny went downstairs to poke up the fire and put water on to boil. No sooner was the water bubbling in the caldron than she was startled by the bang of the knocker on the front door. Tara not being down yet, Destiny went to answer.

Father Clancy stood there, his pale eyes wide in concern. "Mistress Regan, may I come in?"

She led the way to the kitchen, puzzled by his appearance this early in the morning. Seating himself at the table, the priest withdrew a folded paper from his cassock pocket.

"I had difficulty finding you yesterday, but I learned your whereabouts at last. I have a letter for you. Now, Destiny, my dear, why did you tell me Kate was dead? Why didn't you tell me you'd sent her to England?"

Nine

Destiny could only stare at the priest uncomprehendingly. He knew about her deception over Kate! She seized the chair back and stood there swaying.

"Come, now, sit down and tell me about it," Father Clancy said kindly, "and then I'll read you the letter."

"Letter? But who could be writing to me? I know no

one who can write," Destiny said bemusedly. "I don't understand, Father."

"Let me explain. Your sister, Mistress Colgan, had someone write a letter for you, and she had it sent to me, so that I could read it to you. Now, tell me about Kate."

"I didn't say she was dead," Destiny said defensively. "You jumped to that conclusion, and I didn't tell you otherwise."

"But why, Destiny? It's not like you to prevaricate."

She knotted her fingers together tightly. It was no use. She could not lie to him. "Because I thought sending her to England with Shuna would give her a better chance than staying here. And because Mr. McPherson would only marry me if I had only one child."

"I see." There was no reproach in the priest's tone. "So it would be best for you if he never knew of Kate. But tell me, Destiny, whose child is she?"

"Why, mine of course!"

"Posing as Shuna's, I know. But I mean, who was her father? Is she your first- or second-born child?"

Destiny remembered her confession of long ago. Of course he knew she bore Conal Carmichael's child, but he evidently did not know which of her daughters it was, the dark or the fair one. She must be certain.

"Did you not write it down at the time you baptized my babies?"

He blinked. "It appears I did not, or only that I baptized a daughter to Jim and Destiny Regan. No more."

"Then it matters little now, does it, Father? To me they are both beloved children, and I prefer it to be forgotten that they had different fathers."

He shrugged. "True, their parentage is of little consequence now. But I fear the news I bring you in this letter may bring you sorrow. Prepare yourself, my dear."

Destiny had almost forgotten the letter. She sat up, eager and yet apprehensive at his words. "What does Shuna say?"

"I'll read it to you. 'My dear sister, 'Tis sad I am to tell you such sorrowful news, but I must. Nothing but ill has befallen us since we set foot in Liverpool. Mick found us a place in a lodging house run by a Mr. Jacob, but all the people there were poor and looking for work like us. Some of them were very sick of the ship fever, and first Shaun and then I caught it. I am sick abed now as my friend writes. Mick, God rest his soul, was set upon by a gang of ruffians in an alley and sorely beaten and robbed. He died in my arms the next day.'"

"God have mercy!" Destiny exclaimed in horror. "Mick murdered and Shuna ill abed!"

"'Tis a terrible thing," said Father Clancy, crossing himself. "May God have mercy on Michael Colgan's soul. Liverpool is a city of sin and vice, I hear. Let me read on. 'Shaun was with Mick in the alley, and I have not seen him since. I fear the murderers killed him too.

"'Now I am alone but for my friend Big Nick. He speaks English in a strange tongue, but he can write, and so he is writing this letter to you for me. I shall send it to Father Clancy.

"'Kate is with me yet, but I fear she has caught the sickness from me. Big Nick has promised to look after her, but I fear for her little life. I cannot feed her, for I have no money, and the child grows weak and thin and the fever is high upon her. Forgive me, Desty, for I did my best. God bless and keep you. Your loving sister, Shuna.' There the letter ends, with a cross and 'Shuna, her mark' written in the corner," the priest concluded.

He refolded the letter and handed it to a benumbed Destiny just as Tara entered the kitchen leading Rosanna by the hand. She stared at the priest.

"Father Clancy!" she exclaimed. "Why are you here? Is it to remind us it's nearly time for our Easter duties?"

"That, my child, and to bring a message for Mistress Regan."

Destiny was not listening to this interchange. Her mind was racing. If Shuna and Kate were alone and ill, she must get to them and bring them home, whatever the consequences might be. She could not leave her sister and child to die.

But at the moment she had not enough money even to reach them, let alone to bring them home. The fare to England would suffice to start with. She fingered the coins folded in a piece of material and tied by a string about her waist. Not enough.

"Father, could I talk to you alone," she urged, drawing him by the sleeve out into the hall.

"What is it, my child?"

"Can you lend me a few shillings to get to England? I must go to Shuna and Kate. I promise I'll pay you back, somehow."

He looked at her sternly. "Destiny, I am not given to encouraging borrowing—"

"But, Father! I'm desperate! You wouldn't have me abandon my own sister and child in their hour of need! You've read the letter—they could be dying! Please, Father, oh, please!"

He considered for a moment, and then reached into his pocket. "Here, I'll let you have two shillings of my own, for I cannot sanction the giving of church money. Repay me when you can. I can do no more."

"Bless you, Father!" She took the money and saw him out of the door, then rushed back to the kitchen, where Tara was feeding bread soaked in milk to Rosanna.

"Tara, did Mr. McPherson leave you money to buy food?" she demanded.

"He did. There's ten shillings in the cupboard he said I was to give you when you came."

"Then give it me now." Tara put down the spoon and opened a cupboard, took out a pottery dish, and extracted the coins, which she handed to Destiny unquestioningly.

"Here they are, mistress."

Destiny made a quick calculation. With Jim's three shillings and the priest's two, she still needed five shillings for the ship fare. She handed five shillings back to Tara.

"Here, keep this for food for the two of you. Now, sit down and listen to me. You know I am soon to be mistress here?"

Tara nodded.

"And that I could have my pick of any girl in the village as my maid?"

Tara's eyes widened. "You wouldn't dismiss me, mistress, would you? I'm strong and willing and I'm used to the work here."

"I need a girl who is capable of keeping the house sparkling clean, capable of minding babies..."

"That I can do, mistress. I've helped with seven little brothers and sisters before they died."

"Capable of running the house alone, if need be, and still keeping things as neat and orderly as if I was still here," Destiny went on sternly.

"Oh, I can, mistress! I promise I won't let it get as bad as it was again! Oh, please keep me on! We need the money, or 'tis desperate we'd be."

"Do you think you could cope with the house and Rosanna on your own?"

"To be sure, mistress! The baby is sweet as an angel and no trouble at all. I'd manage fine!"

"And have you a discreet tongue in your head? Can you keep secrets?" Destiny added, seeing the girl's puzzled look.

"Oh, that I can! That is," she muttered as an afterthought, "so long as it won't get me in trouble with the master. He has a powerful bad temper when he's aroused."

"Take care, Tara," Destiny scolded her. "Do not speak ill of the master to your future mistress."

"I'm sorry! I didn't mean to!" Tara's white face told of her fear. Destiny knew she could trust the girl.

"Then listen. I have pressing business to attend to which may take me away for some days. A week, perhaps, possibly longer, but I shall return before the master. I want you to take care of Rosanna and carry on cleaning the house, take down the curtains and wash them, and do all you can to have the place ready by the time I return to prepare for the wedding. Can you do it, and at the same time tell no one?"

"I can, mistress."

"Do this faithfully for me and you shall remain my maid. Is that understood?"

"Yes. When do you go?"

"Today."

She was glad that Tara made no protest, accustomed as she undoubtedly was to accepting McPherson's instructions without question. Destiny felt no qualms about taking his money as she kissed Rosanna and set off toward the city and the Cobh road. After all, she was as good as his wife now. The money had been left for her.

As she passed through the village, no one took any undue notice of her. Dressed as she was in just her thick black shawl and carrying no other baggage, she drew no attention. Out onto the city road, then through its paved streets and out onto the Cobh road she went, thinking how full of hope she had been for Kate when they traveled this way only a few weeks ago.

That night Destiny slept in a barn by the roadside. The hay was warm and she was not the only refugee seeking shelter there. An old woman with a youth of fourteen or so lay snoring at the far end, but they were still sleeping when Destiny woke at dawn and set off on the road again. Only once did anyone accost her, a group of men playing pitch-and-toss on the roadside, and even their teasing was desultory.

"You shouldn't be out alone, girleen, a pretty thing like you," one of them called.

"Need a strong man to take care of you, mistress?" another laughed, but she knew it was all banter. Not one of them, judging by their haggard, half-starved faces, had the strength to lay a finger upon her.

The road down to the port was long and steep, and by the time the tall masts of the ships came in sight Destiny was footsore and hungry, for she had eaten nothing since leaving McPherson's house and drunk nothing but a cupped handful of water from a stream.

There were not so many people on the cobbled quay as there had been the day Shuna left, but still quite a number stood about bidding good-bye to relatives and gathering their few possessions to board ship. Destiny made her way to the packet company's office.

"One ticket to Liverpool, sir," she said to the small gray-haired man behind the counter.

He looked at her quizzically. "You traveling alone?"

"I am."

He consulted a sheet of paper. "I've already got a full complement of passengers for today, but if it's only one, I can squeeze you in. Deck passenger?"

"Is that the cheapest fare?"

"It is. More to go in the saloon. Ten shillings on deck. The wind's blowing up, and it's likely to rain, but you find shelter where you can. Under the tarpaulins, if there's room left."

Destiny paid and thanked him, then joined the line of people filling up the gangway of the ship. The deck was already crowded. Under the tarpaulins spread across the deck was a herd of lowing cows. Sailors were allowing a few women with small children to occupy the little space left under shelter, but the men were obliged to remain in the open. From somewhere belowdecks Destiny could hear the sound of squealing, terrified pigs. She huddled near a corner of the tarpaulin where the wind might be less biting, and drew her threadbare shawl tightly about her.

It was an hour before the deck was eventually crammed tight with passengers and the ship set sail. Destiny watched the familiar outline of the buildings on shore as they slipped past and out of sight. Other passengers crowded at the ship's rail, waving good-bye to family and friends, their eyes filled with tears. Destiny felt pity for them, driven by hunger to leave their loved ones behind, their gaunt faces all expressing the sorrow and despair she herself experienced. Pray God she might be successful in her mission and find her sister and child safe!

As the ship entered the open sea, the mass of screeching seagulls abandoned their pursuit and turned back. Destiny felt the rise and fall of the choppy waves and felt suddenly very vulnerable in these strange surroundings, parted from home and from firm land beneath her feet. As night fell a slanting rain came with it, heavy and persistent. All the gray faces about her looked wet and miserable. One woman sobbed quietly.

The wind blew up stronger, and with it the ship heaved and tossed. Before long passengers began to look queasy, and a woman near Destiny suddenly vomited, unable to move to reach the railings. The sweet, heavy smell of vomit made Destiny's stomach turn. Then more and more people began to be sick, and soon the deck was redolent of the stench.

A sailor in a blue jersey and sea boots picked his way among the huddled bodies. He was tall, with a rangy, loose-limbed gait, and seemed to be looking for someone. He stopped and looked at Destiny questioningly.

"You on your own?"

"I am."

He cocked his fair head on one side. "Wet and cold, are you?"

She nodded. He bent his knees and crouched beside her.

"I could give you a place in the warm. Down in the saloon. Nice fire there. You could dry out."

She looked up at him. "It costs more to travel in the saloon, doesn't it?"

"Not if I take you. Come with me."

He straightened and continued picking his way through the bodies, some sleeping, some prostrate from illness, toward the deckhouse. Destiny hesitated, then rose stiffly. She was shivering with cold, wet to the skin, and nauseated by the rank odor. Anywhere was better than here.

Lifting her skirts, she followed the tall figure through the massed sprawled bodies and down a narrow companionway into a corridor where a number of low doors opened off. He opened one at the far end and beckoned her to follow him in. Once inside, he closed the door with a clang behind her and locked it.

Destiny looked about her. This was no saloon, this tiny room with its half-dozen bunks ranged two by two, the upper ones no more than eighteen inches above the lower ones. She looked at the sailor warily, guessing his intention.

"This is not the saloon. Why have you brought me here?"

He smiled confidently. He was not unhandsome, Destiny thought, with his clear blue eyes and full-lipped smile half-hidden by a fair beard. "You're cold, aren't you, girl? I have something here to warm your insides." He poured amber liquid from a bottle into a thick glass.

"I feel ill," Destiny said with an effort to lose his interest.

"Then this is just what you need. Here, have a nip of this. Best brandy in France, that is."

His voice was lilting and warm, and as Destiny sipped the fiery liquid, she began to feel more at ease, relieved at being out of the searching wind and freezing rain. She shivered as she sipped.

"Here, you're frozen! And you're soaking! Take your wet things off," the sailor said in tones of concern. Destiny made no objection as he removed her sodden shawl, but when his hands moved to unlace her bodice, she sat up sharply.

"No! No!"

"You can't sit in them wet clothes," the sailor said persuasively. "Let me dry them out for you, and meantime you can crawl in my bunk and wrap up warm in the blanket. Then you won't catch your death of cold. Makes sound sense, doesn't it?"

Destiny was no fool, but the idea of getting out of those soaking, cold clothes and wrapped in a warm blanket was appealing. "Go on, I won't look," the sailor said.

Half-dazed by the brandy, Destiny slid out of her clothes and under the blanket while his back was turned. The bunk was hard and narrow, but the rough blanket was blissfully warm and dry.

The sailor turned back and grinned. "That's better, isn't it? Now, move over and make room."

Ignoring her pile of wet clothing, he pulled off his jersey and unbuttoned his trousers. Before Destiny could protest, he was beside her, thrusting his great body close to hers.

"I'll soon warm you, my beauty," he was murmuring in that lilting voice, and suddenly there was a sharp rapping at the door.

"Williams! Open up this door!"

The sailor grunted and rose, opening the door without pulling on his trousers. A ship's officer stood there, his narrow face impassive when he saw Destiny in the bunk.

"I guessed as much," the officer said in clipped tones. "Can't wait to get to port to lay a woman, can you? For heaven's sake, man, we'll dock in twenty hours or so."

"I'm off duty," Williams grunted sourly.

"I know, but there's such a thing as discipline aboard this ship. I'll not have you laying the passengers because your Welsh blood is too mean to spend a shilling ashore. There'll be hundreds of dockside Judys willing to take your shilling there, but you have to try to find a destitute passenger who'll have you for free. Get your clothes on, man, and come up on deck. And get that woman out of here."

"Sir," Williams mumbled, "I was going to pay her a shilling."

"Well pay her and get rid of her," the officer snapped, and turned away. Williams closed the door, muttering an imprecation. Destiny lay still, watching him.

"Would you really have paid me a shilling?" she asked. It seemed a colossal sum in return for what she would have submitted to out of pure gratitude.

"What matter now? Get up and get dressed."

"My clothes are still soaking."

"I'll take you down to the saloon. Get up," he repeated. This time he did not avert his eyes as Destiny climbed out of the bunk and began pulling on the clinging cold skirt and bodice. She saw the gleam in his eyes, but he made no move toward her. Instead he jerked away and pulled on his own clothes.

The saloon where he led her was a large room crowded with bodies, some sitting and some lying, but it was warm with its glowing fire at the far end. He pushed a way through and led her to the fire.

"Sit here and dry out. Perhaps I'll see you when we disembark," he said quietly, and left her.

The ship was still tossing fitfully, and a few of the saloon passengers were sick, but it was warm by the fire and Destiny could ignore the smell as her clothes steamed and gradually dried out. Then she grew drowsy and began to sleep. Time and again she awoke, stiff with cramp, but slept again till dawn. If only she could have something to eat to still the gnawing pangs of hunger, she would have been tolerably comfortable. Few of the passengers seemed to eat either.

During the day the wind abated and the ship heaved less violently, and by dusk she could hear voices and scurrying activity on deck. Passengers in the saloon began to rise and gather their boxes and bundles.

"Nearly in Liverpool," an elderly man commented. "Only twenty-six hours in all. Not bad for a rough crossing."

Destiny joined the flock of people crowding toward the companionway leading up on deck, and eventually emerged into cold, misty air. Across the deck they filtered, and above their heads she could see the outline of tall, elegant buildings. This was the fine city of Liverpool she had heard tell of.

As her turn came to put her foot on the gangplank to descend, she felt a touch on her elbow. It was Williams.

"Got anywhere to stay tonight?"

"No," she replied.

"Then wait on the dock for me after you've seen the doctor. Right?"

Nodding, she felt herself pushed, and went down the gangway. Well, she thought, at least I've got a friend of a kind in this strange land. I shall not be alone in the city tonight.

Ten

The quayside in Liverpool was swarming with bodies, both passengers trying to disembark from the ship and runners who waited, pushing and shoving, for custom.

"Carry your bags, missus?" they shouted, often snatching a luckless passenger's baggage before he or she had time to agree. One woman, Destiny saw, watched screaming while a youth snatched the bundle she carried and ran off and out of sight with it. Her cries of "Thief! Thief!" went unheeded in the noisy, swarming crowd.

At the barrier an official waved the passengers into a line. They formed up like so many dull-eyed sheep, waiting to be shepherded through the barrier.

"No passengers leave the dock until the doctor has examined you and pronounced you fit," he called out. Destiny fell into line behind a vacant-eyed man carrying a little boy. Just beyond the barrier a tall gentleman in frock coat and stovepipe hat stood behind the window of an office. He, she concluded as she neared him, was the doctor. Finally it came to her turn.

"Are you well? Put your tongue out, please." Destiny obliged. "Very well. Pass on. Next."

He barely glanced at her. She could have been dying of the ship fever and the doctor would never have known, but Destiny's thoughts were abruptly curtailed when a strong hand seized her arm. It was Williams.

"Hello again." He beamed. "Now, let's get to know each other properly. I'm Caradoc Williams, but everyone calls me Taff."

"Destiny Regan," Destiny replied.

"Pretty," he remarked. "Well, if you've nowhere to stay, I know a good boardinghouse. Costs a shilling a night, but it has everything—bed, blankets, a fire, and all. Not running with fleas and bugs like some of them."

He was taking hold of her arm to go. "Wait a moment," Destiny said, pulling away. "I should tell you I have no money for a bed or for food either, though I'm starving. I'm penniless, Taff, not a halfpenny to my name."

He grinned again, fine white teeth gleaming against his tanned skin. "Not to worry. You already know how you can earn a shilling when you need it. A pretty wench like you need never be short of a shilling or two. Come on, let's eat."

Unprotesting, she let him draw her away from the docks and out into the city's fine main streets. It was late afternoon and the streets were thronged with people, beggars cajoling elegant gentlemen for a penny, and fine ladies stepping daintily down from handsome carriages to make a purchase in a shop. By the roadside a man in a muffler was poking up the red coals in a brazier. Taff stopped, reached into his breeches pocket for coins, and gave some to the man. Then he turned to Destiny, tossing a hot potato from one hand to the other and whistling.

"Here, take this and eat it," he said, turning back to the man for another. Destiny clutched the potato and stared. It was beautiful. A perfect, unblighted large potato, such as she had not seen in two years. She broke it open and stared in rapture at its perfect, unblemished whiteness.

"God, how beautiful!" she breathed, smelling its delectable aroma as the misty steam rose from it in the cold evening air.

"Here," said Taff, dolloping a pat of butter and a sprinkle of salt over it. "Now, get your teeth into that."

Destiny needed no further bidding, sinking her teeth into the glorious, buttery texture. It was like manna from heaven. Greedily she devoured every last crumb of it, and then leaned against the lamppost feeling desperately sick.

"You gobbled it too fast," Taff reproached her as he tossed off the last of his.

"It's just that I haven't eaten for so long," Destiny explained. She was determined not to throw it up. Potato was too rare, too beautiful to waste.

"Better now?" Taff asked after a minute.

"Fine. Thank you, Taff, that was beautiful."

As the food settled and digested in her stomach, Destiny began to feel happier. Now the faintness and hunger were gone she could begin to think more positively. She tugged at Taff's elbow.

"Listen, Taff. I don't want to mislead you. If you are looking for a woman to spend the night with, I am not that woman. I came to England on an errand, a mission which could mean life or death. I have neither time nor inclination to dally."

He stopped and looked at her soberly. "Now, you listen to me. I did not take you for a Judy of the streets, but I like you nonetheless. I want to be a friend to you."

"Then help me. Help me find my child." Before she could stop herself, the words came out in a torrent, the story of the great hunger, Jim's death, and how she was forced to part with her child. She made no mention of McPherson, only of the grief of a mother who learns her child is grievously sick. Taff listened intently.

"I see. Poor Destiny. Look, I'll make no secret of the fact that I wanted to take you somewhere where I could sleep with you tonight, for you're a mighty desirable woman, Destiny Regan. But now I know why you're here, I'll make a bargain with you. I have two days' leave now until my ship sails again for Cobh the day after tomorrow. I'll spend those two days helping you search for your sister and Kate and I'll make no demand on you tonight. But tomorrow night, before I sail, will you pleasure me by way of recompense?"

Destiny clutched his arm. "You'll help me search? Do you know of this boardinghouse of Mr. Jacob's, then? I know my sister was there."

"You haven't said if you agree," he reminded her.

"Yes, yes, anything, only help me find them!"

He smiled, satisfied for the moment. "It's a bargain, then. Yes, I think I heard tell of Jacob's place. It used to be a warehouse, down near the docks. Robert Street, I think. Come on, I'll show you."

Robert Street proved to be a seedy, rundown side street filled with derelict-looking warehouses. At one of them where ragged urchins were loitering in the doorway, Taff stopped.

"This Jacob's place?" he inquired.

"Aye. Boss is inside," one of the urchins replied, jerking a thumb toward the interior. The boy stood up, then seemed to stumble against Taff as he passed. The sailor grabbed him by the shoulders and cuffed his ear.

"You don't catch me that easy, my lad." He grinned as the boy rubbed his head ruefully. "I haven't traveled the world for nothing."

Destiny looked at Taff inquiringly. "Trying to pick my pocket," Taff explained. "Watch out for that in the city. Sensible folk carry only small change in their pockets. Me, I keep my real money in my boot."

He tapped his right sea boot and went on into the dark

recesses of the warehouse. A ginger-headed man, short and plump, emerged.

"Mr. Jacob?" Taff asked him.

"Who's asking?" the man countered defensively. "I'm registered and I've got no more than my quota."

"I'm only trying to find a friend—this lady's sister, in fact. Mrs. Shuna Colgan and her child. Have you a record of them? Perhaps they're here still."

The man shook his head. "Don't recollect the name, but I'm sure she's not here now."

"Her husband was robbed and killed," Destiny prompted.

A glimmer of memory lit the man's eyes. "Oh, her. Yes, she left soon after with a big bearded chap. Foreigner, I think he was. Strange fellow."

"And you've no idea where she went?" Destiny urged. "Didn't she say anything?"

"Not as I can remember," Jacob said slowly. "So many people come and go here. A hundred and fifty a night I board—I can't be expected to remember them all."

There was a strange wheedling tone in his voice which Destiny could not understand. But Taff evidently did, for he slid his hand into his breeches pocket and withdrew some coins. Jacob's plump hand flew up and grabbed them eagerly.

"Oh, yes! Now I remember! She had no more money to pay a shilling a night after her husband died, so I told her the name of a place that's only fourpence a night. No bed, no blankets even, but it's clean enough if you're not too fussy. The big man helped her and the child, as the lady wasn't feeling too well."

"Where's this place?" Taff demanded.

Jacob looked up at the rafters. "Now, let me see. There's several such places. Was it . . . ? No, I think it must have been . . ."

Taff understood his delay and proffered more coins, which were promptly snatched and secreted in Jacob's waistcoat pocket.

"Lewis's, that was it. Pole Street."

Destiny's heart leaped with excitement. At the doorway

she seized Taff's arm. "Taff, let's hurry! Perhaps we'll find Shuna and Kate tonight!"

Taff laid a hand on hers. "Better to wait until morning, Destiny. Look at the rain, and it's growing dark. And you have no shoes to your feet."

"I've never worn shoes in my life," she told him, but looking up at the heavens and the great silver needles of rain lashing down onto the cobbles, she was forced to agree. No sense in getting soaked and frozen again. Taff disappeared inside and reemerged in a moment.

"It's all right. Jacob has promised me a small room to ourselves," he said.

It was no more than a garret, but it contained a large bed with rough woolen blankets. Taff peeled off his jersey and boots and climbed on the bed.

"Come, girl, I'll not touch you. I make a promise, and rough as I am, I keep my word."

Gratefully Destiny laid aside her shawl and climbed up beside him. He pulled the blankets over them and put his arm about her gently.

"God knows what kind of a fool I am, but I do like you, Destiny Regan. You may think I'm being a softhearted fool, but that's not the truth of it at all. Hard as nails, is Caradoc Williams. He'll want his pound of flesh tomorrow."

"Hard as nails," agreed Destiny with a smile, "and God bless you, Caradoc Williams."

In the morning she could not wait to continue the search. Taff paid Jacob his dues and ignored the plump man's knowing winks and tapping of his pudgy nose. He smiled at Destiny sheepishly.

"First time I've been misunderstood like that. And may it be the last," he added ruefully.

Pole Street did not prove so easy to find as Robert Street, and Destiny was obliged to let Taff pause at last to buy some apples and pears from a barrow. "I'm too hungry to go on," he complained. Then he bought a small loaf, still hot from the baker's oven, and split it to share with her. Destiny ate hungrily.

They found Lewis's at last, no more than a shanty with a tilted corrugated roof and tumbling boards blocking the windows. It was a hovel compared to Jacob's place, too small to house many overnight. Surely they would remember Shuna, if she were not still here.

Inside was one large room crowded with truckle beds. A fat woman was folding blankets and piling them on one bed.

"Mr. Lewis isn't here. I'm Mrs. Lewis," she said in answer to Taff's inquiry. "You want a bed?"

"No," said Destiny. "We're looking for my sister. Mrs. Shuna Colgan. She stayed here with a little girl."

"Means nothing to me," the fat woman said with a shrug.

"My sister was ill, and the child too," Destiny said. "There was a man with her, a big black-bearded foreigner."

"Oh, him. Yes, I remember him. Funny chap. Didn't speak much, but when he did, he had a thick, funny accent. Big Nick, he was called."

"That's him!" cried Destiny. "Are he and my sister here still?"

"No," said the fat woman shortly. "She died of the fever. Next thing, Big Nick takes the child away—to a hospital he says, because she's dying too."

Destiny swayed and felt Taff's hand under her elbow, supporting her. "You're sure of this?" she heard him ask. "There's no mistake?"

"No," said the woman. "Sorry if it's your sister, missus. Dark she was, and pretty, rather like you, but she was sick when she came here, and got worse. Little girl was blond as a fairy—she caught it too, and frankly, I was glad when the big fellow took her away. Gets a house a bad name when people die."

"Do you know which hospital?" Taff asked.

"There's so many of them, and he didn't say. Couldn't speak much English, you know. Funny chap, big and black-bearded and strong-looking, like a pirate."

"Thanks," said Taff, and led Destiny outside.

Destiny leaned her forehead against the cold brick wall and moaned. "Oh, God! My sister dead and my child sorely ill and vanished with a stranger! What am I to do now? Oh, Taff, help me!"

"Don't give up hope, Destiny. There are the hospitals to try. Come on, it's not yet noon, and we've time to ask at some of them before nightfall."

She took his arm, glad of his calm, reassuring strength. Thank God at least she had an ally in this terrifying city, with its poverty, greed, and sudden death. She leaned against Taff's strong arm, glad of his undemanding strength, reminiscent of the days when Jim had always been there to comfort and encourage....

At the first big hospital they came to, the clerk took his time about searching the records.

"No." He shook his head at last. "No record of a child named Kate Regan, I'm afraid."

"Try Kate Colgan," Destiny said. "It's possible she was known by my sister's name."

But no trace of Kate emerged, either there or at the next two large hospitals they tried. Porters and nurses were evidently far from eager to help a sailor and a shabby woman.

"Not here," said one pert nurse in a starched apron and cap, smoothing her hair primly. "Try one of the charity hospitals."

"That's it," said Taff, taking Destiny's arm again. "Big Nick would have no money for hospital fees. He'll have taken her to a charity hospital for sure."

All day they searched, walking the streets of the city and out into the seedier suburbs, until Destiny's feet felt raw from the unaccustomed hardness of the cobbled streets. Taff at last insisted he should buy some meat pasties for them both in the saloon bar, and there he engaged one of the customers in conversation.

"Have you tried the little hospital down by the canal?" the old gentleman suggested, having heard Taff's story. "They take in a lot of Irish who have no money."

Instantly Destiny and Taff were off again. It was growing dusk now, and a mist was rising from the river, where an occasional mournful ship's bell could be heard. Along the canal towpath Destiny shivered. It was chill and eerie here, but she felt a mounting sense of excitement. Somehow a sixth sense told her that this charity hospital would be the end of her search. As they neared it, she stopped suddenly.

"Taff, let me go and inquire alone. Wait for me here."

She looked up at him pleadingly. His gray-blue eyes twinkled.

"Very well, I'll wait, but don't try and give me the slip. Remember you're in my debt."

"I'll remember, and I'll repay," she promised, and left him sitting on a low wall.

A middle-aged woman in starched nurse's uniform stood at the reception desk in the entrance hall of the little hospital. She listened alertly to Destiny's inquiry.

"Ah yes, I remember the big man with the black beard. I was on duty the night he brought the child in."

Destiny's heart leaped. So she was right! The chase ended here. "The little one—Kate—is she well?" she ventured, heart pounding with anxiety.

"I don't know. I went off duty then, and I've only just returned. Wait, and I'll inquire."

Just then a young nurse with bouncing red curls crossed the vestibule. The senior nurse called to her.

"Wilkins! What happened to that blond little girl we admitted last week? The tiny one who was very weak with the fever? Is she here still?"

The younger nurse hesitated, cocked her pert young head on one side in an effort to recall. "Oh yes, the Irish one? She died the next night. Buried last Friday down in the paupers' cemetery."

The older nurse looked back at Destiny. "I'm sorry, my dear. Relative of yours, was she?"

Destiny could not answer her. Vision blurred and feet faltering, she made for the door. It was too terrible to understand and accept. Outside in the cold night air a terrifying trembling seized her and her knees gave way. Destiny leaned against the hospital's unwelcoming cold stone wall and wept and railed against God.

It was unforgivable, to heap yet more agony upon her soul. Hadn't she already suffered enough in losing a husband, a sister, and now her precious child? Helpless rage suffused her, and she grabbed up a length of iron piping which lay in the road and smashed it viciously against the hospital walls, against the iron railings of the park, wishing there were something vulnerable she could destroy to assuage her passion. It was the lot of the poor—they could not hit back.

At the corner a fine carriage stood empty. Destiny seized her weapon more tightly and ran toward it, smashing the iron again and again against the paintwork and exulting in the crash of breaking glass. Then she flung down the piping and ran toward the canal.

All was silent and deserted as she neared the wall dividing the towpath from the road. Taff was not sitting where she had left him. From over the wall she suddenly heard the sound of muffled voices.

"Go through his pockets again, Bill. He must have more than that, a sailor just paid off. For God's sake, hurry, and let's chuck him in the canal before anyone comes."

She saw them then, a group of three men leaning over a prostrate figure on the towpath. She drew back in alarm. Ruffians attacking an unwary man, she thought, and then realized to her horror that the fair head lying there was Taff's.

"Help! Murder!" she screamed. The three men leaped in alarm, let fall the limp limbs of their victim, and fled away along the path, over the wall, and off. Destiny ran to kneel by Taff's inert figure and raised his head on her lap. It was no use. The knife that stood out from his chest had sunk deep. Taff was dead.

Destiny's brain clouded and she felt sick. Oh, God, no! This was too much! Husband, sister, child, and now her only friend! Was there no mercy in heaven?

A sudden thought assailed her. If she were found here kneeling by a dead man, it could look very suspicious. Who would believe a poor Irish traveler had not plunged the knife into Taff, perhaps because of an argument over a whore's fee? The thought sobered Destiny's confused brain.

The money. The thieves had complained because Taff had not much money on him. Destiny recalled Taff's words about his boots. It was his right boot he had tapped. With difficulty she pulled the heavy boot down over his long gray socks, and there, sure enough, lay a golden guinea. Unashamedly Destiny pocketed it. It would more than pay her fare home, and Taff would have wanted her to have it.

She stood up, looking down with pity and affection on the blood-soaked figure, and crossed herself. God rest your soul, Caradoc Williams, for you were a good man, she prayed.

The sound of approaching voices startled her into reality. She must flee before she was discovered here. Blindly she ran, clambering over the wall and away down a side street. Tomorrow she must get a ship home, away from this city of crime and misery, even if it was only to a hollow life of pretense to be shared with McPherson.

Eleven

1863

Conal Carmichael was relieved to turn off the hot, dusty London street into the porticoed entrance of his club. In the cool, marble-pillared vestibule, where a waiter deferentially took his hat and cane from him, he could forget the heat and the flies and noise outside, and the general unpleasantness of London in high summer.

Conal moved on, down the few thickly carpeted steps toward the library at the back of the building, the waiter following silently behind to take his orders when he was ready. In the high-ceilinged library, shadowy and cool with its ornate mahogany pillars supporting the massive bookshelves, only two of three gentlemen reclined at their ease. One, a puffy-faced army colonel, snored contentedly in his deep armchair, unaware of the noise he made to disturb the hallowed air.

Conal chose a leather armchair far removed from the others, half-hidden by an aspidistra in a brass pot. He was loath to be drawn into polite social conversation with another of the library's occupants, for he had other matters on his mind. Mindful of the club's rule of silence, he gave muttered orders to the waiter to bring him brandy and water, and then he unwound his length into the comfort of the armchair.

It was relaxing and tranquil here, far removed from the clatter of hansom cabs on the cobbled streets and the piercing cries of street vendors, and had it not been for the worry on Conal's mind, it would have been easy to unwind and doze. After all, he had been at the card tables until three this morning, playing until sleep dimmed his eyes, in a desperate effort to reinforce his dwindling resources, but to little avail. Two pounds and sixpence was the extent of the evening's profit, not even enough to pay his cobbler's bill.

A frown rutted Conal's brow as he sipped the brandy the waiter had unobtrusively placed on the small table beside him. Small wonder that gray hairs now flecked his temples, he ruminated, constantly troubled as he was by shortage of ready money. Life in London society was expensive if one was to live up to the position of a landowner, but the petty rents he collected from his poor Irish tenants were far too frugal to permit the style of living he desired. The few business ventures he had embarked upon to augment his income had not always been successful, and now playing cards for high stakes was the only avenue left open to him, but London gentlemen seemed to be becoming aware of his uncommonly good luck at the tables, and willing opponents with cash were becoming increasingly difficult to find. Some new means must be discovered to pay off the creditors now dunning for payment of their bills—and that very soon if he was not to retreat to the lonely exile of Ballymachree in order to escape.

Conal sipped moodily. He resented having to scratch around for money when life was really for living and enjoying. This accursed business of finding the wherewithal to drink and dine and entertain, to go to the races and play cards, was damnably time-wasting, and his hitherto friends seemed to have sensed that he was in difficulties, for they grew daily more remote and aloof. Even the pretty young ladies who had once fallen easy victim to his charms now grew more inaccessible, seeming to prefer to Conal's wild wooing the dandies who came laden with gifts of flowers and jewels. He glowered at the aspidistra.

A quick, light step disturbed his moody reverie, and Conal looked up to see the waiter's mild blue eyes surveying him.

"Beg pardon, sir, but I thought you might like to know that Mr. O'Keeffe has just arrived. He has gone down to the dining room."

Conal's mood changed instantly. He leaped to his feet, moodiness at once replaced by eagerness.

"Then order lunch for me, Watkins, and lay a place at Mr. O'Keeffe's table," he commanded, and made for the door. It was months now since he had seen Philip O'Keeffe, and his friend's constant quiet warmth afforded him pleasure. It would be no use approaching Philip for a loan, since his money was always tied up in his various charitable works, but he at least would greet him with warmth and not turn aside because Conal was temporarily in difficulties.

Philip's fair head was easily discernible among the dozen or so diners in the graceful dining room, with its gleaming damask table covers and sparkling silver cutlery. He sat alone by the window, and as Conal threaded his way between the tables to join him, he looked up. There was no doubting the honest warmth in his eyes as he recognized his friend.

"Conal! My dear fellow, how splendid to see you!"

Conal felt the firm grip of his hand and then pulled out the chair opposite him and seated himself. Philip leaned across the table eagerly.

"I didn't know you were in London, Conal. How very opportune that you should be here just as I am here for a few days."

"I have rented a villa in Melton Square for the summer," Conal told him, "but truth to tell, I shall be forced to give it up soon and return to Ireland."

"Short of money again?" Philip queried with an amused light in his eye.

"Temporarily. I suppose it's no use asking you for a loan?" Conal replied.

"None at all, I'm afraid. Your estates are far larger than mine, and how you manage to get through all your revenue so quickly beats me, Conal. You must live like a prince," Philip commented. There was no reproach in his voice, only gentle amusement.

"Not so extravagantly as some, but only as a gentleman should," Conal retorted. "You wouldn't happen to know where I could lay my hands on some ready cash, would you? Only as a loan, mark you, at a reasonable rate of interest."

Philip shook his head and smiled ruefully. "I regret not, but I suppose you have already tried Lathom and the others?"

Conal grunted. "He's out of town, and the others are oddly not at home when I call. I'm at my wits' end where to turn next."

The waiter brought the wine list, and Conal leaned back, leaving Philip to read and select. After all, he could not foot the bill for wine, Conal reflected savagely. Life was bitterly unfair. Philip murmured something to the waiter, handed back the list, and then turned to Conal.

"I'm sorry I can't help you, Conal, but I'm only in London for the week on behalf of a patron of mine. If you've already tried all your friends, then I'm afraid there's nothing else I can suggest. Perhaps you would be wise after all to return to Ireland with me when I leave in a week or two."

But Conal was not listening to the suggestion, for one word in Philip's speech had caught his ear and attention. Patron. A patron of Philip's numerous charities implied a man of means, and one with a liberal disposition at that. As the waiter brought and poured a little wine and waited for Philip to taste and approve, Conal spoke casually.

"And who is this patron of yours, Philip? Some titled gentleman, or someone of our acquaintance?"

Philip nodded to the waiter, who then filled the glasses.

"Titled, yes, but no one of your acquaintance. He is a

Russian count whom I have known up in Manchester for some years, and he is making his first visit to London—first visit to the London social world, that is, for he has been here before only on business."

"He is here with you, then?" Conal asked, trying to suppress the anticipation he felt from showing in his voice. A businessman perhaps, but a foreigner, and new to the ways of society, he could prove an easy victim.

"Not exactly," Philip replied abstractedly, his gaze traveling down the menu card in his hand. "I am staying here at the club, and he is at a hotel with his daughter. We meet daily so I can show them the sights of London and do all the fashionable things. The count is very keen to give his daughter a taste of London life because she has had such a sheltered upbringing. I think I'll settle for the veal. What about you, Conal?"

"Roast beef," Conal replied without looking at the menu, for his mind was busy with weightier matters than food.

"And you and he are here for the week only, you say?" he inquired, trying still to hide the eagerness he felt. "So what are your plans today?"

Philip smiled. "This afternoon I am absolved, for they wish to go shopping in Regent Street, but tonight I am to accompany them to Lady Langbourne's ball. Do you have an invitation?"

Conal shook his head, growling. "No. I think I offended the lady, and she no longer invites me to her soirees."

Philip laughed, a gentle laugh of amusement. "What did you do, Conal? Fleece her favorite uncle at cards?"

"No. Her butler found me in the closet with a parlormaid and told his mistress. She won't forgive me for that, since I had been kissing her while her husband's back was turned, not an hour before."

Philip's laughter provoked other diners to turn their heads in his direction. "Oh, Conal! You haven't changed a bit!" He chuckled. "Always one for the ladies with your wild, dashing ways, and they seem to love it. I never had your winning ways, more's the pity."

As the waiter brought the soup and the two men began to eat, Conal reflected that it was odd that Philip had never married. He was a handsome-enough fellow, even if, like himself, he was in his forties now. Such a conventional, easygoing chap, and comfortably off, it was a wonder he hadn't yet taken the conventional course of marrying and having a family.

Philip's circumstances being of less interest than his own, Conal's mind quickly reverted to the question of contriving a meeting with the unsuspecting and wealthy foreigner. Impatiently he managed to wait until dessert was served before mentioning him again.

"Where else do you plan to take your friends during their stay?" he asked Philip.

"Oh, a trip on the river perhaps, to Richmond and to see Kew Palace. And Catherine has expressed a desire to see the great Crystal Palace. Then dinner with one of the count's business colleagues one evening."

No opportunity for Conal to chance upon them, Conal reflected. Then it would have to be Lady Langbourne's ball tonight. Somehow he must redeem himself with her, but that took time, for ladies whose pride had been hurt were slow to soften and relent. And he had no time to spare. He would simply have to gate-crash the ball and rely on her ladyship's natural breeding not to have him thrown out. And if she permitted him to stay, he could always make up to her later. A snatched kiss and a hasty caress behind the tropical plants in the conservatory, and all would be forgiven....

Conal pushed his chair back abruptly and rose from the table. "I have matters to attend to," he told Philip briefly. "I shall see you at Lady Langbourne's this evening."

"Without an invitation?" Philip queried. "But then, I've never known you to fail in getting what you wanted. No doubt you will be there when I arrive, and then I can introduce you to the count and his daughter."

"I'll leave the daughter to you," Conal retorted. "She sounds a tame and uninteresting creature, from what you tell me."

And he had seen Russian women before, Conal reflected, like the woman acrobat last year at the music hall, large-boned and flat of face, with a low brow and greasy black hair. Philip was shaking his head.

"She's far from uninteresting, I assure you. Catherine is refined and highly intelligent, and I find her company a rare pleasure."

But then Philip did not look for the same things in a woman as he did, thought Conal as he left the dining room. The count's daughter was probably plain and as cold as the Siberian snow, and Philip was welcome to her intelligent conversation as long as he left her father to Conal's mercy.

Emerging from the cool interior of the club into the enervating heat of the streets, Conal made his way back to Melton Square and his impressive house overlooking the small park where children played while their nurses watched. A small girl in a white smock tossed her ringlets angrily as her nurse tried to persuade her to bowl a wooden hoop.

"I want Cedric's hoop!" she wailed.

"I've explained, Cynthia, that iron hoops are only for boys, and little girls have wooden ones. Be a good girl, now, and bowl your own." The young nurse's face was flushed with heat and exasperation, but Conal heard no more as he mounted the steps of number twelve, rang the bell, and waited for his butler to admit him.

Once inside, he ignored the butler's outstretched hand waiting to take his hat and flung it instead toward the hatstand. As it fell to the floor, the butler bent to retrieve it, brushing the brim with the heel of his palm.

"Have my best shoes come back from the cobbler's yet?" Conal demanded.

"No, sir."

"Then go and fetch them at once. I am going to Lady Langbourne's ball tonight and want to look my best," Conal said peremptorily. The butler did not move. "What are you waiting for, Perks?" Conal snapped.

"I was wondering about payment, sir. Mr. Hodgkiss has already sent in his bill, which has not yet been paid."

"Then tell him to add it to my bill and submit it at the end of the month as usual. Don't just stand there, man, for I need my shoes!"

Conal heard Perks's barely discernible sigh as he moved away toward the baize door leading down to the servants' quarters. Insolent fellow! He'd get a well-placed boot applied to his behind if he ventured to remind his master of his debts again. It was a sore enough point without the servants reminding him.

Half an hour later Perks appeared in his master's bedroom with the repaired shoes and the murmured warning that Mr. Hodgkiss would accept no more repairs until his outstanding bill was settled. Conal made no comment, since it had become almost a daily occurrence for Perks to tell of yet more pressing creditors, but he gave vent to his resentment by stropping his open razor viciously on the leather strap, with the result that he nicked himself twice while shaving and swore vehemently at Perks. The butler, to his credit, retained his smooth urbanity in the face of his master's unwarranted bad temper, and Conal grew even more irritable. No doubt the fellow was wondering whether he too would receive his wage at the end of the quarter, or whether he ought to be casting around for a new position.

Muttering and cursing, Conal applied pieces of lint to the cuts on his chin and sent Perks scurrying down to the kitchen to have his best linen shirt ironed and his trousers pressed. It was vital that he should look his best tonight, every inch the prosperous gentleman, and he hoped the cuts would not scab and spoil his impeccable appearance. And all this effort was not for the benefit of Lady Selina Langbourne or any other lady, but to convince a foreign nobleman that he was a shrewd and capable businessman who knew what he was about.

At last, at eight o'clock, Conal looked in the full-length mirror and was satisfied. His unruly black locks neatly tamed with macassar oil, a well-cut tailed jacket and trousers and a sparkling white shirt with a stock held in place by a discreetly impressive pearl pin, he looked just what he had planned—elegant, but with that restrained air of opulence that betokened the successful business gentleman. His irritation vanished as he dispatched Perks to call a hansom.

The evening air was still sultry and languid as Conal

rang the bell of Lady Langbourne's tall, imposing villa and was admitted to a brightly lit vestibule.

Several ladies and gentlemen in evening dress and already divested of their cloaks were gathered in groups, talking and laughing. One of them, a young woman in sea-green chiffon, detached herself from a group and came toward Conal. He recognized Lady Selina Langbourne, and there was unveiled surprise in her hazel eyes.

"Mr. Carmichael, I do declare! I had not expected to see you here this evening." Her tone was cautious, not quite hostile nor yet welcoming, and Conal knew it was up to him to reinstate himself in her good graces quickly if he were to remain.

"But I trust you are happy to see me, Selina, as I am to see you." Maybe the use of her first name was presumptuous, but no one could hear, and she had not objected to it that night he kept murmuring it in the conservatory. Women, he found, usually reacted well to the sound of their names, especially if spoken softly and without a smile. It seemed to betoken an earnestness they welcomed, and Selina was no exception.

"I did not invite you, Conal, but you are welcome nonetheless," she murmured, taking his hand and leading him forward. "Come, let me introduce you to my other guests."

The sound of music from the ballroom swelled as she led him to the entrance and gestured to a couple standing there, a fair-haired young man she presented as the Honorable Ernest Something-or-other and his sister Eithne. Conal could not make out Selina's words clearly above the sound of the violins and piano, but the insignificant appearance of the Honorable Ernest and his horsey-faced sister did not warrant his attention, for he had more serious matters on his mind. He would have excused himself to move on in search of Philip, but Selina beat him to it.

"Excuse me a moment, Conal, but I know you and Eithne will find you have much in common," she said, darting him an impish smile and moving away. Conal resisted an impulse to smack her behind heartily, recognizing it was her way of teaching him a lesson, dumping him with the ugliest woman at the ball, but instead he contented himself with muttering something inaudible to the expectant Ernest and Eithne and hastening away from the ballroom.

Along the corridor that led to the salon he caught sight of Philip. Alongside his friend's tall figure there stood a bearded man, undoubtedly a foreigner, and alongside him was a young blond-haired girl. Without doubt these were the count and his daughter, and Conal drew in a deep breath of satisfaction.

At last. The quarry was in sight. Now all that remained was for him to play the game shrewdly, and all his difficulties could be resolved.

Twelve

Conal addressed Philip heartily, as if they had not met earlier today. "Philip! My dear friend!" he cried, slapping him on the shoulder. Philip smiled and turned to the foreigner.

"Count Nicolai, allow me to present my compatriot and friend, Mr. Conal Carmichael." As the count bowed slightly, Philip addressed Conal. "The Count Nicolai Andreyev and his daughter, Catherine."

Conal returned the bow, casting only the briefest of glances at the pretty, smiling girl and fastening his attention again on the impressive-looking foreigner. Behind the count Conal could see one of the many mirrored alcoves in the house, reflecting the glitter of the chandeliers and Conal's own dark countenance. The count and he were not unalike, he noted, both tall and broad and dark of hair and eye. Only Count Nicolai's more liberal spattering of gray hairs at the temple betrayed the fact that he was some ten years or so older, possibly fifty, Conal reflected. The main difference between them was that whereas Conal was clean-shaven, the stranger sported a handsome black beard, elegantly groomed.

As Conal was turning over in his mind how to lure the gentleman away to privacy, the girl suddenly came to his aid. She folded her fan, a pretty feathered pink one that matched her gown, and raised a finger.

"Philip, listen! A waltz! You promised me we should dance the first waltz together," she said softly. Philip bowed and took her hand.

"So I did. If you will excuse us, gentlemen."

And to his delight, Conal found himself alone with the count. Women could sometimes inadvertently do the right thing after all.

The count smiled as he watched his daughter walk away on Philip's arm, then turned to Conal. "Do you stay long in London, Mr. Carmichael?"

Conal noted his quaint accent, guttural and yet not so harsh as the way Germans spoke. His voice was mellow and pleasant, and Conal answered him courteously.

"For the season only. I have rented a villa in Melton Square." If the Russian knew London, he would recognize it was an impressive address, and just to establish his credentials further, Conal added, "But soon I must return to Ireland to collect the rents from my estates." There, now the fellow knew him to be a landowner too. "Do you propose to spend long in London, Count?"

The big man shrugged. "A week or two only, to introduce Catherine to the social life. She has led a very sheltered life and finds London exciting. But soon I too must turn my mind to business again."

This was the opening Conal had been looking for. Trying to sound casual, he said, "And what line of business are you in, Count? It is possible you could further your affairs while here in London."

"I am in mining," Count Nicolai replied briefly, ignoring Conal's later remark. "Would you care for a glass of wine?"

He signaled a waiter who was passing with a silver tray

on which stood several glasses of champagne. Taking two, the count offered one to Conal, who raised it with a smile.

"To business, sir, and long may it prosper."

The count grunted and sipped the champagne.

Ignoring the implied rebuttal, Conal tried again. "Mining, you say. What kind of mining are you in? Tin, copper, iron ore?"

"Gold mining. In America."

Gold? Conal's eyes gleamed. So Philip was right, and the count was indeed wealthy. Conal indicated a couple of gilded chairs and invited the count to be seated. The strains of the waltz still drifted to their ears, so they would not be disturbed yet for a moment.

"Then you might be interested in a little scheme of mine," Conal said casually when they were both seated. "Just one of several, you understand. I have acquired an interest in a tin mine in Cornwall which promises to yield a handsome return. Perhaps I could persuade my partners to let you have a share in it, a small one, you understand, perhaps a thousand or so."

"What is the name of your mine?" The count's tone was peremptory.

Unruffled, Conal answered him. "Wheel Melinda. Because you are a friend of Philip's, and I am always anxious to do him a good turn. A thousand, shall I say? I think I can persuade the others."

"No." The count's reply was curt, and he made no effort to explain, but Conal was aware of the emphatic tone in the older man's voice. He was no fool.

Unabashed, Conal tried again. "No matter, for there will be countless others anxious to have the opportunity. I could offer you another prospect if you are interested, however, so long as you breathe no word of it to anyone else." He leaned forward and lowered his voice confidentially. The count raised his dark brows in query.

"A small, select consortium of businessmen are about to open a new shipping line, exporting cooking pots and clothes and other basic necessities to Africa. Only a few will be offered the opportunity of investing in this scheme, and I should be happy to put your name forward."

"No."

Conal was vexed. Not only was the fish not biting, but he made no explanations for his abrupt refusals. The man might be a foreigner, unused to London ways, but he was too shrewd by half, or just plain unadventurous. When Conal had made his third proposal and had that too equally baldly refused, he was near to shouting out with rage. Instead, he laid his glass aside and suggested they adjourn to the drawing room.

"I believe there is a game of cards in progress. Perhaps you would care to play?" he ventured, making to rise. The count looked up at him with an amused smile playing about the corners of his lips.

"If you wish, Mr. Carmichael, but I warn you I never play for stakes higher than sixpence. My money was come by with great difficulty, and I have no intention of losing it over a card table."

Conal was furious. The last chance of separating the exasperating Russian from his gold was vanishing rapidly, and it was at this moment that Philip returned from the ballroom leading a shining-eyed Catherine.

"Oh, Father! You really should join the dancing," she said happily. "Everyone is having such a wonderful time!"

"No, my dear," the count protested mildly, "I prefer conversation to dancing anytime, though I fear Mr. Carmichael has perhaps found my conversation less than rewarding."

Conal detected the gleam of amusement in the count's dark eyes and felt wrathful. The man, having refused to listen to him, was now mocking him, and that was more than Conal could bear.

The count turned to Philip. "Come, Philip, let us talk of the new wing you wish to add to the hospital if Catherine wishes to continue dancing. Perhaps Mr. Carmichael would care to partner her—he might find that more rewarding than his business schemes." He turned to Conal again. "To be frank, Mr. Carmichael, I think you should step more cautiously than to allow yourself to become involved in worthless ventures. A little precaution could save your pocket."

"Worthless ventures?" Conal repeated in surprised bewilderment.

"I refer to Wheel Melinda. I know for a certainty that that mine is useless, worked out and dead a half-century ago. I learned this when I had my engineers carry out a survey there some years ago. If you are wise, you will discard your interest in Wheel Melinda as swiftly as you may, before you lose money on it. For my own part, I would not invest in it or any other scheme unless I was utterly convinced of its soundness. As I told you, I have no intention of being parted from my fortune, for I intend to keep it intact for my daughter to inherit."

He smiled benevolently at Catherine's fair head, but she had not heard him. Conal glared at the older man malevolently as the count drew Philip to sit in the alcove, leaving Conal with the excited girl. Conal fumed, unsure whether the count's remarks had been intended as well-meant advice or a stinging reproof. Of course Conal had known the mine was useless, but he had not expected a stranger to be aware of it. The older man was too shrewd and quick by half.

He seized a glass of wine from the tray carried by a passing waiter and tossed off the contents, then became aware of the girl's gaze fastened intently upon him. He scowled. He had no time for young girls brought up in seclusion and whose sole aim seemed to be to watch and comment upon others. If she was giving him a silent reproach for not having procured wine for her, well, damn her!

"Why are you looking at me like that?" he demanded curtly.

"I was wondering whether I ought to wait until you invite me, or whether I should ignore the rules of propriety and ask you to dance," she answered clearly. Conal was amused at her directness, but was about to refuse to dance when he caught sight of the ugly Eithne and her honorable brother advancing upon him. Swiftly he took Catherine's arm and led her toward the ballroom.

Lady Langbourne was just leaving the floor with her partner as Conal entered, and on seeing him, she cast him a provocative smile.

"You are marked down on my card to have the supper waltz with me," she purred, and Conal knew at once what she was after, for he had never signed her card. "Perhaps when we have eaten I could show you the rare blooms in my conservatory," she added with a sidelong glance. "You haven't seen them for ages."

Conal felt the blood race in his veins, for his wild nature never failed to respond to the call. But he was in no mood for trifling tonight, and the promise Selina held out of furtive embraces and a snatched kiss was not going to satisfy him after the disappointment of his encounter with Count Nicolai. He resolved to show Selina the earnestness of his intentions.

"I have seen your blooms, Lady Langbourne, but not the unique rose you tell me you have down at the summer arbor. The sun is not yet set, and there is still time."

Dimly Conal was aware of Catherine's wide eyes watching as Selina fluttered her lashes, veiling her green eyes as she replied. "Ah, yes, the rose her majesty's gardener has specially bred for me. Perhaps, if you are good, I shall let you see it. We shall see, after the supper waltz."

She had understood his message and was not going to commit herself—yet. As she sauntered away on the arm of her partner, Conal heard Catherine speak and looked down at her. Her eyes were bright with curiosity, and he guessed that although she had not understood the exchange, she had sensed the charged atmosphere. Young and innocent as she was, her instincts had been aroused.

"Shall we dance, Mr. Carmichael?" she said, and her gaze still rested upon his face as he took her hand and circled her small waist. She was light and fragile as gossamer to hold, and as they moved around the ballroom, Conal still felt the blood pounding in his veins, a mixture of bitterness against the count and frustration regarding Selina. For a moment he experienced an overwhelming desire to crush Catherine close to him, to make her cry out in pain, to punish her obdurate father, but then the feeling passed. Instead, if he had the chance, he would punish Selina relentlessly once he had her alone in the privacy of the arbor. After her tormenting teasing, he would teach her what wild and violent lovemaking could be. Flirtation might be part of the accepted life of society people, but women should learn that they had no right to lead a man on, and especially when he was in need of a scapegoat on which to vent his frustration. He smiled to himself grimly, aware that Catherine was still gazing up at him entranced.

He was looking down into her small, rapt face when the idea suddenly came to him, and he could have kicked himself. Why had he not thought of it before? Even if Catherine had been as ugly as that Eithne, he would be glad to accept her with her huge dowry. That was the answer! The girl was obviously smitten with him, probably the first handsome man she had encountered in London, so the rest should be easy. The count had made it plain his immense fortune was for her, and she was a pretty-enough little thing.

"How old are you, Catherine?" he asked without preamble. She did not seem to notice.

"Seventeen, nearly eighteen."

She answered innocently and with directness, and Conal gave her his silent approbation. She would do well as a wife, honest and undemanding. Life could go on for him as it had before, and she would never question him. A fire of excitement throbbed in his veins as he contemplated the thought. Easy now, capture the little bird softly, he told himself. A sudden direct move could frighten her out of reach.

"Catherine," he murmured softly, holding her a little closer. He heard her sigh with pleasure. A good start, but how was he to follow up his advantage in a crowded ballroom?

He would have to get her away from here, into one of the many smaller rooms set aside for cards and conversation, but just as the dance ended and he was planning to lead her away from the lights and chatter of the ballroom, the count and Philip appeared in the doorway. On seeing Catherine, the count came to her and took her elbow.

"It grows late, my dear, and I fear we must leave," he said kindly. Conal saw the girl's face fall with disappointment.

"So soon, Father? I was enjoying it so."

"I know, but the hour is late for you, and I have papers to attend to. Besides, you must be fresh and rested for the outing tomorrow."

The smile returned swiftly to her pretty young face. "Ah, yes! We go to visit Richmond and Kew tomorrow. You will accompany us, won't you, Mr. Carmichael? I am told it is so pretty there."

Conal bowed slightly. Despite the moment of inward fury when it seemed the count would snatch her away from him and he reacted as violently as a spoiled child whose precious toy was taken away, he clutched instead at the offer she held out. A sunlit day in the beauty of Kew, which he knew well, would be sure to offer some further chance of pursuing the girl's affections. He would have to play the ardent swain for the day, but the rewards could be well worth it.

"I should be delighted, Catherine." He spoke her name lingeringly and saw the pink flush that came to her cheeks. As he watched her father lead her away, he was not discontented. He had made some mark on the girl, and until he could pick up the chase again tomorrow, there was still the delectable Lady Langbourne to comfort and pleasure him tonight. Without a word to Philip, he went off in search of her and more wine.

In the morning Conal awoke with a blinding headache, a muzzy head, and only the dimmest of memories of a frenetic hour in the arbor by moonlight. As the butler drew back the heavy chenille draperies of the bedroom window and allowed the brilliant sunlight to stream in, Conal groaned and buried his face in the pillow.

Then he suddenly remembered. Unsteadily he rose and splashed his head with cold water from the jug on the washstand and then shook his head vigorously in an effort to clear the heavy, dull ache. Droplets of water flew everywhere from his shaggy head, but after breakfast, when Philip called for him in the carriage, Conal was beginning to feel almost human again. It was essential to have a clear head today if he was to succeed in his plan, which could cure his problems forever.

Catherine and Count Nicolai were waiting by the jetty when Conal and Philip arrived, and Catherine, looking as fetching and fragile as a fairy in her pink summer gown and bonnet, was aglow with anticipation. Conal made sure that it was his hand that helped her climb into the boat and that the seat for the rower was left vacant for Philip.

"It is much cooler here on the river with the breeze," Count Nicolai commented as the boat pulled away from the bank and headed upstream. Conal did not reply, for he was studying Catherine's fine profile. She turned her head and saw his slumbrous, impolite stare and lowered her lashes demurely.

The Thames was alive with craft of every description, and it seemed that half London's population was seeking escape from the hot, dusty streets on the cool, sunlit surface of the river.

Droplets of perspiration were banding Philip's brow by the time Kew Bridge came in sight. It was with relief that he pulled the rowing boat to the shore.

"Here we are, Kew Gardens," he announced as he leaped out and began to tie up the boat. Catherine gazed in admiration at the throng of people sauntering about the great park, which spread right to the water's edge.

"Is that the Kew Palace you spoke about?" the count asked Philip as he stepped ashore, indicating the huge, gloomy building nearby. Philip nodded.

"Busy once, during George the Fourth's reign, but empty and unoccupied now," he commented. Catherine held out her hand to Conal to help her step ashore. He gripped her hand firmly and held on to it seconds longer than necessary, and was gratified to see her warm smile. Matters were progressing well.

"I should like to look closer at the palace. Would you care to accompany me, Catherine?" the count said.

Catherine shook her head. "It looks a mournful place. I should prefer to walk under the trees, Papa."

Conal seized his chance. "You are right, it is a sad place, for Queen Charlotte died there. Philip will take your father to see it closer, and I shall accompany you along the promenade to the conservatory. We can all meet there later."

He cupped her elbow and led her away, giving the count no opportunity to demur.

Philip's voice followed him. "Very well, our time is our

own until lunch, which I have booked at the Star and Garter on Richmond Hill at one."

Catherine found the gardens a sheer delight, exclaiming with wonder at their serenity and unexpected surprises. She declined to enter the humid heat of the enormous conservatory, preferring instead to wander along the many secluded walks and inhale the fragrance of the blooms. The many temples hidden away in quiet corners filled her with delight, particularly the tall Chinese-style pagoda that towered as loftily as the surrounding elms.

"It is so magnificent and stately, I can imagine the royal family once holding court here," she breathed in admiration. Here and there an artist sat painting the beauties of nature about him, while families of every stratum of society walked leisurely about, resplendent in their Sunday-best clothes. As the sun climbed higher, Conal grew anxious to remove Catherine farther away from the danger of intrusion from Philip and the count.

"Kew Green is also a very pretty spot, with its church and old houses," he told her. "Let me take you there."

"But what of my father and Philip?"

"You heard Philip say lunch is booked at one o'clock. We can meet them there," Conal said with an air of finality. She did not argue, and he knew she was enjoying being alone with him.

Kew churchyard also offered delights to Catherine when she discovered that the famous landscape painter Gainsborough was buried here, and she bent to touch his gravestone with reverence.

"I think Gainsborough chose a more suitable place to rest, here in a country churchyard surrounded by the trees he loved, than so many of his great fellow painters who lie in the crypt of St. Paul's," she murmured softly. Conal sensed in her words the romantic yearning that young women so often evince, and resolved to respond accordingly.

"And where would you like to lie, Catherine, when your turn finally comes?" he asked softly.

She sighed deeply. "Oh, I don't know. Not in Manchester's grim gray churchyard. Somewhere wild and free and beautiful."

He nodded. "I share your view, and so I shall lie in my beloved Ballymachree, where my ancestors have been laid to rest for generations." What a hypocrite he was, he laughed to himself. Ballymachree meant no more to him than any other spot on earth, and who cared where one was buried anyway? But the mention of Ballymachree in reverent tones had the desired effect. Catherine looked up at him admiringly.

"You are so fortunate, Mr. Carmichael. Tell me about Ballymachree."

So as he took her hand and led her out of the churchyard and along under the cedars, he described in glowing terms a fairy-tale valley with its impressive mansion, where he, as lord of all he surveyed, was wont to live. Catherine ventured to say she wondered why he ever forsook such beauty.

"Ah, needs must, when I have so much business to attend to," he replied sadly, feeling inwardly pleased at his performance. Catherine was surveying him with compassion now, and once a woman felt this, it made the task of rendering her pliable infinitely easier. She was no doubt thinking by now that such a sad and lonely man needed a wife to comfort him. In case she was not, he pressed the point.

"Ballymachree lacks only one thing to complete its beauty," he murmured so softly she had to incline her head to hear. "If only there was a loving mistress for my mansion, to grace my table and comfort my days, then I should be a fortunate man indeed. But until now I never found her." He stopped there, knowing the value of leaving some words unsaid. The gentle tinge of pink on her cheeks indicated that she understood the rest, and she drew her hand away from his to point out a leafy lane.

"Where does that road lead?"

"To Mortlake. I would take you there one day, for it is full of interest. Did you know that the great Queen Elizabeth's astrologer, John Dee, lived there once?"

He knew the tale would appeal to her romantic young heart, so he told her all he knew about Dee, including the time Queen Elizabeth had the Earl of Leicester take her swiftly to Dee's house to beg his help when a waxen image of herself was found in Lincoln's Inn Fields with a pin piercing its heart. Catherine was entranced, and Conal found himself grateful for the rainy day he had recently been kept captive indoors and had whiled away the hours reading Hall's *Book of the Thames,* which had included a fund of such stories.

On Richmond Hill Catherine stood enraptured by the surpassing beauty of the scene below, the river winding its glittering way among fertile woods and dense foliage. Conal pointed out the distant outline of Windsor, far beyond Richmond Park, and heard Catherine's deep sigh of contentment.

"Come," he said, taking her hand again, "let me show you the Shrew Ash, famed for centuries for its magical properties."

"Is it far from here, for we are to be at the inn by one," she replied, but he could discern the note in her voice that betrayed her eagerness to fall in with him.

"Not far. Come."

On the way he told her of the old superstition about the great old ash tree near the pond. He had read in the book how the tree, in which it was believed a shrew mouse had once been plugged in alive, had thus attained magic powers. Its twigs could be used to touch the affected parts of sick and injured cattle and pigs and cure them instantly.

"In fact, only recently a young mother brought her sick child here, and at the hour of sunrise she broke off a twig and touched her baby with it," Conal told her. Catherine looked up with wondering eyes.

"And was the baby cured?"

Conal shrugged. "I did not hear the end of the story. Come, I'll show you Richmond Green."

By dint of capturing Catherine's attention with anecdotes of the village and pointing at the grave of the famous actor Edmund Keane, and the old gateway which was all that remained of the ancient palace of Sheen, Conal succeeded in making Catherine forget the hour. He pointed above the gate.

"See the arms of England there," he said, "supported by the dragon and greyhound? Edward the Third died here. Henry the Seventh rebuilt it after a fire, and he and his son Henry the Eighth lived there. Queen Catherine of Aragon gave birth to a son here, and Anne of Cleves also lived here. Good Queen Bess herself died here, so you can see it is a historic place."

He felt her shiver and thought it was the reference to death that chilled her, but Catherine looked up at the sky. "It grows cold, and I think we shall have rain," she remarked.

Not until that moment had Conal realized that the sun had vanished behind a bank of gray cloud. Drops of warm rain began to fall even as she spoke. "It must surely be time we met the others?"

"More than time. It is nearly two," Conal replied. "I kept you late on purpose because I did not wish to share your company. Nor shall I, for I may never have the opportunity again."

He spoke roughly, unable to repress the anger he felt at the prospect of losing her before his aim was accomplished. As the raindrops fell harder and Catherine began to look about her for a place to shelter, he pulled her to him and seized her shoulders.

"Do you hear me, Catherine? I have waited nearly forty years, and now I've found you, I will not let you go. I want you, Catherine, I want you for my own, and the thought of letting you go drives me to despair."

She was staring up at him speechlessly, the rain clinging to her golden ringlets so that she sparkled like a bejeweled fairy, and he felt a grim desperation to possess her. Not for her beauty or her body, though they too would be pleasant to own, but for the mountain of gold she would bring as her dowry.

"Please, Conal, I think there is going to be a storm," she whispered. Glancing up, he saw she was right. The air held that heavy, yellowing intensity which threatened a swift and heavy downpour.

Muttering, Conal took off his jacket and flung it over her shoulders before hurrying her downhill toward Kew. She looked puzzled.

"Are we not going to the Star and Garter? Philip and my father will be concerned for us."

The rain was dashing down now, and Conal began to run, pulling her after him. "Too far, and uphill. We'll shelter in Kew Gardens until they come back to the boat," he shouted above the hiss of the downpour. Suddenly the heavens opened as if to spill their entire contents on Kew Gardens, torrential rain lashing their faces and soaking their clothes.

The gardens by now were deserted, and Conal ran toward the shelter of the Chinese pagoda. There, under the wide, curving roof of the lowest section, he stopped. Catherine, panting and breathless, leaned against a pillar while water poured from her hair and sodden clothing. Her delicate pink gown clung closely to her slender body, and Conal found himself admiring her lithe young figure.

No one else was about. Evidently the other pleasure-seekers in Kew had chosen elsewhere to shelter, and Conal took advantage of their privacy. Drawing her close to him, he buried his face in the hollow of her neck.

"Catherine, beautiful Catherine, I must have you for my wife or I shall go mad," he muttered hoarsely close to her ear. She did not draw away, and he could savor the fragrant freshness of her, warm and wet and vital. She would be a delight to possess, he reflected, for a time at least. Even if he grew bored after a month or two, she was the kind of woman it would be easy to deceive. It would be easy to abandon her in Ballymachree on the pretext of business in London, where he could enjoy again the delights of willing arms like Selina Langbourne's—or her parlormaid's. But first of all he must secure Catherine, and her money.

"I shall go mad," he repeated in a croak. "I was robbed of my senses the moment I laid eyes on you."

She looked up a him wonderingly, and he knew the ecstatic light in her clear eyes was not this time for the beauties of Richmond or Kew. Like most women, she was responding to wild, swift wooing and the first knowledge that she could awaken fierce passion in a man. The knowledge of such power made them all a little intoxicated.

"But, Conal, you ignored me when first we met," she countered gravely. "I thought you had no time for me."

"Only because I could not bear to look at you, wanting you as I did. But my desire was too strong for me to go on pretending," he replied quickly, pleased at his own quick thinking. She smiled, shaking her curls so that he felt the droplets flick his face. He was not lying altogether, he thought, for at this moment he did truly desire her, warm and wet and sweet-smelling as she was. Somewhere in the recesses of his memory a flicker moved, a flicker of a recollection of another encounter with a woman, when there had been heat and wetness and the fragrant scent of wet earth. But it was all a long time ago, and he did not try to recall who the woman was.

Catherine's young body was warm and firm as he slid his arms about her, and she yielded to his kiss without demur. After a moment he let her go and stood back to look at her with a somber gaze.

"Catherine, my beloved, tell me you will have me, or my life is ended," he muttered brokenly, and had the satisfaction of hearing her quick gasp.

"Oh, Conal! You must not speak like that!" she cried.

"It is true," he moaned. "If I cannot spend the rest of my life loving you and caring for you and heaping you with all I possess—my lands, my mansion, my money—then my life is to no avail and I might as well end it today if you refuse me."

He broke off with a sound that he hoped sounded like a sob. A slim, damp hand seized his.

"Oh, Conal! Of course I will marry you! How could I refuse a man who loves so swiftly and with such intensity?"

It was all Conal could do not to smile broadly. With candid directness she had accepted him, wasting no time in the mincing coquetry a London lady of fashion would have affected. He had her now, and all that remained was to dispose of the count's objections, for he would be sure to recognize Conal's intentions, shrewd man that he was. The best course, Conal decided, was to attack him via his vulnerable spot—his daughter. Conal he could refuse, but his beloved daughter he could deny nothing.

Catherine's small face was glowing with radiant happiness. Conal laid a finger gently on her cheek. "Beloved, you have made me the happiest man on earth. But I fear your father may not share our happiness, and may even try to stop our marriage," he said quietly. Catherine's smile changed at once to a vexed look.

"Why should he stop us?" She frowned. "Why should he object? My father seeks only my happiness, and he will be glad that I have found the man I want to marry."

"He may say I am too old for you, or that I am an adventurer after your money," Conal said.

"Nonsense! He will be glad I chose a mature man and not a flighty young one. And he knows you are already a man of substance, for I heard him ask Philip, who told him of your vast estates in Ireland and your many business commitments in London."

Conal frowned. So he was right, the old boy had been shrewd enough to check up on him. Catherine saw the frown and smoothed it away with her fingertips.

"Do not be unhappy, my love, for I shall soon convince Papa that all I need is you to make me happy, and he will be anxious then for our wedding. You will see."

Conal felt mollified, convinced that she was right. "Then when shall I speak to him, to ask for your hand?" he demanded, wanting to have the matter over and settled as soon as he could.

Catherine slid her slim arms about his neck. "Give me a few days. Speak to him at the end of the week, if you will. By then he will be eating out of my hand." She was smiling mischievously, and Conal knew in that moment that she would win her way. The gardens lay heavy with the freshly fragrant smell of rain-sodden roses and wet earth, an intoxicating combination that filled Conal with a heady feeling.

And the heady sensation was not only from the flowers but also from his own sense of triumph. As they waited, hand in hand, for the storm to abate, he watched the rain dancing and bouncing up from the ground, and felt a matching sensation of exultation within him.

When at last the rain ceased and he knew the count and Philip must now be coming back downhill, he took Catherine in his arms for one final, secret kiss. But the gilded vision that hovered before his eyes was not her golden curls but the vista of piles of glistening golden sovereigns.

Thirteen

Destiny kicked off her shoes and sprawled in the long, lush grass to wait for Rosanna. Even after all these years of wearing shoes, it was still a relief to kick them off now and again and feel the warm, soft summer grass under one's feet.

She stretched slowly and sinuously, like a cat reveling in the warm sunlight, and recalled those days, fifteen years ago now, when McPherson had first insisted she should wear shoes.

"You may not be used to them," he had snorted in answer to her protests, "but you'll damn well wear them and like them. I can't have my wife trailing about barefoot like a peasant! Whatever you were, you're now the wife to the bailiff of the Carmichael estates, and you'll live up to the standard."

It had not been kindness on his part to insist, to dress her in fine woolen gowns and thick stockings, but simply a matter of prestige. A bailiff was no gentleman, but he was well above the level of the poor tenants, and he was determined to make the difference clear, to live at a level halfway between peasant and gentry. So the intervening years since their quiet wedding had been relatively contented for Destiny, well-clothed and fed and able to watch her surviving child, Rosanna, grow in strength and security.

Relatively contented only, she mused, plucking a blade

of grass and biting it between her teeth. There had been constant conflict with McPherson, from the marriage day itself. Not that Destiny thought life would be supremely happy with him, but his sudden rages had been quite unexpected. The first had been the moment he had taken her home from the church ceremony.

"Take the child to the kitchen, Tara. Destiny, come into the parlor." She had followed dutifully, thinking he made not a bad figure of a man in his best green coat. The door closed behind her, McPherson turned suddenly and struck her a vicious blow across her cheek. Destiny gasped and staggered.

"What the devil do you mean by robbing me?" he roared. "You couldn't wait till I was gone to England to rob my maid, and you not even my wife! I'll have no sneak in my house, do you hear! You will do as I tell you, and no more!"

Destiny stared at him, rubbing her cheek. The fury leaped in her, but she controlled herself.

"What do you mean?"

"You know what I mean! Tara told me you took five shillings and went away, and when you came back, you made no account of it. I'll have every penny accounted for in this house, do you hear? I'm a generous man, but you'll account for every penny or risk a hiding else. What did you do with my money?"

He towered over her, his blue eyes like a madman's with rage and his sandy hair bristling. Destiny spoke calmly.

"A relative of mine was sick. It was my duty to go to her." It was the truth, after all.

"A relative? A thousand more of your poor peasant folk lie sick and dying, and would you expect me to pay for them all to eat? Where did you go?"

"To Cobh." That was partly true, at least. He must never know about England.

The wild light in his eyes began to fade. Her calmness seemed to have a soothing effect on his rage. Instead of hitting her again, he seized her shoulders and shook her roughly. Destiny fought down the instinct to scratch and kick, and let him shake her without resisting.

"Never again, you hear? Nor do you leave this house and go anywhere without my permission!"

She refrained from reminding him that she had not been his wife at that time and was still free to come and go as she wished. No point in enraging him further, now she had promised to love and obey. She recalled how the words had stuck in her throat when Father Clancy was waiting for her to say "I will." For several long seconds she had stood, dumb and powerless to speak, before at last the words had issued from her lips in a strangled croak. The thing was done. Now she was at the mercy of this cold, wild man she had taken for husband.

Destiny rolled over on the grass, still chewing the green grass stalk, and recalled how McPherson's strange, cold domination had manifested itself again that same day, on their wedding night. She spat out the grass juice with distaste as she remembered his tall, nightgowned figure and his sandy hair sprouting from under the tasseled nightcap. He watched her without speaking as she undressed on the farther side of the great double feather bed.

The cold blue eyes flickered as he surveyed the gleam of her skin in the candlelight, and then suddenly, as she was reaching for the cream cotton nightgown laid ready on the counterpane, he sprang at her. Fierce fingers sank into her arms, and with the weight of his body he flung her down on the bed. Hands feverish with desire clawed at her, and Destiny cried out in protest.

"Wait! I'm not ready."

"But I am. I've waited a long time, and I'll wait no longer," he muttered.

"No!" She tried to stay him, but he was too strong. Helpless, she lay back. Again and again he tore into her, panting, and his normally pale-skinned face reddened with lustful exertion. It was not long before he groaned and stopped. Destiny lay motionless, filled with revulsion. As once before, long ago, it had been unprovoked rape, but McPherson had aroused in her none of the fire in the blood that Conal had done. She banished the disgust of the moment from her mind by recalling the sweet savagery of Conal Carmichael.

McPherson grunted and rolled over. "You are my wife

and I shall use you as I will," he muttered by way of explanation. Destiny despised him. He would never be able to stir in her the exultant passion, the desire to respond, that Conal had done.

McPherson was eyeing her thoughtfully. "You're a cold fish," he remarked. "You lay like a piece of cold cod on the fishmonger's slab. You disappoint me. I hope next time you'll find more enthusiasm."

Destiny shrugged. If he spared no time to arouse a woman, how could he expect ardent response? In any case, she felt nothing for this man but cold dislike and revulsion.

"You'll have to do better than that," he remarked, and pulling the covers over him, he turned over and went to sleep.

And so it had continued, Destiny reflected. In the early months he had assaulted her often, always rapidly and without preamble, and always he commented coldly afterward on her failure. After that, he began to approach her less frequently. Once he had even beaten her for her unresponsive submission, slapping and punching her until red weals rose all over her skin, but when he discovered that even such an effort did not rouse her to anger, he did not repeat it.

"God, but you're cold," he said bitterly. "I thought you a woman of fire and passion, and I was prepared to wait and even marry you. You cheated me, Destiny."

After that he relapsed into moody silence, treating her as a servant and with little respect. But Destiny bore it in silence. Fury and dislike seethed in her, but she hid her feelings in return for the security McPherson afforded her and the child.

Nowadays he rarely touched her, either in bed or to lift his hand against her, but unpredictable as he was, she knew he could erupt into one of his rages at any moment and hit her again. She did her best not to provoke him, to keep house well and earn a kind of grudging respect. He was proud of her, she knew, for in the fifteen years of their marriage she had grown to be an attractive, handsome woman who caused many a second glance when she passed by. He clothed and shod her well, and a constant healthy diet had ensured that she retained her strong white teeth and firm, youthful figure. Destiny placed her hands about her waist. Yes, at thirty-five she still had the slender shape she admired in Rosanna.

Rosanna was a lively, laughing girl of rising eighteen now, carefree and optimistic despite her cold stepfather's domineering manner. Only rarely now did the girl relapse into those strange, withdrawn moods of her childhood, when Destiny had found it hard to understand her. After those odd moods the child had often spoken of strange visions she had had, and Destiny had hushed her. The villagers of Ballymachree, no longer having any reason to like Destiny and her child, would have construed Rosanna's moods as evidence of second sight or witchcraft even. Nor did McPherson know; in his cold, practical way, he would have pronounced the child unbalanced. So only Destiny knew of Rosanna's periodic trances, her strange, faraway look, and her incomprehensible words.

But the last attack had been over a year ago. Nowadays Rosanna was perpetually lively, especially when McPherson was out of sight, and she brought a glow of warmth and happiness to her mother's life. Capable and hardworking as he was, McPherson had been glad to seek work for Rosanna at the big house, and today was her first day. Any minute now she should be coming over the fields home.

Destiny abandoned her musings and sat upright to watch for her. Shading her eyes against the sunlight with an upraised hand, she caught sight of the girl. Rosanna's slim figure came toward her, walking with long-legged grace across the meadow. She was beautiful, Destiny thought with pride, her honey skin and raven-black hair contrasted sharply with her white bodice. Rosanna smiled and flung herself prone beside her mother.

"How was it?" Destiny asked her.

"Hard work—that housekeeper stands over us like a hawk. But exciting, Mammy. You've never been in the hall, have you? It's a beautiful house, all shining polished floors and fine furniture and marble statues and a fountain in the garden. And the big hall where the gentry eat when Mr. Carmichael is there—it's enormous, with rafters and a huge fireplace six people could stand inside upright." Her young voice was filled with eagerness and enthusiasm.

"I know. I've seen it," Destiny murmured.

"You did? I thought you'd never been there."

"Once. Long ago. We had to pay the rent, and most of the villagers could not pay."

Rosanna made no answer. She had heard tell of the lean years, the bad years in the forties when half the village had died of the hunger. There had been poor harvests since, but none so cruel as those years.

"You won't remember, but you were there. You were only a baby then," Destiny went on. She did not mention the other baby, the blond little angel whose life was destined to be so short. Not once in fifteen years had she spoken of Kate, and Rosanna had grown up not knowing of her dead sister. Destiny herself tried not to remember her, nor Shuna nor Jim, for the memory was too painful still, and only served to revive her hatred for Carmichael.

"Is Mr. Carmichael expected home yet?" she asked Rosanna. " 'Tis a long time since he was here."

"No," Rosanna replied. "Mrs. Kidd, the housekeeper, says he has no fondness for Ballymachree. She says he spends most of his time in London."

Nor do the villagers of Ballymachree have much fondness for him, Destiny reflected. Since the hunger, when he had used them so cruelly, he had come but seldom to visit his Irish estate. He still exacted his rents, but left McPherson to see to it and to take the money to him in London.

"Did you get along all right with the others up at the hall?" Destiny asked. The villagers who worked there might have been unpleasant to a girl risen from peasant to the bailiff's stepdaughter.

"No trouble," Rosanna answered, "except that some of the fellows cast a fanciful eye at me. The footman, for instance. Now, he's a fine, raring fellow all anxious for the chase." Rosanna was smiling broadly, exhibiting her fine white teeth.

"I hope you didn't encourage him," Destiny reproved her.

"Not I, unless you can call a slap on the face when he pinched my behind encouragement." The girl laughed. Destiny clicked her tongue.

"Such behavior, and on your first day, too. Mrs. Kidd will have her eye on you from now on."

"She didn't know of it, nor would I be the one to tell her. I can handle the lads, Mam, have no fear of that."

Yes, she would, Destiny thought as she rose and brushed the grass from her gown. Rosanna was a fine, mettlesome girl, and it would take a rare man indeed to tame her. But that was the way Destiny would have it. No need for her daughter to yield submissively to a man in return for survival, as she herself had done.

Rosanna pulled the pins from her thick black hair and tossed her head, letting the abundant mass of hair fall free in the breeze. Together the two women walked toward the house.

"Is Father at home?" Rosanna inquired, and Destiny could hear the stiffness in her daughter's voice. Though the girl never criticized or complained of McPherson, she knew the girl disliked him as fiercely as she did.

"No. He's down in the city and won't be home until dark."

After supper, when Tara had cleared the dishes from the table and gone into the scullery, mother and daughter sat by the fire sewing and talking of the day's events. Mostly it was Rosanna who talked, recounting in lively fashion the mannerisms and quirks of the laundry maids and stableboys and footmen she had met, mimicking their walk and their voices so comically that Destiny had to put down her needle to wipe the tears of laughter from her eyes. They were contented thus, mother and daughter, when McPherson's oppressive presence was far away. If only it could always be like this, Destiny thought. When McPherson's heavy tread was finally heard in the hallway, Rosanna rose quickly.

"I'm for bed, Mam. It's late, and I must be up early for work."

Destiny heard her exchange polite greetings with her stepfather in the hall, and then McPherson came in. He flung his riding crop on a side table and tumbled into the chair Rosanna had just vacated.

"Where's my dinner, Destiny?"

"Tara will bring it presently. I've kept it hot for you."

"Presently? I want my meal now, dammit, woman. Go fetch it for me."

Dutifully Destiny rose. Later, when he had eaten and drunk and fallen asleep by the fire, snoring loudly, she put away her needle and cotton and went upstairs to bed. The lamp still glowed in Rosanna's room, casting a thin strip of light under the door. Destiny went in. Rosanna was standing at the window in her nightshift, her elbows on the sill and her hands cupping her chin.

"Still awake, macushla? You'll never be up at cockcrow if you don't get your sleep," she reproached her gently. Rosanna looked like a child standing there in her shift, with her hair loose and flowing, and maternal pride and protectiveness filled her.

"I was thinking, Mam, that's all. Whenever I look up there," Rosanna said, pointing up the hill toward the glen, "it reminds me of a dream I had once, long ago. I was a child, and it was a strange dream that comes back to me whenever I see that hill."

"A dream? What kind of dream, child?"

"A nightmare, I think, though I cannot remember all the detail. All I remember is being held high in the air, as if by some great black bird, and my feet can't reach the ground. I'm frightened, and the bird screams out and makes me scream. And I remember blood and the wind howling, and that's all."

Destiny had laid her hand affectionately on the girl's shoulder. At her words the hand stiffened and lay still. With a sick stab of conscience Destiny recognized the dream, but it was no dream.

"Put it out of your head, my girl, and get to sleep. You'll have Mrs. Kidd angry if you're yawning over your work tomorrow. Don't forget to say your prayers. Good night and God bless."

In her bedroom Destiny undressed and washed slowly, thinking of Rosanna's words. Though the child did not recall it, it had been no dream but a hazy memory of a night long ago, the night Destiny came home from England. Racked with grief as she was over the deaths of Kate and Shuna, and Taff's murder, there had been room in her heart to feel fierce, cheated rage against the cause of all her misery. If it had not been for the callous cruelty of Conal Carmichael, her life would not have been so laden with grief. He was the cause, the heartless, unfeeling brute who had caused the death of hundreds more. And footsore though she was after the long walk up from Cobh to Ballymachree, Destiny could not rest.

She had gone to Tara's room, where the maid snored alongside the sleeping toddler, and the sight of the little one's innocent sleep had made Destiny weep afresh. Snatching up the child, she had taken her out into the night and climbed the hill to the glen where it had all begun. Rosanna, fearful of the darkness and the wind's howl, had cuddled close against her inside her mother's black shawl.

And up there, recalling the tyrant's lustful embrace and her guilty response, Destiny had cried out aloud in her misery.

"May God curse you, Conal Carmichael," she had cried, but the wind bore her words away and lost them. "May your bones melt and rot, and your children be maimed and die! May you never find peace, but roam the world in misery as you have made others do!"

The child had whimpered, staring at her in ignorant terror. Destiny shook the child and held her aloft so that the wind whipped her thin little shift about her scrawny legs.

"Say it after me, Rosanna! The devil's curse on Conal Carmichael!" The child stared and cried out in terror. "Say it, Rosanna! Curse Carmichael!"

"Curse Carmichael," the baby voice repeated, and wept again, flailing her arms about, but Destiny held her higher.

"May he die in agony, stewing in his own blood! He will, we'll see to it, macushla, you and I will let loose his blood, or may we rot in hell for eternity. Cry it, Rosanna, Carmichael's blood in exchange for ours! Carmichael's blood!"

"Blood!" the child screamed, and Destiny crushed the little body to her, crooning words of comfort.

"That's right, mavourneen. We'll have our revenge one day, I swear it. Come, I'll take you home to bed."

Strange, thought Destiny as she clambered into bed and waited for McPherson to come up, strange, but I thought Rosanna had not remembered that night, for she has never mentioned it since. If she believes it a childhood nightmare, then it is perhaps better that way.

After all, Destiny's hatred of Carmichael seemed to have dimmed over the years. Sometimes it burst forth, but only very occasionally now. Perhaps his long absence had mellowed her, for fleeting memories of him were always mixed with a powerful desire. There had never been another man for her who could arouse that same wild exultancy, and now there never would be. A wistfulness filled her. It would be so beautiful to experience a man's love and passion once more, the kind of ecstasy she had almost forgotten.

McPherson stumbled up to bed, cursing his wife for leaving him asleep.

"Stiff as a board I am, after riding all day, and then falling asleep in that damn chair. Move over."

Peeling off his breeches, he climbed into bed. His shirt still smelled of the day's sweat. Destiny turned away in distaste, then felt his fingers fasten on her thigh.

"No," she said quietly, removing his hand.

There was a moment's silence, in which she wondered if he would hit her. Then he sighed.

"Suit yourself," he said, turning over with a crash that made the great bed shake. "If you won't, there's others who will. And from the satisfaction I get from you, it's not worth the effort anyway."

Destiny turned her face into the pillow. He could do as he pleased, so long as he left her in peace and to her dreams of ecstasy.

Fourteen

Some weeks later, when full summer was spreading its bounty of sunshine and nocturnal rain to carpet the valley of Ballymachree with abundant acres of yellow potato flowers, Destiny was amazed to hear Tara's news.

"Married?" she repeated in surprise. "To whom, and when?"

"As soon as possible, ma'am, and to Brian Mulcahy, of course. You know I've been keeping company with him these five years and more," Tara replied with a blush.

Destiny stared in astonishment. True, she had known that Tara went to meet her young man on her evenings off, but she had never brought him back to the doorstep even. The girl was turned thirty now, but although she was some five years younger than her mistress, she had not weathered well. Her body, thin and emaciated when Destiny first came to this house, was scrawny and shapeless still, despite the amount she ate, and her thin, wiry hair was beginning to show strands of gray. It was usual for couples to marry late in these parts, waiting to amass a little money and goods for their home, but Tara was already growing rather old for rearing a family. Destiny was puzzled.

"I'm very glad for you, Tara, and I hope you'll be happy, but why have you not told me before?"

Tara's eyes slid away from hers, and she fidgeted first with her cap and then smoothing her apron. "We just decided last night. Brian's calling the banns right away, once you've agreed to let me come in days only. You won't mind me sleeping out, will you, ma'am? It's not as if Miss Rosanna was still a baby."

"No, of course not, Tara." But secretly Destiny wondered. Tara was never usually secretive, but naive and free with her inmost thoughts as a rule. Destiny suspected there was more to this sudden decision, but resolved to hold her tongue and not pry into the maid's personal affairs. She should be glad of the girl's luck, plain and shapeless as she was. She took Tara's hands in hers and congratulated her. Tara dimpled and blushed again.

"And as a wedding gift I'll give you my iron kettle and stool and all the things I brought here with me long ago," Destiny added. Tara's eyes widened in pleasure.

"Them things you love so much? Oh, ma'am, I couldn't! You scour and polish that kettle every week, though you never use it—I know how you treasure it."

"I treasure you too, Tara. You've been a loyal servant and I'd like to show my gratitude. And I'm glad you'll still work for me, for I'd find it hard to grow used to a new maid."

"Never fear, ma'am, I'll be here at daybreak and you'll never know but I slept here." Tara's eyes glowed with enthusiasm, and then for a fleeting second Destiny thought she could glimpse a shadow in their depths, but what it betokened, she could not tell. Only a sixth sense warned her that there was more to this than met the eye. But then her mind reverted to domestic matters.

"Come, now, Tara, there's the baking to be done. The master brought in a fine brace of rabbits that will make us a splendid dinner, and there's the apples from the Carmichael orchard for a pie. Make haste now and get a good fire roaring."

Destiny was in the kitchen with Tara, up to her elbows in flour, when McPherson came in. Droplets of sweat clung to his sandy eyebrows as he flung himself down on the rocking chair. Tara went out into the yard to empty the pail of apple parings. Destiny poured a jug of ale and offered it to her husband.

"Did you know Tara was to be wed?"

McPherson's blue eyes stared. "Tara? Who the devil would wed a cow-eyed idiot like Tara?"

Destiny laid a warning finger to her lips lest the girl should hear. "Brian Mulcahy. And she's not a bad catch, either, plain as she may be. She'll cook and mend for him well, and she's not yet too old to bear him children."

"Have you sacked the girl?"

"I have not, nor shall I."

McPherson laid aside the jug and stood up. "If working for us is not good enough for her, she can get out of here. I want no servant who's got half her mind on her own house. Get rid of her at once."

"That I shall not," Destiny said firmly. "She's been a good and loyal servant these many years, and she's willing to stay. She pleases me well."

McPherson glared. "Did you not hear me, wife? I am master here and I say she goes."

"And I am mistress," Destiny retorted, "and it is a mistress's responsibility to see to servants. Am I not right?"

Two pairs of eyes glared defiantly at each other for several seconds; then McPherson's gaze moved to the window. Destiny knew she had won, for he would always do as the gentry did. "Very well," he concurred, "but keep the imbecile out of my sight."

Destiny made no comment, unreasonable as his remark might seem. She was accustomed to her husband's truculent manner.

"By the way," McPherson added in a curiously nonchalant manner, "there's a lad up at the hall who needs a home for a month or so. I said he could stay here. I knew you wouldn't mind."

Destiny looked up quickly. There was something odd in his averted gaze, his casual manner, and his unusual generosity. He never invited people to the house, claiming always that this was his private haven where he could put his feet up and relax so long as his privacy was uninvaded. This sudden breach in his normal behavior was curious.

"What lad? Who is he?" Destiny asked.

"Oh, just a boy who helps in the stables sometimes. Name of Liam. He's an orphan and has no home of his own."

"Poor little thing! How old is he?"

"Eleven, I think. You don't mind?" McPherson's eyes

were probing hers, and Destiny was puzzled. Why should her hardhearted husband become so full of concern for an orphan boy?

"Of course I don't mind. We have so little company here. Rosanna will be glad."

McPherson picked up his riding crop. "I'll be off up to the hall, then. Dinner at six sharp tonight."

Orders given, he strode out again, leaving Destiny very puzzled, but she was glad, whatever his reason for inviting the boy here. Perhaps then he would be willing to open the door thereafter to other visitors, to the life and warmth that company brought. This house had been in isolation too long. Rosanna had grown up ignorant of the company of others until she began work at the hall.

But now it was different. Each evening the girl came home tired but excited, talking animatedly and with a starry-eyed expression of a way of life she had never formerly known. Everything thrilled her, from the starched apron she had to wear to the magnificent silver she had to polish. One evening she came home even more excited than usual.

"Such a raring fuss Mrs. Kidd is in, Mam! Everything in the house is to be spring-cleaned and polished because the master is coming home! She's like a crazed hen clucking round after her chicks, chasing us and complaining that we haven't done the job well enough and it's all got to be done again. Lord knows, I've never liked the sound of Conal Carmichael, but I hate him the more for all the work he's giving me!"

Rosanna was laughing, but Destiny could only feel the sudden lurch inside her. Conal coming home, after all these years? Surely McPherson knew, yet he had not mentioned it.

"Is there tea in the pot, Mam? I'm parched," Rosanna said.

"I'll brew fresh. Why do you hate the master so?" Destiny said, rising to put the kettle on. She was curious. Conal's name never passed her lips, so Rosanna's dislike of a man she had never met could not come from her mother.

"I don't know," Rosanna replied thoughtfully. "From what I hear tell of him, he's a blackhearted villain, but my feeling goes deep. Almost as though it was in my blood and I was born hating him. What's for supper tonight?"

She had dismissed the subject, so Destiny did not prolong it. It was evident Rosanna did not connect her nightmare with Destiny's curse on Carmichael that night, but some of the emotion must have remained. So be it. Rosanna had reason to hate Carmichael, even if she did not know the reason, and Destiny was glad she was not alone in the hating.

"Scrub the taties for me, will you, macushla?" she said to her daughter. She placed the bowl of potatoes on the table. Even now the sight of fine, unblemished potatoes filled her with a warm glow. They would always represent security and freedom from fear. If only Jim could have lived to enjoy the sight and the same security...

As Rosanna washed the potatoes and put them on to boil, Destiny shredded cabbage. "By the way, your stepfather has invited a young boy to stay here with us for a while," she told Rosanna. The girl looked up sharply.

"He invited a guest here? Of his own free will? Wonders never cease. Who is he, Mam?"

"An orphan from up the hall, he says. Name of Liam. Do you know of him?"

Rosanna dropped her knife with a clatter. "Oh, no! Not him! What does he want him here for?"

"Why not, girleen? It'll be company for us."

"He's no company, Mam! He's a boy, a small boy, and a strange one at that. He's a cripple, Mam, and not all there, I'm thinking. He makes my flesh creep. I can't stand the sight of him!"

"Hush, now, Rosanna! That's no way to talk of a poor little boy! Be charitable, child, and remember he has no parents of his own. A little warmth and love will do him good."

"You can't love him—he's a strange child, with strange ways. Oh, Mam! Don't let's be having him here."

Destiny tossed the cabbage into the skillet. "Your stepfather has invited him, and that's all there is to it.

You can pay no heed to him if you've a mind, but I'll be glad of his company, once Tara has gone. He can have her bed then.". .

"He's no company, Mam—not the kind you'd want, anyway. He's moody and quiet most of the time, and wild and wicked at others. Lord knows why they keep him on at the hall for all the work he does! I think he's simple, or plain crazy. I don't know why they keep him at all. But he's not the sort you'd want here, that's for sure."

"We'll see," Destiny replied placidly. "You can be wild and willful too, Rosanna, so you've no call to be criticizing a child. You'll learn more tolerance as you grow older."

"Like you, Mam?" Rosanna flashed her a wide, engaging smile. "Well, don't say I didn't warn you, that's all."

But despite Rosanna's warning, Destiny could not help feeling a pleasurable anticipation. It would be so pleasant to have a child about the house again for a time, someone to tend and care for. There was so much love burning inside her, crying out for expression, and so little opportunity to give vent to it. McPherson was completely unlovable, Rosanna too grown to submit to hugs and caresses, and there was no one else. She tried not to let memories of Jim and the fair child with the velvet brown eyes intrude on her thoughts. Both were long dead, though never forgotten.

Strange, she thought, that she had never borne a child to McPherson in spite of his many onslaughts. It was almost as though Providence was guarding her against further heartbreak, and she was grateful. Just for a little while, though, it would be nice to have a child about the house, and she prepared for Liam's arrival contentedly.

But the child she visualized was not the one who arrived on McPherson's horse with him a day or two later. McPherson dismounted and lifted the boy down from the saddle.

"Well, here he is. Liam Dooley, greet my wife, Mrs. McPherson."

Destiny looked at him, wild black tousled curls surrounding a faintly olive-skinned face where black eyes glowed with distrust and hostility. Looking into their depths, she felt a faint stirring of half-recognition, but instantly the feeling faded. He was small for eleven, skinny and leaning at an angle as he stood. Glancing down, she saw why. He was clubfooted. McPherson prodded him.

"Go to your hostess, boy, and bid her good day," he commanded, but the child stood motionless, animosity staring from his eyes.

"Leave him to me, husband," Destiny said kindly. "Soon he'll not feel so strange with us."

"Then I'll about my business," McPherson said as he remounted. "Keep a close eye to the lad and don't let him get away. Above all, keep him out of sight of the hall." So saying, he rode away.

"Come, Liam," Destiny said invitingly, holding out her hand. The boy glared at her but did not move. He was ragged and filthy, his dark hair matted, and scratches on his face and hands indicating that he probably had lice. Destiny ached to get his filthy clothes off him, to bathe him in the big tub and wash that thick mop of hair till it shone. Whoever had had charge of him until now had evidently cared little about his cleanliness and appearance, though he looked moderately well-fed. True, he was thin and small, but not as emaciated and potbellied from hunger as she remembered village children used to be in the hungry years of the famine.

Since he would not respond to her offered hand, Destiny turned toward the house. "Follow me, Liam, and I'll find some bread and cheese for you," she said instead. At the mention of food, his eyes glinted and he moved a tentative foot. Destiny led the way. At the door she turned. He was limping awkwardly toward her. Satisfied, she went in. He followed her into the kitchen and sat, uninvited, at the table.

"Here, now, bread still hot from the oven," she said, cutting a thick wedge from the warm loaf. Without a word he seized it and began devouring it hungrily. Likewise the wedge of cheese she gave him vanished instantly. A mug of milk he swallowed thirstily, then hobbled away from the table toward the corner. The kitten lay asleep on a scrap of blanket. Liam whacked the sleeping kitten sharply, causing it to waken and mew in alarm.

"No, Liam! Don't hurt the puss!" Destiny remonstrated, but he ignored her, pulling its tail hard until the little creature squealed.

"No, Liam! That's wicked!" Destiny cried, pulling at his arm. To her amazement, the boy rounded on her with hate in his black eyes, raising his arm as though to hit her. Destiny gripped him fast.

"Now, look here, young man, we'll have no shenanigans in this house, do you hear?" She wrinkled her nose in distaste at the rank odor of sweat and dirt that rose from his clothes. "I'm the mistress in this house, and I'll have no tantrums here, and no filth. So it's soap and water for you, my lad."

To fill the tin bath would only give him the opportunity to escape, she realized, clinging to the small, wriggling body, so there was no help for it but the pump. Marching him firmly out into the cobbled yard, she held him forcibly under the tap while she pumped. He writhed and muttered but did not speak, and gradually Destiny could see the filth fade, leaving him fresh-faced and with soaking curls clinging about his face. With no soap he was still not as clean as housewifely instincts demanded, but at least the worst was gone, she consoled herself.

"Now, inside by the fire till you dry out," she commanded. Muttering still and casting dark, malevolent looks at her, he hobbled obediently inside. During the rest of the day she could feel his murderous eyes on her back as she worked. This was not the way she had intended to befriend him, but the boy had evidently had little discipline and needed to learn who was in command.

By the time McPherson came home from work for his supper, Destiny was exhausted from watching over the boy. Twice he had tried to let the chickens out of the run into the lane, and it was no boyish mischief that prompted him. There was malice in the child, and Destiny could not understand him. McPherson listened to her comments about the boy.

"Just keep an eye on him and see he comes to no harm," he remarked when she had done. "It's important to keep him quiet and safe."

Destiny stared. Normally her husband would have

raged at such an account of a child's disobedience and bad behavior. "But why?" she asked. "Why must he be here, and not at home? Whose child is he?"

"Mrs. Dooley's."

Destiny knew of Mrs. Dooley, who had died not long ago. Nurse she had been up at the hall. She had never married. "Mrs." was a courtesy title, granted to her because of her position. Destiny bit her tongue and kept silent. If Liam was the nurse's illegitimate child, there would be reason to keep silent about it. He had evidently been suffered to live at the hall and work in the stables when old enough, but discipline he had had none. Whoever took charge of him after his stay here would have a hard job of it.

"Rosanna is late home tonight," she commented as she served up McPherson's supper.

"Working late because Mr. Conal is coming home tomorrow," he replied between mouthfuls of stewed mutton. "There's a lot to be done in preparation."

"Bringing guests with him, is he?"

"A large party, I understand. After all, there's to be great festivity at the hall soon."

"Festivity?" repeated Destiny, uncomprehending.

"To be sure. Feasting and merrymaking, oxen to roast and all. It's not often there's a big wedding in the county."

"Whose wedding?" Destiny questioned, her heart beating faster.

"Why, I thought Rosanna would have told you. Perhaps Mrs. Kidd hasn't told the staff yet." McPherson stuffed a forkful of potato into his mouth. Apprehension seized Destiny.

"Told me what? For heaven's sake, who's to be married? Surely not Conal Carmichael after all these years?"

Surely not Conal, she told herself stubbornly. He must be close on forty now, and as confirmed a bachelor in his ways as any man on earth.

"Why, to be sure, Master Conal," McPherson said without interest, reaching for more salt. "He's to be married again in a few weeks."

Fifteen

McPherson's words hummed in Destiny's brain, making her so dizzy that she was forced to clutch the back of his chair for support. McPherson went on eating, unaware of her turbulent thoughts.

Conal to marry? And *again,* he had said. Destiny felt a kind of possessive jealousy—up till now she had somehow and irrationally seen herself as the only woman Conal Carmichael had ever desired. But now there was another, a lady of his own station undoubtedly, and Destiny found it hard to swallow. And there had been one before this new bride. Though the thought hurt, Destiny was curious.

"Again, you say? I did not know Mr. Carmichael had been married at all," she said in a tone as indifferent as she could contrive. "Strange, but I think it was not known in the village."

"Nor should it be now," McPherson replied as he pushed his plate away and sat back. "I spoke without thinking. One word, and the secret is out. The master did marry once, years ago, and regretted it. He wanted no talk about it in Ballymachree and bid those of us who knew to keep silent. So I tell you now, keep your mouth shut, wife, for now above all he would wish it forgotten when he is bringing a new bride home."

"I'll not speak of it outside these doors," Destiny promised. "But tell me, who was she and where is she now? He never brought her here."

"A lady of breeding in London. She had no wish to visit Ireland, for she was of a delicate disposition and believed the damp air here would be bad for her health. As it was, she died a year after the wedding. No use at all to Carmichael, except for her money and estates in England. He came into all that."

Poor girl, whoever she was, thought Destiny. She gained little from Carmichael's greed, only suffered, as his tenants had done. Destiny visualized a fair, fragile blossom of a girl, perhaps that sister of Philip O'Keeffe's who used to visit Ballymachree years ago. At least the creature had not had long to live and repent her error.

"And the new bride?" she continued, still in an offhand tone. "Is she an English lady too? Shall she live in Ballymachree?"

McPherson shrugged and reached to the mantelshelf for his pipe and tobacco. "She's to be wed here at least, but who's to say where they will live? Not English, though, by all accounts. She's the daughter of a Russian aristocrat, I'm told, a countess."

"A countess?" Destiny marveled. That was next to a princess, she thought. Conal had done well for himself indeed. Still the strange, hurtful pangs persisted. "Is she beautiful?"

"I don't know," McPherson snapped irritably. "I've never seen her."

Destiny left the subject alone. It was apparent that McPherson was angry with himself for letting slip the one vital word that had breached the secret of Conal Carmichael's first marriage. But why had it been kept secret from Conal's Ballymachree tenants? she wondered. Surely not solely to avoid the cost of the festivities a landlord usually provided for his tenants on the occasion of his marriage? Conal was tight-fisted, but surely he would not break with tradition.

Suddenly recalling that all this time she had left Liam alone and unsupervised up in Tara's room, Destiny forgot about Conal and went anxiously to see all was well.

Liam was sitting cross-legged on the floor between Tara's bed and the truckle bed that was his. He stared balefully at Destiny as she entered, and did not move. Then she saw what he was doing. On his lap lay the patchwork counterpane she had spent all the winter months laboriously stitching, its myriad hues of green and gold and scarlet contrasting sharply with his dark hair and skin, and she gasped. He had torn the segments apart, one by one, and a scattered heap of cotton remnants lay about him. He bent his head and went on tearing the quilt apart, dropping patches defiantly before her eyes.

Destiny leaped on him and cracked her hand hard against his thin shoulder. "What do you think you're doing, you wicked child?" She seized him and dragged him to his feet.

He bared his teeth and hissed at her, for all the world like a cat cornered by a dog. Destiny was alarmed, never having encountered such a reaction from a child before, but she held on to him firmly.

"Do I have to watch you all the time to stop you from mischief?" she demanded. "Remember you are a guest in my house and behave accordingly. I'll be kind to you and care for you well, but how can I like a boy who is so destructive? Don't you want to be liked?"

He gave her a disdainful look, shrugged off her grip, and walked away to the little window. Destiny was nonplussed. It was as if he cared nothing for the rest of the world and its opinion of him. She tried another tack.

"Go down on your knees, Liam Dooley, and pray to God for forgiveness for your bad behavior. This is no way to treat your benefactors, but the good Lord will forgive your sin if you are truly penitent."

He ignored her. Evidently he had no respect for heaven's opinion of him either. Destiny sighed and controlled her frustration.

Not so Rosanna. When she eventually came home from the hall, she ate her supper in the kitchen, declining Destiny's invitation to have it in the parlor where Destiny and her husband sat by the fire, and later went up to her room. Within seconds she was down again, throwing open the parlor door so suddenly that Destiny leaped in surprise.

Rosanna was fiery-faced, her eyes glittering with rage, and the fingers of her left hand were clamped firmly on Liam's ear. The boy was wriggling and whimpering.

"I found this brat in my room, Mother, and do you know what he was doing? You know that length of blue lace I bought at the midsummer fair? Well, he was tying it in knots! It's ruined! And I meant that lace for my Sunday petticoat."

Her face was scarlet with justified indignation. Both women looked at McPherson, awaiting the inevitable outburst, but it did not come. McPherson puffed on his pipe unconcernedly.

"Well, what am I to do with him?" Rosanna demanded. McPherson removed his pipe.

"Leave him be. Send him to his room."

Rosanna gaped. "Is that all? You would have beaten me soundly for such a trick. Is he to go unpunished?"

"I told you, let him go to his room," McPherson repeated impassively. Rosanna colored up furiously.

"That I will not! He was in my room, and he could have been thieving for all I knew! He's a filthy, horrible brat, and I don't know what possessed you to bring him here. But I'll teach him not to skulk in my room like he does about the stables. Take that, boy, and remember to stay out of my way in future!"

Rosanna dealt him a hefty clout, making Destiny leap to her feet. "Rosanna! You heard your father! Let the boy alone. Liam, go to your room."

The boy wriggled free and ran, leaving Rosanna to vent her fury upon her mother. "Mother, how could you? You would not have let me behave so! Just because he bids you . . ." She flung a disdainful gesture toward McPherson.

Destiny held her breath as her husband rose to his feet, fearing the blow he would aim at Rosanna, and she moved nearer her child. But McPherson did not raise his hand. Instead he spoke, softly but emphatically.

"Listen to me, you cackling women. That boy is to be cared for and guarded closely, but no one is to lift a finger to him. You hear me, both of you? Else you'll have me to answer to. Mind him well and see no harm befalls him, for our lives could depend on it. Now, I'll hear no more. I'm for bed. Are you coming, wife?"

He left the two women, who stared at each other, mystified. Destiny knew the same question that rose in her mind was uppermost in her daughter's, too. Why should their lives depend on caring for a crippled, neglected bastard?

"Come, girl, let's to bed," she said, taking Rosanna's arm. The girl evidently understood the implicit refusal to discuss the matter, for she shrugged and moved to the door.

"He's up to something," she muttered, "and whatever it is, I want no part in it. I hate McPherson and I always will."

She ran up the staircase, leaving Destiny to blow out the lamp. Strange how the girl always referred to her stepfather by his surname, Destiny mused. She had always known that Rosanna detested him and would not acknowledge him. She hardly ever called him "Father," preferring instead to call him nothing except occasionally "sir." She never spoke of her real father either, though she knew of Destiny's first marriage. Still, she could not expect her to like a man she herself despised.

During the next few days Rosanna seemed to forget both McPherson and Liam, relapsing instead into an unaccustomed gloom. Destiny watched her apprehensively. It was unlike the girl, usually so lively, though there had been times before when she had gone into these silent periods of absorption. Destiny tried to make her talk.

"Leave me be, Mother. You sound just like Mrs. Kidd. She's been nagging me all day to pull myself together or she'll complain to McPherson. She's no cause to grumble—I do my work," Rosanna muttered.

"But what is it, child? What's troubling you?" Destiny persisted. Rosanna shrugged.

"I don't know. Nothing special."

"Is it Liam?" The boy was being as provoking as ever.

"No. Just a strange feeling. Oh, I can't explain it, Mother. You know how I used to feel sometimes long ago? That I wasn't alone, that someone is with me and I don't know who? It's just that again. And I keep thinking I see things that aren't there—carriages, ships, lights, strange streets—oh, Mother, I sometimes think I'm going mad!"

Destiny put her arm about her daughter's shoulder.

"That you're not, my girl, and well you know it. Like you say, you've had these feelings before and they've passed, haven't they? They will again."

But Destiny could not feel the comfort she uttered. The girl's strange moods worried her, for she had believed them over and finished. As a child Rosanna had endured them often, and had genuinely believed she had seen what she experienced. As she grew older, the visions came less often but had worried Rosanna more. Always she had felt the same thing—that someone was with her, a companion she liked and trusted at first, but in later years she had become apprehensive about the unseen companion.

The master of Ballymachree rode into the village and up to the hall on a fine sunny afternoon, a procession of carriages following his up the hill. Destiny listened and watched from afar, hearing the sounds of laughter and the clink of horse harness and seeing the colorful line of carriages with mixed feelings of excitement and envy. Though she saw none of the occupants, she knew Conal had brought home his new fiancée, and she longed to catch a glimpse of him.

Was he still as handsome and manly? McPherson and Rosanna would see him at the hall, and she could ask them later, but she yearned to see him for herself. If only Liam could be trusted to be left alone for a time, she could walk up through the copse toward the hall and peep through the bushes, but the boy was as terrible a problem as ever. Not one moment could he be left alone but some harm was done. With a sigh she let the idea slip away. She would have to wait in patience till Rosanna came.

She came at last, but not bright-eyed with excitement as Destiny expected. She wore a dazed, bemused expression as she took off her cloak.

"Well?" Destiny demanded eagerly. "Did you see Mr. Carmichael? How did he look?"

Rosanna sank dreamily onto the kitchen stool. "She came, Mother. She has come at last."

"Who, girl? I was asking about the master."

"She's beautiful, Mother, like a princess in those fairy

tales you used to tell me. Gentle-eyed and kindly, but she looks so sad. I never thought she would come."

"What are you talking about, Rosanna? I'm asking how the master is after all this time, and you prattle about a girl. Is it his fiancée you speak of?"

"Pale and gold she is, Mother, like the angels in the church. I have felt her near me often, and now she has come."

Destiny looked at her daughter anxiously. The girl was still in one of those strange moods after all. She'd get no sense out of her.

"Is it Mr. Conal's fiancée you speak of?"

Rosanna nodded. "She's like a princess."

"So she is, I hear tell. A Russian princess, come from far away. She's no companion of yours, Rosanna."

"But she is; I felt it as soon as I saw her in the great vestibule, and I swear she felt it too. For a second she looked at me, and there was such a great swelling inside of me, and I saw her eyes, Mother. She stared at me, and I know she felt it too."

"Nonsense, girl. Probably your cap was askew, that's all. Come on, now, help me with the vegetables for supper."

So Destiny was obliged to await McPherson's return to inquire about Conal.

"He's well enough," her husband replied laconically. "Very proud of his fine new wife-to-be, that's plain to see. A handsome girl, but she looks too delicate for the likes of him."

For the first time Destiny allowed Liam to join the family downstairs for supper. He had been tolerably quiet and well-behaved during the day, and she had lectured him soundly about the need for good behavior at supper if he was to avoid McPherson's displeasure. The boy had listened without his usual scowl, but Destiny still wondered how he would conduct himself.

McPherson took little notice of him at first, but when Destiny served the beef, the boy lifted it in his hands and tore at it with his teeth. McPherson snorted.

"Can't you eat better than that, boy? Has no one taught you your manners? Use your knife and fork."

The boy glared at him for a second and then continued to devour the meat from his fingers. McPherson rose to his feet, and Destiny held her breath. Rosanna had endured many a beating from McPherson for far lesser crimes.

"Dumb insolence!" McPherson roared, and Destiny waited breathlessly for the inevitable clout. It did not come. Instead McPherson took the boy by the shoulder and dragged him from the table to the door.

"Go to your room, boy, until you have learned the virtue of obedience," McPherson roared. The boy shot him a glance full of hate and scattered away. Again, fleetingly, Destiny sensed a flicker of familiarity in that look, but instantly the feeling vanished. She stared at McPherson in disbelief. She had never known him show such restraint before. When he was angered, a blow came easier to him than verbal remonstration. Age must be mellowing him.

Next morning Liam seemed in far more tractable mood. Though he still never spoke, he helped Destiny wash the dishes and followed her out into the yard when she took up the bowl of corn to feed the chickens. McPherson was still in the house, and Destiny felt glad to escape out into the warm sunlight, away from the heavy atmosphere his presence always produced.

"Would you like to feed the chickens, Liam?" she offered. Best to take advantage of his quiet mood to get him used to the idea of cooperating. He took the bowl from her in silence and began scattering the corn.

Poor child, she thought, watching the thin little figure limping about the yard. Because of his lameness and unprepossessing appearance, no one had had time for him, to tame him and love him. That was all he needed—time and love. She felt her heart swell with pity for him. After all, she too had had delicate blossoms to fend for once, and one at least had survived to bloom into beauty.

She brushed an unbidden tear away and lifted her head. From the distance came a sound of galloping hoofbeats. A single horse, riding early. She felt her heart quicken. Only one rider from the hall ever rode out so early, and that sound she had not heard for many a year.

Shading her eyes against the sun, she saw him at last,

careering wildly down the hill from the direction of the glen. He crouched in the saddle, black hair flying, and looking for all the world like a demon riding out from hell. Destiny's heart plunged and throbbed. Then for a second he and the horse seemed to hover, and then fall.

She heard his cry, but it was one of anger, not alarm, for she saw him leap to his feet and remount. The horse walked on in a lopsided tilt. It was lamed, but Conal seemed not to care. She saw his whip rise and fall, and the horse's tottering attempt to obey.

Liam had emptied the bowl of corn, cast it aside, and wandered haltingly out into the field to watch the rider with disinterest. From behind her Destiny heard McPherson's raucous call.

"Wife! Come here! Where's my ledger?"

Disappointment filled her. Conal was obliged to come this way in order to reach the hall by the shortest route, but wifely obedience obliged her reluctantly to go indoors.

"Where the devil have you put my ledger, woman? I know I left it here," McPherson stormed, his sandy hair bristling.

"Here it is, husband, in the drawer," she said calmly, retrieving it for him. McPherson muttered something incomprehensible. He himself had put it there.

"The master is out riding on the hill. I think his horse is lame," she added. It was an excuse to get back outside. McPherson leaped up.

"Lame?" he ejaculated. "He'll be furious! I'd better go."

He strode quickly toward the door; then a thought struck him. "Where's the boy?"

"Liam? He's outside."

McPherson seized her shoulder. "Then for God's sake fetch him in, woman, before the master sees him." Roughly he pushed her before him. "And keep him out of sight."

But it was too late. Liam stood in the field, near the great five-barred gate that kept the cows from straying into the next field. Conal was riding toward the gate, beating his limping horse in angry frustration.

"Open the gate, boy!" Destiny heard him call. The boy

stood motionless. McPherson let go of her arm and hurried across the field.

"You hear me, you cretin? Open the gate!" Conal roared again. Liam made no move. Conal's horse approached the gate and stopped.

"I'll open it, master!" McPherson called, but Conal's face grew redder with anger. He was beautiful still, Destiny thought as she hastened after McPherson. Age had only silvered his temples but not thickened his fine body or coarsened his features. He was a magnificent man still and, God forgive her, he still made her blood pound.

"Open the gate, or I'll flay your stupid hide off you!" Conal raged, but the boy still stood his ground. McPherson rushed forward and opened the gate. Conal's horse limped slowly through and stopped. Destiny saw Conal raise his whip.

"I'll teach you not to obey your master, you dumb peasant," Conal hissed, and she saw the arc of the whip as it flashed and bit into the boy's shoulders. Liam reeled back under the blow but made no cry. McPherson leaped forward and snatched at his master's bridle.

"No more, master, no more!" he cried. Destiny could only watch the scene, transfixed. That Conal should react violently was predictable, but not McPherson's protection of a crippled child. He, who had supervised the eviction of scores of children to their certain deaths, to protect a village idiot?

Conal hesitated, surprised. "You tell me not to chastise an unruly peasant?" he exclaimed. "Are you going soft, man?"

"Chastise the villagers all you will, master, but not this boy," McPherson said breathlessly. There was something shifty about his look that Destiny could not understand. Liam stood a few yards away, glaring at both men. Then, without a word, he hobbled toward Destiny and slid his hand into hers. Destiny gripped it firmly.

Conal had watched his awkward gait. "I see. Mother's little runt of the litter, is it? You have gone soft, McPherson. Who is this woman?"

"My wife, sir."

Conal's black eyes gleamed. "You've not done badly

for yourself. A fine body of a woman, McPherson, but can she bear you no better sons than that?" He pointed his whip disparagingly at Liam.

"He is not our son, sir. He is the boy Mrs. Dooley brought up."

McPherson's words were quietly spoken, but Conal's reaction was alarming. The mockery in his eyes died suddenly, and was replaced by a look of venomous hate. Destiny only caught a glimpse of the terrible look before he wheeled his horse about and limped away.

She looked down at the boy, and her heart leaped. In his black eyes stared the selfsame expression of hate. Instantly she recognized it, and the world skidded. The boy was so like the master, she was a fool not to have recognized it before.

Sixteen

Conal Carmichael led his fiancée out of the hall onto the balustraded terrace. Her fingers rested lightly on his arm.

"There, what do you think of my Irish estate, Catherine?" he said, indicating with a broad sweep of his arm the rolling acres below. She inclined her head graciously, so that the blond curls clustered there caught and reflected the sun's rays.

"Beautiful, Conal," she replied calmly. "Very beautiful countryside. And those masses of yellow flowers in the fields—what are they?"

"Potatoes, my dear. The peasants live on them." He regarded her face in profile attentively. She was beautiful, it was true, with that glacial kind of beauty the Russians were famous for. She could prove to be an ice queen, he mused, but she would soon thaw under his fire. Not that she inflamed him in the way other women had done. He preferred his women dark and fiery, but Catherine's aloof beauty held a challenge he could not resist.

"Do you think you will be happy to live here after we are married?" he asked. Not that it mattered whether she was happy or not, once he had secured her father's fortune, but until the knot was tied, she must believe him capable of making her happy. She drew her hand away, speaking in that same calm way. "Your Ballymachree seems a very pleasant place in which to live."

He wished she sounded more enthusiastic. Never mind, he thought. A Russian aristocrat who brought both beauty and wealth to him was the most important thing; her enthusiasm was not necessary.

Catherine Andreyeva, daughter of Count Nicolai Andreyev. He reveled in the thought of introducing her to his Irish neighbors as he had already done to his London friends.

"Let me show you over the hall now," Conal said to the girl. She turned obediently. He smiled. She was a submissive cow, presenting no future problems for him. So long as she bore him sons to perpetuate the Carmichael line, that was all he would ask of her. And the getting of them would be a pleasant task, he mused, for she had a slender, graceful body and her gown clung closely enough to reveal the shapely curves of womanhood.

She duly admired the Oriental rugs and chinoiserie his father had collected on his travels, picking up a small jade statue of a goddess.

"A beautiful piece," she murmured, "so smooth a texture."

She spoke little until he took her to visit the orangery. Lifting her delicate nose to sniff the scent, she asked casually, "Is your friend Philip O'Keeffe to come to our wedding?"

"Philip? Oh, yes, he travels from England next week. I had forgotten you had met."

"Such a charming man, so gentle and polite. I fancied him a clergyman when first we met," she commented.

Conal laughed. "He might well have been, so philanthropic as he is. He's always involved with caring for the less fortunate, his hospitals and so on."

"A kindly man. I hope he will be our neighbor, for I understand he has estates near here."

Conal raised his brows. Strange that Philip should be noticed by a woman, he thought—Philip, who never raised his voice or projected his views; Philip, who all these years had remained a bachelor. Still, it was surprising what attracted some women. If Catherine was expecting the same docility from her husband, she was doomed to disappointment.

He was following her down a corridor in the hall and thinking how pleasing was the fragrance that accompanied her, when a maid approaching them stood back to let them pass. After they had passed, Catherine turned.

"Who was that girl?"

Conal turned to look. The girl had vanished from sight. "I don't know. I didn't see her. Just one of the maids. Why?"

Catherine shrugged and flushed. "Oh, I saw her yesterday, and I had the strangest notion that I had seen her before, that's all. But I can't have, can I?"

"Impossible. The staff at Ballymachree Hall all live locally. She probably reminds you of someone you met once."

"Perhaps."

She let the subject drop. Silly woman, he thought, and hoped she was not going to be one of those sensitive women always having premonitions or fits of the vapors. It was hard enough as it was to maintain an unaccustomed facade of politeness.

He sighed. It was not going to be easy to maintain the game for a few weeks more, but he had succeeded already in these past months in London. He was not going to give up now, with the prize almost in his hands. Just a few weeks more . . .

Catherine Andreyeva sighed with relief when her affianced husband made his apologies. The sandy-haired bailiff had entered the parlor and muttered something in his ear before Conal turned to her.

"So sorry, my dear. An urgent matter to attend to. One of my horses has gone lame."

Relief filled her as he strode away. He was a handsome-enough fellow, but he left much to be desired. His polite manner, which had impressed her so much in London, now seemed but a veneer hiding a more irascible nature beneath, and she was beginning to feel uneasy about marriage to this man.

There was a discreet knock at the door, and immediately it opened. Catherine saw the black-haired maid standing there, her pretty face pink with embarrassment.

"Forgive me, miss. I thought there was no one here." She turned to leave.

"No, wait," Catherine said. "Come here. What was it you wanted?"

"Only to put more coal on the fire. I'm parlormaid, and it's my job." The girl hovered uncertainly before her, her blue eyes probing hers with curiosity.

"Then do so. What is your name?"

"Rosanna, miss."

"A pretty name. For a pretty girl, if I may say so."

Catherine could not take her eyes from the slim figure as she bent to lift coals from the hod with a pair of iron tongs. It was strange, but once again she had the curious sensation of knowing the girl already.

"I feel we have met," she said haltingly, aware that it was impossible. And it was more than that; it was as if they had once known each other well. She bit her lip, conscious of having been impulsive, of revealing herself to a girl whose station was far removed from her own. The girl's reaction was startling.

"I feel it too, miss!" The girl let the tongs fall and turned to her with an expression of delight. "I feel I've known you all my life, that you've always been there! But how odd that you should feel it too!"

Rosanna flung herself on her knees before Catherine, clasping her hands together as if in prayer. "I can't even say your name properly, but I've known you forever."

"Catherine. Catherine Andreyeva," Catherine told her

in a whisper. "And I'm glad you share my sensation. I thought I was crazy."

"Not you, miss! You're a beautiful Russian princess, far too good for that evil Mr. Conal!"

"Hush!" Catherine said, laying a finger to her lips. "Someone will hear you! And you are wrong. I am no princess, but the daughter of a count, that is all. And surely you are wrong about Mr. Carmichael—he does not seem evil to me."

"But you don't know him! He's callous and cruel. My mother told me," Rosanna cried vehemently. "He let his tenants starve and threw them out of their homes to die! He's heartless and wicked, and I'll not let him make you unhappy! I'll die first!"

Catherine smiled. The girl's ardor was captivating. "I shall be glad of a loyal friend here in Ballymachree, Rosanna, but you must not speak so wildly of your master, or you will find yourself in trouble."

"You'll let me be your friend?" The girl's dark gaze was eager. Catherine took her hands gently in her own.

"If you'll tame your wild ways and curb your unruly tongue, I will, and gladly."

Rosanna seized her hands and kissed them. "I've waited so long for you to come, Mistress Catherine. My life is yours, and I'll defend you to the death if you'll call me friend. Nothing shall ever harm you while I am near."

Catherine squeezed her hands. "Then I'll ask Mr. Carmichael if you can be my personal maid instead of parlormaid. Will that suit you? I'm sure he'll not object."

Rosanna leaped to her feet, her eyes aglow with delight and her cap askew. "Maid to a princess? Mother will be delighted! I always told her you'd come, but she never believed me." She twirled about the room happily until Catherine restrained her.

"Go about your duties now, Rosanna, until I have a chance to speak to your master. I'll send for you if he agrees."

"He'll not deny you anything, miss—not until you're wed, that is," Rosanna replied thoughtfully. "After that ... Miss Catherine, must you marry him? Why don't you run away? I know I would," Rosanna said angrily. "You are rich, aren't you? You could keep your own house?"

"In my station it is expected of me to make a good marriage. I have little choice in the matter, now we are betrothed."

"Well, I wouldn't let anyone force me into marriage, especially to one as evil as Conal Carmichael!" Rosanna flared. "I'd want a man I could love and respect, and how could any woman love him?"

"That's enough, Rosanna," Catherine cut in gently. "Go about your duties, and remember you promised me to curb your tongue. You must be discreet if we are to be friends."

"Very well, miss." There was a reluctant note in Rosanna's voice as she bobbed a curtsy and withdrew. Catherine was content. A fiery friend she might be, but her patent love and loyalty would be invaluable in the trying days ahead. And it was curious how they both shared that strange sense of affinity when half a world divided them. Curious, but comforting.

So many thoughts whirled in Destiny's brain that she found it hard to concentrate on the tasks of baking and cleaning that day. Tara had finally packed up her belongings and moved out, in readiness for her nuptials, and the boy Liam's dark gaze reminded her constantly of Conal. Was the uncanny likeness between man and boy a pure coincidence, or was there a family skeleton in the Carmichael cupboard? All day Destiny pondered over the possibilities, and then Rosanna came home with her exciting news.

"Personal maid to the countess?" Destiny repeated in disbelief. "How did you come by such a position, and you not working there but three weeks yet?"

"Countess Catherine herself arranged it, and the master did not mind at all. She likes me, mother. She feels we've always been friends too."

"Tush, girl. She a princess and you but a poor peasant girl. Don't be getting ideas, or you'll be in for disappointment. The likes of them care nothing for the likes of us," Destiny reminded her.

"Countess, not princess. And I'm no peasant, either. I'm stepdaughter to the bailiff of the Carmichael estate, and that's halfway to gentry," Rosanna retorted proudly. "And whatever I am, I see no difference between her and me, nor does she. We're friends, Mother, and if you could see her, you'd like her too."

"That's as may be, but you be careful. One move out of turn, and the master will kick you out of there as soon as look at you, and what will you do then?"

Rosanna shrugged. "We'll face that when it comes. He won't get rid of me so easy, Catherine will see to that."

Destiny sighed. Her daughter was young yet and explosive and had a firm faith in the future that her mother was loath to shatter. She was a good girl, loyal and loving and kind, if only she could keep control of her rebellious streak.

McPherson was far less communicative when he came home. For the most part he ignored Destiny's questions until she had inquired about the lame horse for the fourth time.

"For heaven's sake, stop nagging me, woman! Can't you see I'm tired?" he snapped irritably. "The master went down to the stables and shot the horse himself. There, now, are you satisfied?"

That was typical of Conal, she thought. Either things conformed instantly to his desire or he had no more time for them. He had too little patience to wait for the horse's leg to be set and wait while it was recovering. Useless, it had to be dispensed with.

In an effort to draw McPherson out to tell her more, she told him Rosanna's news.

"Lady's maid to the countess?" he repeated thoughtfully. "She's done well for herself. That girl could go far if she plays her cards right."

Rare praise from a bitter man. Encouraged, Destiny went on to tell him of the countess's obvious liking for Rosanna, and from there she led on to speaking again of Conal. McPherson's small eyes moved shiftily. She could see he wanted no reference to the incident in the field. She was determined to find out the truth, even if it provoked him.

"Husband, what is Liam to Conal Carmichael?" she asked with an air of innocence. Instantly she saw the light blaze in McPherson's eyes.

"Nothing, woman, why should he be? Go fetch me my supper. I'm starving."

Destiny rose to go. "A body cannot help noticing the resemblance between them. Are you sure there's no kinship?"

"I told you. He's the Dooley child."

"You told the master he was the boy Mrs. Dooley brought up. I saw how the master looked."

McPherson leaped to his feet. "You see more than is good for you, woman! I warn you, wife, you keep your thoughts to yourself, and if I hear you so much as breathe a word to anyone else, I'll flay the hide off you! Do you hear me, woman?"

He seized her shoulder roughly, his pale blue eyes glaring down into hers with venom. Destiny shrank from his grip.

"I hear you, husband."

He let her go, and she went out into the kitchen. So she was right, she thought angrily. The boy was Conal's child, the result of his first marriage undoubtedly, and Conal had refused to recognize a stunted, crippled son. He had cast him off as useless, just as he had rid himself of a lame horse. The bastard, she raged inwardly, the heartless, cruel bastard!

Rosanna brought news a few days later.

"The wedding festivities are to begin," Rosanna said breathlessly. "There is to be a big ball for all the fine guests, and a smaller one first for the tenants. Imagine, Mother, all the villagers dressed in their best will be entertained in the great hall, with lashings of food and ale for all."

"I'm glad to hear the master is following the tradition," Destiny commented, trying to fight down the strange feeling of anger and jealousy that troubled her.

"You must wear a fine gown and outshine them all," Rosanna went on enthusiastically. "And then you'll see the countess and her father and all the guests. Mr. O'Keeffe has arrived today from Carrigaline."

"Philip O'Keeffe? I remember him from years ago. He was a handsome young man," Destiny remarked.

"And he is still. And his manservant, Bob Fellows, is a lively young spalpeen too," Rosanna said with a laugh. "He's already asked to partner me at the ball."

Her eyes sparkled mischievously. Destiny smiled. "He's quick off the mark, and he not here two minutes yet. And what of all the Ballymachree lads who've been eating their hearts out for you?"

Rosanna tossed her black mane of curls. "Is it my fault if they're slow? They'll have to take their chance if they want to get anywhere with me, Mother."

Destiny laughed. It would take a rare man indeed to handle Rosanna, and she would be in no hurry to choose. For one thing Destiny was grateful—Rosanna would not have to sacrifice her liberty to a man in return for security, as her mother had done.

The night of the tenants' ball came at last, and Destiny felt excited. Tonight she would see Conal again, not this time in her workaday gown, but in a splendid silk one she had specially made for the occasion. She turned this way and that before the mirror, admiring her own reflection.

The deep pink of the gown showed off her creamy skin and glossy dark hair to perfection. And her slender figure was still that of a girl, she reflected proudly. She looked ten years younger than her age and could easily be taken for Rosanna's older sister.

Even McPherson made begrudgingly appreciative comments. "You're not a bad-looking woman, at that, Destiny McPherson," he muttered, and she could see he was proud to take her arm and accompany her into the vestibule of the hall.

The great hall was decorated with flowers, the scent of roses hanging heavy on the warm evening air. Tables laden with roast duck and ham and beef bordered the room, and in the middle the villagers clustered in embarrassed chatter. A fiddler on the dais struck up a jig, and soon all shyness vanished as the dancers began to whirl and caper.

McPherson fetched Destiny a tankard of ale, and together they sat to watch the dancing. A few of the villagers nodded to her, but none came to talk, Destiny noted. She was still an outcast, neither peasant nor gentry-born, but it troubled her little. She watched the great double doors anxiously, awaiting the arrival of Conal and his fiancée. He must come down soon to receive the good wishes of his tenants.

She did not see him at first. He must have entered alone by a smaller door, for suddenly she looked up and there he was, standing in front of McPherson. Her husband rose quickly and offered the master his seat. Conal sat down beside her, ignoring McPherson completely and sliding his arm along the back of her seat.

"How ravishing you look this evening, succulent enough to devour," he said with a broad smile that made her heart race. He looked magnificent, a gleaming gold fob stretched across his brocaded waistcoat and his wild hair tamed back smoothly about his tanned brow.

"So you remember me?" she asked, wondering whether he could possibly remember that time long ago when he had found her so desirable.

"But of course. It was only the other day I met you with McPherson in the field. My bailiff chose himself a handsome woman indeed, for I swear I could carry you off myself this instant."

She glanced up. If McPherson was listening, he was studiously avoiding the impression of having heard. Fleetingly she thought how typical it was of him—he would pawn anything, even his wife, to gain an advantage. But the thought faded quickly, for Conal's hand rested on her shoulder, making her heart beat faster still.

"I would dance with you, so as to put my arms about you," he murmured, "but I am expected to dance the first dance with my bride-to-be. But I could show you the miniatures in the music room if you've a mind?"

McPherson had moved away, and Destiny realized it was left to her to act as she chose. She could hear her own blood pounding in her ears, and her body longed to be taken in his arms again. But something—pride perhaps?—made her delay, to question him.

"Conal, do you remember the cave up the glen? Long ago, on a summer's day?"

His sultry look of desire narrowed for a moment to the effort of recollection. "The cave? I remember the cave, and one day I sheltered there from a storm. There was a girl, a vital, passionate thing." His black eyes widened. "Was it you? My God, I recall it now! Was it really you? Then come to the music room with me and let us celebrate our meeting again."

His voice was husky with desire, and Destiny felt her old animosity melting into a desire to equal his. She was ready to rise and follow, but McPherson reappeared suddenly.

"Mr. Carmichael, the countess is ready."

A look of irritation crossed Conal's features. He pressed Destiny's hand and rose.

"Another time, my dear."

He was gone, leaving Destiny with a gaping void of disappointment. McPherson took her arm as the great double doors opened, the fiddler stopped playing, and the dancers ceased their eddying whirl to focus their attention on the newcomers.

Conal stood there, his hand cupping the elbow of a slim, fair woman at whose other hand stood a graying, distinguished gentleman with a huge beard. Conal raised his hand.

"Villagers of Ballymachree, may I present to you Count Nicolai Andreyev and his charming daughter, Countess Catherine Andreyeva, your future mistress."

There was intense pride in his voice, and the villagers clapped and cheered. Destiny had no eyes either for Conal or the count, for her attention was riveted on the pale, statuesque girl in cream brocade who smiled gravely on the assembly. There was no mistaking her angelic mien and her gentle, velvet brown eyes. Kate had come back from the dead.

Destiny sank senseless to the floor.

Seventeen

When Destiny recovered consciousness, she was lying in her own bed and Rosanna was bending over her.

"Are you all right, Mother?" Rosanna asked anxiously as her mother's eyes flickered open. "I saw you fall—I was just behind the countess. Was it the heat, Mother, or the drink?"

Destiny struggled to sit up. "I'm all right, mavourneen." As her brain cleared, she remembered—Kate, now called a countess and greeted as Conal Carmichael's bride-to-be. Caution warned her not to speak of her shock—not yet. " 'Twas only the heat. Did your stepfather bring me home?"

Rosanna nodded. "With my help. The countess bid me come with you, once she knew you were my mother."

The door opened and McPherson entered. His pale blue eyes registered not so much concern as anger.

"For God's sake, wife, what ails you? You fainted like some woman near her time." His eyes narrowed. "You're not with child, are you?"

Destiny shook her head. " 'Twas the heat, husband, that is all. And the hall so crowded and all."

"Well, a fine fool you made of me. Mr. Carmichael laughed till the tears came, saying I should not give you ale if you could not take it. He thought you drunk! A laughingstock you made of me before them all, and I'll not forget it."

He stormed out, leaving Rosanna to laugh away her mother's concern. " 'Twill do him no harm to be laughed at, and he with no sense of humor at all. What matter what the master thinks, either?—he has his mind full of his wealthy bride."

"He must not marry her, Rosanna!" Destiny cried. "You must stop her—tell her he's no good for her!"

"I've already told her, and she said she must do as she is betrothed to him. 'Tis nothing to do with us, Mother. We cannot stop it, though God knows I'd gladly see her far away from that evil brute."

"Then tell her again, persuade her, promise to help her run away! Please, Rosanna, get her away from him!"

Destiny had seized Rosanna's hands, and her dark eyes were full of pleading. Rosanna knelt beside her, her blue eyes troubled.

"What is it, Mother? Why do you take on so about a foreign girl who means nothing to you?"

"It means evil, Rosanna, if this wedding is allowed to take place. I know it, I feel it in my bones! It must be stopped!"

Rosanna stroked her hair. "There, now, Mother, you're not yourself tonight. 'Tis nonsense to talk of me running away, and with no home but Ballymachree. Go to sleep now and rest, and in the morning you'll feel better. You're far from well, for I've never known you like this before. Sleep now, Mother, and God rest you."

But far into the night Destiny lay awake, long after McPherson had tumbled into bed and pointedly turned his back on her to show his displeasure. Thoughts whirled in her brain, making sleep impossible. Too much was happening, too fast for the brain to keep up.

But among the tumbling thoughts of Conal fathering a crippled child and the unexpected return of Kate, one thought was uppermost. Kate had survived and come home, and whatever else happened, she must be prevented from marrying Conal Carmichael.

"I've always known her." Rosanna's words, seemingly so inexplicable and irrational at the time, now began to make sense. Of course there was an affinity between the two girls, half-sisters as they were. Though they had different fathers, her own blood flowed in their veins. Somehow, despite the years between, when both girls had forgotten each other, some spiritual link between them had persisted.

That accounted for Rosanna's strange visions—the lights, the carriages, and all the trappings of a fine life she could not possibly know. Destiny wondered whether Kate too had had glimpses of her sister's poor way of life. It was strange, mystical even, no doubt the hand of God working in strange ways incomprehensible to man.

And suddenly another piece of the puzzle fitted into shape in Destiny's mind. How had Kate come to be the daughter of a count? Why, of course, Count Nicolai must be the Big Nick Shuna had spoken of in the letter—the Big Nick who actually wrote that letter. And that letter lay still at the bottom of a drawer in the great chest in the bedroom.

The last thought that troubled Destiny before she finally fell asleep was the memory of Conal's closeness that had made her whole being vibrate with longing for him. How could one hate a man so and at the same time yearn for him? It just did not make sense. Everything in her screamed out at the contradiction raging inside her. She wanted him, but she was determined to keep him from her child. Life was going mad.

Destiny awoke before dawn. McPherson had already risen, doubtless to hurry to his master. He was the last person who must know about Kate, Destiny decided, for he would be sure to use the news to his advantage. Rosanna too must be kept ignorant of her sister's existence for the moment, for in her honest, forthright way, she would be sure to blurt it out. Destiny must continue to keep her secret until she had found a way to rescue Kate from Conal's clutches.

She heard the click of the front door as Rosanna let herself out quietly to go to work. Destiny rose, dressed, and went downstairs to discover whether McPherson was still about. The house was empty. She opened the front door and looked out into the yard. Only a dusty mother hen clucked her way across the cobbles, pursued by three chicks. Of the master there was no sign. Destiny was alone to think and plan, for Liam was still abed.

* * *

Rosanna exclaimed in delight at her mistress's pale blue silk nightgown as she climbed out of bed, yawned, and stretched luxuriously.

"Oh, miss, what a beautiful gown! You look like a fairy!"

Catherine smiled. "You should see the marvelous clothes Papa has bought me for my trousseau. They make my everyday clothes look like rags. Come, brush my hair for me, Rosanna."

Rosanna picked up the silver-backed brush from the dressing table as her mistress seated herself before the mirror and began brushing her long, flaxen hair with gentle strokes. Catherine stayed her.

"Brush it firmly, Rosanna, much harder than that, or it will not shine."

The maid smiled. "I have much to learn to be a good lady's maid, but I'll learn fast, you'll see. But there's things I need to know, like what I should call you, for instance."

Catherine reflected for a moment. "In company I think you should call me simply 'mistress,' but when we are alone together you may call me 'Catherine.' But only when we are quite alone, mind you. It is not usual for ladies to permit their maids such a liberty, but I feel we are close friends, you and I, and there is no pleasanter sound than one's own name spoken affectionately by a loving friend."

"Catherine." Rosanna spoke the name gently, with an infinitely caressing sound that made the fairer girl smile. It was like the sun suddenly shining out and dispelling a cloudy day, Rosanna thought warmly. Her new friend—and yet not new, for she felt like a lifelong soulmate—was so beautiful, so kind, and at the same time so defenseless, like a newborn kitten, that she aroused a swift surge of emotion in Rosanna. She longed to cradle this fragile Catherine, to protect her vulnerability against the world. Especially against that uncouth Mr. Carmichael.

"Catherine, must you wed the master?" she asked. Catherine sighed.

"We went through all that. Papa agreed to it after much persuasion, and though I confess I no longer care overmuch for the gentleman, I have no choice in the matter. *Che sarà, sarà.*"

"But why?" Rosanna said explosively. "I would not marry against my will, I'd run away first. Oh, Catherine! Let's run away! I'll take care of you, I promise!"

She laid an entreating hand on Catherine's shoulder. Her mistress smiled again and patted the hand. "Rosanna, I know you would, but it cannot be. I made up my mind to marry Conal, and now that everything is arranged, I cannot change it. I must confess, though, I wonder if my mother would have agreed to this marriage if she were still alive."

"Was she kind and beautiful like you?"

Catherine shook her head. "I cannot remember her, for she died when I was a baby."

"Poor Catherine. You with no mother and I with no father but the beast my mother calls husband, we share one misfortune at least," Rosanna commented.

"But you have a mother and I a father whom we love," Catherine pointed out, "so we are mutually fortunate in that."

"Yet you would sacrifice your happiness to a man everyone detests!" Rosanna flared.

"It is for the best, Rosanna."

"I can't believe it! Oh, Catherine, do let's run away from here!"

Catherine turned sharply on her stool, her expression stern and angry. "Rosanna! I cannot allow you to behave thus. Do not speak so foolishly again or I shall be angry with you, do you hear?"

Rosanna flushed and hung her head. "I'm sorry, Catherine. I did not mean to anger you. It's just that I want to protect you. I can't bear to think of you and Mr. Conal . . . Oh, I'd give anything to get away from Ballymachree, to look after you! I'd cook and wash and clean for you, Catherine! I'd do anything for you!"

Catherine took Rosanna's hands in her own. "I know you would, Rosanna, but it is not to be. Now, put that idea firmly out of your head. And I think I detect something that tells me there is more to it than simply protecting me. What is it, Rosanna? Why are you so anxious to flee from Ballymachree?"

Rosanna stared at her, perplexed. "How could you tell?"

"I don't know. A sixth sense, perhaps, or just the affinity we share. Tell me."

Rosanna looked away in embarrassment. "I hardly like to. It doesn't seem right."

"Rosanna, the truth." There was a commanding tone in the fairer girl's voice that Rosanna could not disobey.

"It's my stepfather. I hate him."

"McPherson? Does he beat you, is that it?"

Rosanna shook her head. "Not anymore, not very often. He used to when I was a child, but not now. He threatens, that's all."

"Then what is it?"

Rosanna's country-pink cheeks deepened to red. "I think he fancies me," she said awkwardly. "I don't encourage him, you understand, but I can see the way he looks at me, all leering and sly. You know how men look at you that way, don't you? Or perhaps you don't, you so innocent and all, but I recognize it. I've seen the way the village lads look when I walk by, and they shout out and tease me about the way my hips sway when I walk. Well, McPherson looks at me the same way, and once he even touched me here"—she indicated her bodice—"as he passed me."

Catherine's brown eyes were wide in shock. "I don't know the look you mention, but I understand. The men in my circle don't speak as freely as your village boys, though I would sometimes prefer that they did. It's often hard to know what people in society are really thinking behind all their polite smiles and small talk. But I do understand, Rosanna, and am sorry. Are you sure, though?"

Rosanna nodded and, encouraged by Catherine's understanding tone, went on hurriedly. "Last night I even heard him outside my bedroom door, and I lay terrified that he might come in. He did once, when I was undressing for bed."

Catherine gasped. "What did you do?"

"I told him to get out, but he laughed and said he was

master of the house and could come and go wherever he pleased, whenever he pleased. He did go, though, when I threatened to call Mother."

"And last night?"

"I heard his hand on the knob, but he didn't open the door. I knew it was him by the heavy sound of his breathing."

"Why didn't you call your mother?"

Rosanna looked shocked. "I couldn't! She must never know, especially as I think I'm not the first he's tried his tricks on."

"Not the first? Rosanna, what are you saying? I know he's Conal's trusted steward and bailiff, but even Conal would dismiss McPherson if he's not behaving respectably."

Rosanna looked miserable. "I can't upset Mother by getting him into trouble and causing him to lose his post, so promise you won't tell. But I think he bothered our maid, Tara, too. I heard him walking about in the night, and then I heard her cry out. There was quiet after, but in the morning Tara told my mother she was leaving to get married. I don't think Mother ever suspected, and I can't tell her about me now. I'd rather just go away."

"I'm sorry, Rosanna, but you and I both have to stay. We can't be cowards and run away, can we? But I'll stand by you, just as I know you will by me. We'll help each other through."

"I swear I'll kill that McPherson if he ever lays a hand on me, so I will," Rosanna muttered.

"Then heaven help him if he tries. Go now and fetch me a gown from the press, for it's growing late and I've promised to walk in the orangery with Philip after breakfast. He's a handsome man, don't you think?"

"He is, to be sure. And his manservant thinks he's a handsome fellow too," Rosanna answered with a smile.

"Is he the young man I saw you talking with in the stableyard yesterday?"

Rosanna nodded. "We were just passing the time of day," she said with a blush.

Catherine laughed. "And a lengthy discussion you had about it too, for you were still there twenty minutes later.

No, not the pink gown today, Rosanna. I have a fancy to wear the green. And pass me my pearl necklace, will you? By the way, there's a day dress of mine there that I don't want anymore—the violet wool one—perhaps you'd like it? We're about of a size, you and I."

"For me?" Rosanna gasped. "Oh, I couldn't possibly take it, Catherine. I've never owned such a dress in my life!"

"Well, now you shall. Take it when you go home tonight. Now, pass me the rose water, will you?"

Without thinking, Rosanna thrust the pearl necklet in her apron pocket and she did as she was commanded.

All day Destiny felt restless. It was almost more than one could bear, to hug a secret close to oneself that one yearned to cry out and tell the world. And more than that, she longed to see her child again, to drink in Kate's beauty and grace and revel in knowing that she was alive and well. Somehow she must contrive to see her, not to tell her what the girl evidently did not know, but just to watch and love her from afar.

But how? That was the problem. In all these years Destiny had never had occasion to enter Ballymachree Hall until the night of the tenants' ball. She had no good excuse like McPherson and Rosanna to go there.

"Come, Liam, help me shake up the feather beds and change the sheets." The boy rose from the table and followed obediently. He was surprisingly docile and willing these days, she thought, though he still made no effort to talk.

Divine Providence must have recognized the desperate need in a mother's love, she realized much later, for the opportunity she sought arrived unexpectedly that evening when Rosanna came home. She flung aside her cloak wearily and began pulling off her apron.

"Here, Mother, wash and starch my apron for me, will you? I forgot to give it to the laundry maids."

Destiny took the crumpled apron and felt something bulging in the pocket. In amazement she pulled out a string of pearls.

"Heavens above, Rosanna, where did you get this from?"

Rosanna started. "Oh, Lord! I forgot! I must have put it in my pocket when my lady changed her mind about which gown she was to wear. How stupid of me!"

Destiny was alarmed. The necklace must be very valuable indeed. "You'd better take it back to her at once and explain, my girl, or it could be thought that you have stolen it!"

Rosanna sighed. "She'll not think that of me, Mother. She knows me too well. And I'm tired. I'll explain in the morning."

Destiny saw her chance. "Tomorrow isn't good enough, my girl. This must go back to its owner tonight, before McPherson finds out. You get your dinner and I'll take it up."

Before Rosanna could argue, Destiny picked up her cloak and was gone. The evening sun was dipping low behind the beech trees surrounding the hall, and soon it would be time for the gentry's dinner. There was no sign of McPherson riding home yet, and she arrived in the hall's driveway without seeing him. That was lucky. He would never allow her to enter. Destiny made for the servants' entrance.

The surprised-looking maid bade her wait. "I'll tell Mrs. Kidd you're here." In a moment she returned and led Destiny through a passage to the housekeeper's parlor. A forbidding-looking lady dressed in severe black with a white lace cap and a bundle of keys at her waist bade Destiny come in.

"I am Mrs. Kidd, Mr. Carmichael's housekeeper. May I inquire what your errand is with the countess?" she asked sternly. "It is not our habit to allow strangers to visit our guests."

"I am no stranger, ma'am. I am Mistress McPherson, wife of Mr. Carmichael's bailiff, and my errand is confidential. Your guest would not wish me to noise her business abroad," Destiny replied calmly, though inwardly her heart fluttered at her own temerity.

The housekeeper sniffed and evidently approved Destiny's refusal to breach a confidence. "Wait here, Mistress McPherson, and I'll see if the countess will receive you."

Destiny sat on the edge of the horsehair chair and waited for what seemed ages. Finally Mrs. Kidd returned. "Follow me," she said tersely.

She led Destiny upstairs, through a baize-covered door into the great vestibule, and up the great winding staircase with its wrought-iron balustrade. Along a corridor she stopped and knocked at a door.

"Come in," a musical voice called. The housekeeper entered first.

"Mistress McPherson, ma'am."

As the housekeeper withdrew, Destiny saw the figure of her child seated in an armchair by the fire. There were no candles lit, and in the firelight's glow the girl looked more ethereal and enchanting than ever.

"Come in and be seated, Mrs. McPherson," Catherine said in a kindly tone, indicating the chair opposite and smoothing out the gray silk of her boudoir negligee. "You are Rosanna's mother, are you not? I am delighted to meet you."

"And I you, my lady." Destiny spoke the words with emphasis, aware that the girl would not understand how she felt. Her heart swelled with love and pride for her, so graceful and healthy she looked. Dear God, you were kind to me after all, Destiny breathed inwardly, for you did take care of my child all these years. Forgive me for doubting you.

"May I inquire the nature of your errand, mistress?" Catherine prompted gently. Destiny gathered her wits. Quickly she poured out the tale of Rosanna's absentminded mistake.

"So I have brought your necklace back, my lady," Destiny concluded as she took the necklace from her pocket. "I hope you will not be angry with Rosanna."

Catherine smiled. "Not I, Mistress McPherson, for I love your daughter well and trust her implicitly. She could have returned it in the morning as she said, but I am grateful to you for your consideration."

Destiny looked into the gentle depths of the girl's velvet brown eyes and felt a tear prick her eyelids. If only she could yield to the craving inside her to take her child in her arms and hug her close with joy! But no, she must keep silent and content herself with feeding her eyes on her.

Catherine rose. "I do not wish to appear impolite, Mistress McPherson, but in a few minutes the gong will sound for dinner, and I have still to dress. Will you excuse me?"

With a wrench Destiny tore herself away. Loitering in the corridor, reluctant to leave the vision too swiftly, she wondered at her own restraint. How had she stopped herself from exclaiming out loud that she was overjoyed to see her own flesh and blood alive and well after years of believing her dead? The ache inside her persisted, the longing to declare the truth and hope to see a little of her own immense love reflected in those velvet eyes.

And, she remembered with a start, there was so much more she should have said while she had the chance. She should have warned the girl not to let herself be wed to Carmichael, to run away rather than let that beast get hold of her. She had meant to add her arguments to Rosanna's in order to convince the girl of her mistake, and now the opportunity was lost.

Destiny hovered, caught up between returning to Catherine's boudoir or leaving. It would be weak to go away without even trying to dissuade Kate from this disastrous step.

Destiny was turning to retrace her steps when she heard the sound of a heavy step and stiffened. At the far end of the corridor loomed the tall, broad figure of Conal, his dark head gleaming under the light of the lamp in the wall socket.

"Mistress McPherson!" he exclaimed in his vibrant, deep-toned voice. "This is an unexpected pleasure!"

"I . . . I came on an errand for my daughter," Destiny stuttered, wishing her heart would stop leaping. "I am just leaving."

"Not without seeing the miniatures I promised you." Conal smiled, his teeth white and gleaming in the half-light. "Here we are, just by the music room. Let me show you."

Uninvited he took her arm and steered her toward a nearby door. "I do hope you are fully recovered from your mishap the other evening?" he inquired as he ushered her inside and closed the door.

"I'm fine, really, it was just the heat."

"These summer evenings are indeed close," he murmured in agreement. "Here, let me remove your cloak."

His hands rose to her shoulders and Destiny felt her cloak slide to the floor. His hands remained on her shoulders, and despite the warm night air, Destiny felt her whole body begin to tremble.

Eighteen

Conal's grip on her shoulders tightened. Destiny broke away.

"What a beautiful room!" she exclaimed, stooping to retrieve her cloak. "Turn up the light so that I may see it better. Where were the miniatures you spoke of?"

She heard Conal's chuckle in the gloom. "Does it matter how beautiful the surroundings, mistress, when you and I both know our blood runs swifter when we are close to each other? Come here. I'll show you the grand piano and the caskets later. In the meantime all we need is the sofa here."

His fingers reached eagerly out to her in the half-light, and Destiny could see clearly the ardent gleam in his black eyes. For a second she forgot the world and her reason for being here as her heart pounded in response to that look of desire.

But then his eager hands brought back reality. The thought leaped to her mind that perhaps, if she pleased him, she could cajole him to do what she so earnestly wanted.

"What do you want of me, Conal?" she asked gently. He seemed not to notice she had used his first name.

"You know what we both want," he murmured, his strong hands caressing her body through her thin summer gown. "I sense you desire me just as much as I desire you."

He pulled her down on the sofa beside him and leaned over her. Destiny raised her fingers to his face, longing to kiss him and draw him close. "I have long wanted you," she purred softly. "Ever since that day in the cave. Do you remember?"

"How could I ever forget the only woman who ever responded with the fire and passion every man dreams of in a woman?" His voice was a croak, his touch more urgent. Destiny fought to ward off the tide of passion that rose in her, clinging to reason and the purpose of her visit.

"I can give you all the love you want, Conal Carmichael," she promised in a whisper. "You have no need of a pale, puny wife while I am here. Let her go, Conal, and I will satisfy all your needs. Send her away. Get rid of her."

He moaned and pulled her bodice down but did not answer her. Destiny laid a hand over his. "You hear me? Get rid of her and I will come whenever you want me. Or come to me when you will. I will never deny you." Her voice was urgent, but so was his need. Destiny sat up suddenly.

"What's wrong?" he demanded, his eyes darkening angrily. "You're jealous, that's what it is! You want to think you're the only one!"

"A woman's pride, Conal," she answered swiftly. "You don't need her, too."

"You stupid bitch!" he snapped. "I need her for her money and position! You cannot offer me those—only your body. But can't you see, we can still meet when I'm married. Men in my position keep a mistress as well as a wife, and no one objects."

For a moment he looked sullen, and then he added persuasively, "Not even McPherson will stand in the way, for he knows on which side his bread is buttered. He'll be grateful to you, in fact. Come, put your arms about me."

She was wasting her time, Destiny realized. She was foolish to believe for a second that she could seduce Conal away from his bride. She could not save Kate from him this way. Reason should have told her so, but the yearning in her veins for him had fooled her for a moment. Despite reason, however, she surrendered to his kiss and felt the heat in her blood rise again. His body pressed hard against hers, strength and desire throbbing in the muscles of his back. She felt herself slipping again into the vortex of exultancy and craving that she remembered so well in the cave. She welcomed his hands, his caresses, the feel of the evening air on her bared skin. His body covered hers, and he moaned softly.

"Damn!" He jerked upright as the reverberating sound of a gong filled the air. Destiny sat up slowly.

"The dinner gong," she said, unable to believe his sudden arrest of passion.

"Yes," he said coldly, rising and straightening his clothes. "I must take my fiancée into the dining hall. Another time—what is your name?"

"Destiny."

"A curious name. Well, good night, Destiny. Until another evening."

With alarm Destiny realized he would go. She leaped up swiftly, all passion gone. "Conal Carmichael, don't marry that girl," she said urgently. He looked at her curiously.

"Why not? What's she to you? I think you meddle too far, Mistress Destiny."

"You must not marry her!" Destiny raced on breathlessly, heedless of her words. "It would be terrible misfortune if you do!"

"Misfortune?" he queried. "How so?"

"I don't know—I just feel it in my bones. I have second sight, you know, and I know beyond a shadow of doubt that you will bring tragedy upon yourself if you wed her!" Destiny cried. He smiled in amusement.

"A witch, are you? A witch who would curse me out of spite? A woman betrayed, is that it?"

His look of scorn angered Destiny. "I have cursed you, Conal Carmichael, in the past, and I shall again. You bring nothing but misery to all you touch. Let the girl go, or I'll go to her myself."

She glared up at him and saw the glitter of angry scorn in his eyes. "And do you think she'd listen to the likes of you? Out of my way, woman, for I'm late for dinner already."

He turned to go. Destiny hissed at his averted back. "I can make her listen! I'll tell her about your first wife! And about the kind of brat you spawn—poor, twisted little runt. I'll show her Liam! Then she'll know what kind of man she's marrying!"

Destiny was unprepared for his violent reaction. Conal swung around sharply, and raising his arm, struck her a savage blow across her face that sent her reeling.

"You dare to threaten me?" he roared. "Speak to her of that, and that's the last thing you'll ever do!" he hissed, his handsome face contorted to a vicious mask of rage. "I'll flay you, I'll kill you! Or worse, I'll mark your beauty so that no man will ever desire you again! Now, get out of here before I thrash you as you deserve!"

"I hate you!" Destiny whimpered, picking herself up from the floor and gathering her fallen cloak. "I hate and despise you, Conal Carmichael, and one day my curse will come home to you, God willing."

"Out, you witch, you evil harridan!" he roared as she fled. Down the corridor she stumbled, crying hot tears of rage and frustration. She had had her chance and had mishandled the situation badly, she knew. Now he would never let Kate go.

The moon was rising palely behind the trees as Destiny crossed the fields toward her home. A light glowed in the parlor window. McPherson was home. She hoped he would not scold her for not being there to give him his supper. After all, Rosanna was there to see to him.

She did not see Liam's small figure sitting on the wall until she was unlatching the gate. His small oval face gleamed white in the moonlight.

"Liam, boy, why are you out here?" she asked, lifting a

hand to help him down. To her surprise, he answered her question.

"The master is angry," he said shortly, and taking her hand, he limped slowly beside her toward the door. Destiny could feel the tension in the air the moment she entered. No wonder the child had sought refuge outside.

McPherson was sitting alone in the parlor, his pipe tightly clenched in his fist and his expression cold. Uncleared dishes still lay on the table. Of Rosanna there was no sign.

Destiny tossed aside her cloak and busied herself clearing and stacking the dishes. "I've been up to the hall on an errand," she said brightly in an effort to appear normal. "Has Rosanna gone to bed?"

"She's gone out to look for you. Liam, go to bed," McPherson said curtly. The boy limped out. McPherson's face suddenly contorted redly. "That girl has got to go, do you hear me? I'll have no disobedient girl throwing tantrums in my house! The sooner she gets herself wed and leaves here, the better!"

"Why, what's amiss?" Destiny said in surprise. It was evident Rosanna had gone off in a temper, to leave the table still littered.

"You ask me what's amiss?" McPherson shouted. "I come home to supper and find you gallivanting off out, and that girl hands me defiance and insolence and you ask me what's amiss? Let me remind you I'm the master here and I will be obeyed. Your place is here to see to my needs, not running off to take a peek at the fine gentry folk up there! You're getting ideas above your station, madam, just because you were taken to the hall once. Get this pigsty tidied up at once, and upstairs to bed with you, my lady. Your day's work is not yet over."

With a sigh Destiny retreated to the kitchen to wash the dishes. It was evident that he was not going to tell her what he and Rosanna had quarreled over, but simply punish her for Rosanna's transgressions.

She dallied over the dishes as long as she could. It was growing late, and Rosanna was still out. Destiny began to grow worried.

* * *

178

Rosanna's forehead furrowed in perplexity. She had let herself into the hall by the servants' entrance, unnoticed by the staff, who were busily occupied in rushing up and down the back stairs serving dinner, and she had searched the upstairs rooms in vain. There was no sign of Mother.

Curious, thought Rosanna, for she had not met her on the way here. One thing was certain, however, and that was that Mother had been here, for the pearl necklace lay there on Catherine's dressing table.

Several of Catherine's clothes also lay about the room, scattered on the bed and over chairs. Whichever maid had helped her mistress dress for dinner had not completed the task properly, and instinctively Rosanna began to gather up the fallen garments and put them away. A petticoat edged with lace and a crumpled handkerchief were too soiled to put away; they were for the laundry, Rosanna decided, and closing the bedroom door after her, she headed for the laundry closet near the main staircase. From below, behind the closed doors of the dining room, she could hear the sounds of laughter. The gentry were evidently in high good humor tonight.

She dropped the discarded clothing into the wicker laundry basket and then noticed Catherine's nightgown and petticoats freshly ironed and folded on the slatted shelves above. Catherine would be needing the nightgown shortly. Rosanna picked up the neat pile, oblivious of the sound of a closing door and footsteps on the stairs until a voice behind her made her start.

"Well, upon my soul, a pretty damsel in my hour of need."

She turned quickly. The master himself, Mr. Carmichael, stood leaning nonchalantly against the doorjamb, a wry smile on his handsome face.

Rosanna blushed. She was accustomed to dealing with the banter of youths of her own kind, but this was the first time she had encountered a gentleman, and he the master too.

He stood upright, and closed the cupboard door behind him. In the confined space he stood close to her. "What are you doing here, little one? Waiting for me?"

"Forgive me, sir. I was just fetching my lady's clean

laundry before going home," Rosanna stammered, making to pass him, but he blocked her way.

He smiled, reaching out a hand to take the laundry from her and replace it on the shelf. "You would not run away and leave your master in sore distress, would you?" he teased.

"Oh, no, sir, but I thought you were all at dinner."

"They are at dinner, but I could not eat. Nor could I endure their trivial gossip any longer. You see, my blood is on fire, little one, and I need a pretty little companion like you to dowse that fire." He put an arm about her and pulled her close. Rosanna struggled to free herself. He threw back his head and laughed.

"I like a girl with spirit, but do not hold me off, little one. The others will go on eating for a time yet, but they will not stay there all night. Come, don't you know it is an honor for a maid to have the attentions of her master?"

Rosanna kicked him savagely. "His attention maybe, but you can keep your hands to yourself. You can dismiss me if you want, but you'll not lay me just because you're the master!"

A look of amazement leaped to Conal Carmichael's eyes, and he bent his knee to rub his shin as Rosanna pushed past him. As she rushed angrily along the corridor toward the servants' stairs, she heard his chuckle of amusement behind her. Who the devil did he think he was to take liberties with a decent girl? she raged inwardly. Handsome or not, and the master or not, he was not going to make free with her.

At the foot of the staircase she almost collided with a dark figure in the shadows. He moved forward into the light, and she recognised Bob Fellows, Mr. Philip's manservant. Beside him stood an enormous gray wolfhound, which bared its teeth and growled at her.

"Quiet, Sultan!" Bob snapped, and the dog slunk back behind him. "I'm sorry, Rosanna, I didn't mean to startle you," he added more gently. "Were you just leaving?"

Rosanna's anger faded instantly, all her resentment of Carmichael's selfishness for the moment forgotten. Bob Fellows was not only handsome and courteous, but he had also made it plain already that he considered Rosanna a lady to treat with respect and attentive charm. What woman could fail to respond to him after Carmichael's brusque boorishness?

"I finished ages ago," she told him, "but I came back on an errand. And you? Isn't that the master's dog you have there?" She pointed uncertainly at the gray hound behind him.

"It is, and Mr. Philip bade me walk him, for Mr. Carmichael does not exercise him as much as a big dog needs. I was just about to take him up the glen and let him run loose. Perhaps I could walk with you, if you will permit?"

Rosanna accepted his arm with a smile as he opened the door and helped her down the steps. The night air was coolly refreshing after the heat of the day, and the moon was showing a pale still face over the trees. After her recent rage she was in no mood to hurry home yet, and it was a perfect night for a stroll up the glen with a handsome man she found attractive. Just so long as he kept that evil-looking hound Sultan on the leash and well away from her. The dog had the same cunning, avaricious look as his master, and she trusted neither.

"Aren't you afraid that creature might turn on you and bite you?" she asked Bob as he helped her over the stile to cross the fields. He threw back his head and laughed.

"Not I, I'm used to dogs. I train Mr. Philip's hounds, and that's why he asked me to walk Sultan. There's nothing I can't do with dogs. They seem to trust me and respond quickly. I'll show you."

Sure enough, when Bob released the dog up in the glen and let him run, the dog came running back to his command. Within moments Bob had him coming to heel to order, and then sitting and lying on command. He patted the dog's great shaggy head in approval.

"Good boy. Now you can run for a while. Go, boy go." The dog loped off into the bushes. Bob turned to Rosanna and took her hand. She did not withdraw it. "You see? It is easy if you have confidence," he said. "I'll teach you how to control Sultan if you like. Perhaps you'd like to come out with me now and again on a fine evening, and I'll show you how it's done."

"I'd like that," Rosanna replied. Not that she cared about being close to that huge, evil dog, but it would afford an opportunity to be alone again with Bob, and the prospect was pleasing. It was so still and peaceful up here in the moonlit glen, and Bob's gentle, courteous manner was proof that not all men were as selfish and vile as Carmichael and McPherson. God! How she loathed those two men. She frowned angrily.

"What is it?" Bob asked. "You look so angry."

"I'm sorry," she apologized quickly. "I was angry before I met you. I was beginning to think all men horrible because the master embarrassed me. He trapped me in the laundry cupboard, and I had to duck him. Perhaps it's only gentry who behave so. You are always polite, and I'm enjoying your company." She smiled again to prove it.

"I'm glad, for I enjoy yours too, Rosanna," he responded, pressing her hand more tightly. "I can understand how you feel about Mr. Carmichael, but I'm afraid it's in his nature. Not my master, though! Mr. Philip always behaves with propriety."

"I do not know the gentleman, though I have seen him in my mistress's company, and she seems to like him. I saw them sitting together in the library today, reading poetry. I truly believe she prefers his company to Mr. Conal's."

"Then she shows good taste," Bob replied. "A pity she is to marry Mr. Carmichael so soon, or perhaps they could have become better acquainted. Mr. Philip has remained a bachelor too long, in my opinion, and I never saw him blossom in a lady's company as he does with your mistress."

He sounded sorrowful, and Rosanna looked at him in surprise. Catherine and Mr. Philip? "When is the wedding to be?" she asked Bob. "Have you heard a date mentioned yet?"

It was his turn to look surprised. "But of course, you weren't on duty tonight, so you won't have heard. One of the parlor maids came down to the servants' hall and told us she had heard Mr. Conal at dinner telling the count that he was tired of waiting and would have the priest perform the ceremony tomorrow."

"Tomorrow?" Rosanna's brain began to spin. "So soon? Did my lady Catherine agree to it?"

"She was not consulted, according to the parlormaid. Mr. Conal demanded it of the count, and he had no choice but to agree. I think you'll have to be at work early in the morning, Rosanna, to help your mistress prepare, so I'd better take you home. Sultan!"

The dog came running from the bushes at his call. Bob fastened the leash to the dog's collar and handed the leash to Rosanna. "There, you take him. You'll find he'll obey you if you speak confidently enough. Don't let him pull you."

Rosanna took the leash reluctantly. She would have preferred to retain Bob's hand, but had to content herself with the feel of his hand under her elbow as they walked through the wood. "Heel, Sultan," she called whenever the hound tried to pull away, and in time she was relieved to discover that the creature obeyed. By the time they reached the field near home, she even patted the dog's head as Bob had done, and was gratified when Sultan sat obediently, as though anxious to please her.

At the gate Bob brushed a kiss lightly on her cheek. "Tomorrow night?" he asked. Rosanna felt a leap of pleasure, and then hesitated.

"We'll see. There's much to be done tomorrow," she said, and hurried indoors. Today had been such a strange day of turmoil and surprises that she could not safely trust her own feelings.

Destiny was lighting a candle from the kitchen oil lamp in readiness to go up to bed when at last she heard Rosanna come in.

"So there you are, macushla," she said in a relieved tone. "I was worrying where you'd got to at this hour of the night."

"No need to worry over me, Mother. You know I can take care of myself. I was walking up the glen with Bob Fellows. He's a fine young man, Mother. You'd like him.

Not a bit like that lecherous Mr. Conal. If he hadn't been the master, I'd have cracked his face for him today."

Destiny felt anxious. "Mr. Conal made advances to you, girl? What did you do?"

Rosanna laughed dryly. "Oh, I got away from him, but it might not be so easy another time. I don't know, I'm not even safe up at the hall. Out of the frying pan into the fire."

"What do you mean?" Destiny asked. Rosanna was biting her lip, and she turned away quickly.

"Oh, nothing, I was rambling. But Bob told me something, Mother, a piece of news you won't like to hear."

"I don't like what I've heard already," Destiny said in vexation. "I want no daughter of mine being the toy of that wicked Mr. Conal. You must keep out of his way." It was impossible to explain to Rosanna the mixture of revulsion and jealousy she felt.

"But listen, Mother. Tomorrow Mr. Conal and Catherine are to be wed. He'll wait no longer, and he's made it clear tonight that he wants the wedding tomorrow. Poor Catherine cannot escape now."

Destiny stared at her in horror. "Tomorrow? Oh, God, no! He must not! We must stop him somehow!"

"But how, Mother? 'Tis too late now to talk of running away. But I'll protect her, I promise. I'll ask her tomorrow if I can go to live in the hall, for she needs me by her, and then I'll promise I'll do all I can to see no harm comes to her. You can trust me, Mother."

But Destiny was not listening, staring at her daughter in terror. Conal Carmichael sought to marry one of her daughters and bed the other, and come hell or high water, she must stop him. Especially since one of the two girls he threatened was his own child.

Nineteen

Destiny awoke with a start, wondering what the troublesome thought was that had nagged her into sudden wakefulness. Her first thought was one of relief; mercifully McPherson had been asleep when she came to bed, so he had not troubled her. Her second thought as she stretched out her arm was that he was already up, and then suddenly it came to her. Today Conal was to wed Catherine, unless somehow she could prevent it!

Leaping out of bed, Destiny washed and dressed in frantic haste. Rosanna and McPherson were already gone, Rosanna no doubt at this moment helping her mistress to don her wedding gown. Destiny seized her cloak and hurried out, down the hill toward the church. She did not even know at what hour the wedding was to take place, but as she neared the old gray stone church, she could see the villagers in their Sunday-best clothes already assembling there.

They were smiling and chatting among themselves, but though they eyed Destiny curiously, none spoke to her. She pushed her way past them, into the already crowded church, and found a space in a pew near the back. Conal was seated near the altar, awaiting his bride, Philip O'Keeffe sitting with bowed head beside him. How totally unalike they were, she thought, the fair head of the one captured in a golden shaft of sunlight through the stained-glass window above, and the other dark and brooding as the devil himself. A devil who should not have her beloved daughter in his clutches, not if Destiny could help it.

The whispering congregation's sudden silence told her that the bride was coming, and in the arched doorway she saw the tall figure of the bearded count, resplendent in top hat and a tailed coat, and the slender girl in oyster satin leaning on his arm.

Destiny caught her breath. Catherine looked angelic, an ethereal vision of perfect womanhood with the sunlight dancing on her golden hair and the aura of chiffon about her flowered cap. Brown eyes gazed soberly down the aisle to where her prospective husband stood waiting, and Destiny felt a pang of tenderness for her child and the apprehension in her eyes.

Destiny could only stare in admiration at the lovely, wistful creature who advanced slowly down the aisle toward the altar and the tall dark man who was to be her husband. All around could be heard the gasps and murmurs of approval, and Destiny felt powerless to move.

Father Clancy stood at the top of the altar steps, above the couple. Philip O'Keeffe stood behind the bridegroom, and Count Andreyev behind Catherine. The priest raised his hand.

"Brethren, we are gathered together to witness the joining of this man and this woman in holy matrimony," he intoned.

"No, no!" Destiny heard herself cry out, and found herself pushing her way out into the aisle. "No, he cannot marry her!"

Heads turned, and the congregation muttered its disapproval of so sacrilegious an interruption. Neither bride nor groom moved. Only Father Clancy looked up from his book and peered uncertainly toward her.

"Father Clancy, do not marry them!" Destiny cried out. "He cannot marry her!"

"Why, Mistress McPherson," said the priest, recognizing her voice. "Whatever is the matter? Pray be seated and let us continue in peace."

"No, Father! Conal Carmichael cannot marry my daughter! I will not allow it!"

This time the motionless tableau at the altar sprang into life. Catherine's fair head turned to face her, bewildered and alarmed. Philip O'Keeffe's head turned in openmouthed astonishment. The count turned slowly to deliver an inscrutable stare, and Conal Carmichael spun around to glare at her with ill-concealed fury.

"Be silent, woman!" he roared, "or I shall have you thrown out! Is this your idea of petty revenge?"

"No revenge, Conal," Destiny replied loudly. "Only seeking to see justice done."

"Justice?" he snapped. "What are you blathering about? Michael, Seamus, remove that idiot woman from the church!"

Two footmen began to move, but Father Clancy intervened. "There will be no laying of violent hands on a body in my church, Mr. Carmichael. This is the house of God. Mistress McPherson, do you know of any lawful impediment to prevent this marriage?"

"I do," Destiny proclaimed proudly. "The lady is not the count's daughter to give away, but mine."

"What rubbish!" Conal said irritably. "For heaven's sake, Count, put the lie to this woman's rambling."

All eyes turned on the count. His face grew visibly pale behind the dark beard, and he shook his head and remained silent.

"He cannot," cried Destiny, "for he knows I speak the truth. And more than that, Conal Carmichael, you remember the glen and the cave on a hot summer afternoon, do you not, for you admitted as much not three days ago?"

He colored up hotly. "What nonsense is this, madam? Do you hope to humiliate me publicly? Where is your husband? I'll see to it he gives you a sound beating for this!"

"I am here, sir." To Destiny's surprise, McPherson appeared from the back of the church and took her arm. "Come, wife," he said shortly.

She wrenched her arm away. "Not until I have spoken my piece!" she cried, conscious that every pair of eyes in the church was fastened upon her in wonder. "Carmichael remembers the cave, and me, and what we did. Well, know this too, Conal Carmichael! I bore you a child as a result of that day, a fine, beautiful girl child that you knew nothing of. I loved and cherished her, and she is mine! And I'll never let you lay hands on her!"

Turning, Destiny ran from the church, hearing McPherson's heavy footsteps close behind. Let him fume, let him beat her, she did not care so long as the marriage did not take place. And to marry them was more than Father Clancy could do now.

McPherson caught up with her and seized her arm roughly, spinning her around to face him. "What madness is this, woman? Why do you utter such dreadful lies? You have but one daughter, Rosanna, and she was Jim Regan's child. Do you try to ruin us both with your foolishness?"

"You think so?" Destiny cried exultantly. "Well, you were wrong. I had two daughters, one by Jim and one by Carmichael, but you said you would take me if I had only the one child. So I sent Kate away, fool that I was, but now she's come back, and she has a right to know the truth."

"What truth? That she is Carmichael's daughter?" McPherson's small eyes were wide in disbelieving wonder.

Destiny was about to spit out an answer when the idea came to her. To confess which child was Conal's would be to leave the other exposed to his wiles. Destiny ignored McPherson's last question and answered the first.

"Why, the truth that she is my daughter," she said coolly, feeling a mounting sense of exultant power. "If she can persuade the count to confess the truth, she will soon discover she is not his child."

Below them, down the hill, figures were emerging from the church—the gaily dressed ladies and gentlemen from the hall, the bride in her oyster satin on the count's arm—and the coaches were hastily lining up to carry them away. Destiny smiled grimly. For the moment, triumph was hers, for the wedding had clearly been abandoned, but she knew this was not the end of it. For the moment she could enjoy a grim satisfaction in knowing she was protecting both her children from him, but the battle was not over yet. Conal would not let Destiny conquer him thus easily. He would fight back.

* * *

Conal Carmichael paced angrily up and down the library floor, a fierce frown marring his forehead. Sitting watching him in silence were a pale-faced Catherine and her solemn father. Philip O'Keeffe stood motionless behind Catherine's chair, and Father Clancy stood nervously twitching the folds of his cassock by the fire.

"Can't you see, Count Andreyev, it was all just spite on her part," Conal rumbled. "You heard her—I dallied with her once, many years ago when I was but a youth, and she cherishes a wild notion that that makes me hers forever. Only the other night she was here begging me not to marry Catherine, promising me her own charms instead. I turned her down, of course, and that's why she plans this in revenge. A woman scorned, and all that."

"Perhaps," said the count reflectively.

"But can you be sure she did not bear you a child as a result of that . . . dalliance," Philip O'Keeffe intervened. "Can you be sure she is lying?"

"If she did, no one ever heard of the child," Conal exploded. "Of course she's lying. And Catherine, of all people? I can't understand why you did not deny her wild story at once, Count."

Catherine looked up at her father. "You did not because it could be true, isn't that so, Papa? I could be her daughter, could I not?"

"Nonsense!" Conal roared. "You a lady of society and she but a village wench as she was before she married my bailiff? I think her rise in station has gone to her head and given her notions of grandeur, claiming to have mothered you."

"But it would explain so many things I could not previously understand," Catherine went on quietly. "The strange feelings I have had of having been here before."

"The French call it *déjà vu*. It is not uncommon," Conal replied.

"And of having an affinity with the place, and more than that, with people here. My maid in particular."

"Affinity? What romantic woman's talk is this?" Conal demanded impatiently.

"Your maid? Rosanna?" It was Philip who spoke, his gentle, even voice a strong contrast to Conal's angry roar.

"Yes, Philip. And Rosanna is Mrs. McPherson's daughter. If what the lady says is true, then Rosanna is my half-sister, and the mystery of our affinity is resolved. In the circumstances, I cannot and will not marry you, Conal."

Conal spun around angrily to face the count. "The lady is willful, it seems to me, sir. You know this whole story is a pack of lies calculated by a scheming woman to prevent my marriage. I suggest you treat this matter with the scorn it deserves and order Catherine to marry me at once."

The count looked at the younger man's fiery dark face with composure. "I regret that in the circumstances I can do no such thing. At any time I would not command Catherine to do anything against her will, and in this case, where the circumstances are still unclear, I consider it my duty to withhold judgment until all is known."

Conal's expression darkened further. "Unclear? You know the circumstances of your own daughter's birth, do you not? You can emphatically put the lie to this woman's claim?"

The count regarded him coldly. "No, sir, I cannot. Catherine is my adopted daughter, though I wish she could have learned of it in pleasanter circumstances."

Catherine's blond head, still veiled for the ceremony, turned upward to stare at him. "Adopted, Papa? When, and where?"

"Fifteen years ago, in Liverpool. You were about three at the time."

"And you never told me?"

"I thought the circumstances of my finding and adopting you too harrowing a story for your ears. I often meant to tell you. Forgive me, my dear."

Tears brimmed in his black eyes, and Catherine reached up a hand to take his. He clasped her hands in his and bowed his head.

"This is ridiculous!" Conal snorted, starting to stamp up and down the room again. "In a moment you will begin to believe Catherine is really that bitch's child! Father Clancy, I appeal to you to bring some semblance of reason to this charade! The woman has produced no real evidence why the wedding should not go on, has she?"

The priest shook his head. He was visibly shaking. "No, no real evidence, but a suspicion which has some evidence to back it up. In the circumstances, I feel I could not perform the ceremony, even if the lady and her father were agreeable."

"Could not? Would not?" Conal stormed. "What defiance is this, priest? Do you not hold your living from me?"

"I do, sir, but there are too many strange mysteries in this case."

"The only mystery is Catherine's true parentage, but that is of little consequence! Destiny McPherson is certainly not her mother!"

"But she could be," the priest replied in a small, worried voice. "For now I remember it, fifteen years ago."

"What? What do you remember?" It was Catherine who spoke, her pallor relieved by a sudden spurt of color to her cheeks.

Father Clancy clasped his hands as if in prayer. "It is against my vows to reveal the secrets of the confessional, but I wonder whether it would not be a greater sin to let this marriage go on. Oh, Father! Forgive me and guide me what to do for the best!"

"Speak, man! Out with it." Conal's voice had shrunk to a whisper.

The priest swallowed hard. "Destiny Regan, as she was then, confessed to me that she was to bear a child which was not her husband's. It was only just after the birth of her first child."

"Did she tell you the father's name?" Philip O'Keeffe asked anxiously.

The priest nodded miserably. "She did. She said it was Mr. Carmichael."

The silence in the library for the next few seconds was almost tangible. Then Conal turned away.

"She was lying."

"In preparation for today?" Philip cut in. "It seems unlikely."

Catherine was sobbing quietly. Philip laid a comforting hand on her shoulder. A sudden idea occurred to Conal.

"Wait a moment, you said the woman had another child. A girl?"

Father Clancy nodded. "Rosanna, the lady Catherine's maid."

"And which was the firstborn child?"

"I don't know."

"Have you no records?"

"Only the date of each birth, or rather the baptism."

"No names?"

"Only that it was a girl child."

Conal's frown was swiftly replaced by a smile of satisfaction. "Then don't you see, there's no proof. She could have borne my child, but it could equally well be this Rosanna. All we have to do is discover which was born first. My child, if mine at all, could only have been the second one."

"That's true," the priest agreed. "So if we learn the order of birth of the two young ladies, we can at least eliminate the first from being your child. May we send for your maid, my lady?"

"By all means," Catherine agreed quickly. "Philip, be so kind as to ring the bell and bid the parlormaid send for Rosanna."

Philip obeyed, and while the maid went off in search of Rosanna, Catherine looked thoughtful. "My birthday is November 12, 1845," she remarked quietly. "We shall soon see as to Rosanna's."

At that moment a knock came at the door and Rosanna entered. She bobbed a curtsy and stood awaiting her mistress's order.

"Rosanna," Catherine said quietly. "You were in the church today and heard your mother, did you not?"

"Yes, my lady, and a real shock it was to me, too. I had no idea," Rosanna replied.

Conal cut in sharply. "Enough of this. All we want to know from you, my girl, is your date of birth. Do you know it?"

"To be sure, I do. I was born on August 18, 1845,"

she replied confidently. "I am nearly eighteen years of age."

"Impossible!" snapped Conal. "There, you see, there is only three months' difference in their ages. The woman was lying. Even a saint could not perform a miracle like that!"

Father Clancy clicked his tongue in disapproval. Catherine smiled at Rosanna.

"Thank you, Rosanna. You may go now. I shall call you later."

Rosanna, frowning, bobbed and withdrew. The count coughed nervously and stepped forward.

"It is no use relying on these dates to solve the mystery, I'm afraid, for Catherine's birthday, which she has always celebrated in November, is a purely arbitrary date, chosen by me."

Philip stepped closer to him. "What are you saying, Count Andreyev? That you do not know Catherine's real age?"

The count nodded. "I judged her to be about three years of age when her mother died and left her to my care. That was in November, 1848, so I chose to give her that date. It was better than nothing."

Conal leaped toward him, his dark eyes bright with excitement. "Her mother—she died, you say? Then Destiny McPherson was not her mother!"

"I took the woman to be her mother, for the child was in her care. But I remember a letter she had me write for her before she died, a letter to a relative here in Ireland. I do not recall the name or even the address, but it was to a woman, telling her of the child. So my friend need not necessarily have been her mother. All I know is that the child was left alone, sick and destitute. The woman and her husband were both dead. I adopted Catherine as my own."

Catherine's eyes glistened with tears. "And a dearer, kinder father there could never have been. God bless you, Papa."

Conal slapped his thigh impatiently. "And we are still no nearer the truth. Either of these girls could be the elder. I see no reason to believe any of this nonsense, except that Catherine is an orphan. But I do not mind. She is now your adopted daughter and heiress, Count Andreyev, and I am still willing to marry her, whatever her origins."

"Even though the maid Rosanna could be your daughter?" Philip asked quietly. "Or worse still, Catherine?"

"It cannot be considered," Father Clancy pronounced. "There is a dreadful name for the sin you would commit in taking your own child to wife, and I cannot condone that."

Catherine leaped up and ran sobbing from the room. Philip hastened out after her.

"Then, by God, the McPherson woman must be made to tell the truth," Conal growled. "And I'll get it out of her if it kills me."

Twenty

It was noon before McPherson came home. Destiny was alone in the house, for Tara had not turned up for the day's work, and Destiny gave it little thought. She had probably taken the day off to go to the big wedding, but in any event Destiny's mind was in too much turmoil to care. She tried to calm her whirling brain by setting about the ordinary daily tasks of the house.

"Do you realize what you've done, woman?" McPherson demanded when he strode into the kitchen. "They're all at sixes and sevens up at the house, the master locked away with the count and the priest and roaring like a mad bull, the lady Catherine weeping like a baby, and Rosanna trying to comfort her. Mrs. Kidd has prepared meals no one will eat, and all the maids are terrified of the master's fury. And you've done this, with your wild tongue."

"I did what had to be done," Destiny replied quietly.

"And do you think Conal Carmichael will let you get away with it? You stand there ironing like nothing had happened, and any minute the master could come crashing in here and give you the hiding of your life! And well you deserve it!"

"And what will you do if he does? Will you protect me against him?"

McPherson's close-set eyes stared at her in surprise. "Is that what you want of me? To set up against a man as powerful as he? Do you think I'm mad too, woman?"

"So you'll let him beat me."

"I'm no fool. I know on which side my bread is buttered. Mark my words, if I see him coming up here, and he still in a black rage, I'll make myself scarce and you'll have to fend for yourself, my girl. Use your wayward tongue then to save yourself if you can, but don't look to me to fight him. You're on your own, Destiny McPherson."

"As I always have been," she replied calmly. "You disappoint me, McPherson, but I'm glad at least I know where I stand."

She replaced a cooling iron on the hob and lifted the hot one, spitting on it and hearing the hiss that showed it was ready for use. Liam opened the door, and seeing McPherson, stood uncertain.

"I'll be off to my work," McPherson grunted. "I don't want to be here if he comes, nor any complaints from him about me slacking. Have some sense if he does come, Destiny. You've had your moment. Do whatever he wants, and it will be the better for both of us."

Seeing she would not answer, he turned and pushed past the boy. Liam came in and seated himself quietly in the corner on the floor.

"Here," said Destiny, handing him an earthenware bowl of water. "Make yourself useful and damp down those clothes in the basket for me, will you?"

Liam took the bowl and began sprinkling water from his fingertips onto the linen. Destiny smiled at him, and had the gratification of seeing an answering twitch at the corners of his lips. Poor little fellow, she thought, ignored and neglected for so long. All it needed was for someone to take notice of him and give him a little affection, and he would soon lose his uncouth, backward appearance. What a loathsome creature Conal Carmichael was, to cast off and neglect a child who needed attention so much!

There was a sound outside, and Destiny looked up from the steaming shirt she was pressing. The door opened and Rosanna burst in.

"Mother, the count is here to see you, and Catherine is in the carriage outside."

"Bid him come in, and welcome, and my daughter too," Destiny said calmly, laying aside the iron. "And you take Liam outside awhile, will you?"

Rosanna held out her hand to the boy, and he rose and limped out after her. Seconds later a tall, burly figure filled the doorway.

"Come in, Count Nicolai," Destiny said politely. "I was expecting Mr. Carmichael to come, not you. Is my daughter Kate coming in?"

She eyed him squarely, challenging him to deny Catherine was her child, but he simply shook his great shaggy head. He was a fine-built man, she noted, broad and strong as a blacksmith, handsome too with his graying black hair and solemn dark eyes.

"Catherine awaits in the carriage, for she is a little upset," he said slowly.

"She does not deny me?" Destiny asked anxiously.

He shook his head again. "She believes you, though until this day she believed herself mine."

"Then I'm glad," Destiny said in relief, "for blood recognizes blood. My child Rosanna knew her half-sister at once, though she did not know why then. But why are you here, Count?"

"To satisfy myself you are truly her mother, and now I see you closely, I do not doubt it. You are so like the woman I took to be her mother."

"My sister, Shuna, God rest her soul. She took my Kate to England, or the child would have starved to death else. I had no choice, though I loved her better than my own soul. Do you believe that, Count?"

"I do, for I have loved her no less, though she was not my blood. Shuna had me write a letter once, and I realize now it was to Catherine's mother, though I had forgotten the address. I sent it to a priest, I recollect, though I understood little English in those days and wrote only the words that Shuna spoke. Did that letter come to you?"

Without replying, Destiny went upstairs to her room, ransacked in a drawer, and returned with a sheet of paper in her hand.

"Is this the letter, Count?"

He read it in silence for a moment. "It is, and there is Shuna's mark. I remember how I had to hold her up while she made it, for she was so weak. She died a few days later in my arms."

"I know, Count Nicolai, for I went to Liverpool to find Shuna and Kate, and they told me of Big Nick, who cared for them."

He smiled. "Big Nick. Ah, yes, I remember. I spoke only a few halting words of English then, and I think they took me for some big, wild barbarian. The truth was that I was driven from my home in Russia, had landed in Hull, and was walking across England to Liverpool to take ship to America. Then I met your sister. I was penniless."

"But you are a rich man, so I've been told," Destiny said.

"Not then. I could not care for Catherine. I took her to a hospital when she was sick of the fever, and when they said she would recover, I left her there. I knew the man who ran the hospital also had an orphanage where Catherine would be cared for until I could come back for her. So I set sail for America."

"I traced you and her to that hospital, but they told me my child was dead," Destiny said, tears brimming as she remembered that night and Taff's death.

"Some mistake, evidently," the count said gently. "What a blow for you."

"Yet you came back and took her from the orphanage, and by some miracle, brought her back to Ballymachree."

He smiled, the smile irradiating his great, bearded face with warmth and tenderness. "The ways of the Almighty are indeed strange. When I had made my fortune in the gold rush of forty-nine, I came back. I sought out Philip O'Keeffe and reclaimed my Catherine. I adopted her and took her to live with me in Manchester. I gave her the best, Mistress McPherson, and a good education with the best tutors I could find."

"Philip O'Keeffe?" Destiny said in perplexity.

"He manages the orphanage where she was, among his other charitable institutions," the count explained. "We remained friends, and I saw him from time to time in London, but he never saw Catherine again until he suggested last winter that I bring her to London and he would introduce her to his friends. That is how we came to meet Mr. Carmichael."

"I see," said Destiny. Now the miracle of Catherine's return to her own village was explained. Suddenly she remembered herself. She had a guest in the house and had as yet offered him no refreshment.

"Let me fetch you a drink, Count," she said quickly. "I have no wine, I fear, but I have an excellent draft of ale you might enjoy."

"Thank you, no," he said quietly. "You are very like your beautiful sister, Mistress McPherson."

His look held hers, admiring and yet respectful. Destiny laughed.

"I wonder so handsome and rich a man as you never married, Count," she said lightly, and instantly regretted her words when she saw the sad look that clouded his dark eyes.

"I could not. I only ever loved one woman, and she died in my arms fifteen years ago."

Destiny could have kicked herself. She longed to apologize, but the harm was done. As if to spare her feelings, the count took her hand gently in his.

"I shall tell Catherine of how you sought her in England, how you loved her, though I think she knows it already. And when she is calmer, I shall bring her back to talk to you. Are you agreeable?"

Destiny responded to the pressure of his hand. "I

would love to hug and kiss her now, but if you think it wiser to wait..."

"And in the meantime keep clear of Mr. Carmichael, for I fear he will come and try to make you retract your statement in the church. He may try to make you deny your words."

"Deny my own child? Never!" Destiny said proudly. "But surely he does not want to marry her still?"

"He will if he can, for my money."

"But why did you ever agree to the marriage? Kate does not love him, surely?"

"I believed her besotted with him, and added to that, she knows marriage to a respected landowner would secure for me the recognition my money alone could not win. An émigré is always an outcast in London society until marriage into the gentry redeems him. I think she wanted to do that for me, bless her."

"Outcast or not, you're always welcome here," Destiny said warmly, and felt the count's hand tighten on hers before he let go.

"Thank you, Mistress McPherson. Now I must take my leave, but I promise to return again soon, bringing Catherine."

She watched him go, calling to Rosanna to rejoin her mistress. As Rosanna climbed in the coach, Liam came back into the kitchen and sat down again, this time at the table. With a start Destiny realized it was past lunch hour and the boy must be hungry.

"Move the irons off the hob, Liam, and I'll heat up a bowl of soup for you, boy," she told him. When the soup was bubbling, she poured it into a bowl for him and watched while he broke bread into it and ate hungrily. Poor boy, in the excitement of the day she had forgotten to feed him until now, and he had had the patience to wait without complaint. She patted his dark curls in a gesture of affection, and he jerked his head away to glare up at her warily. She sighed. He had not yet lost his defensive manner. It would take time.

The boy—Conal's child! In her turmoil she had forgotten Conal's earlier marriage. The count and Kate did not know of it yet, for it was doubtful Conal had told them.

Should she have told them, made it plain that Conal already had a son and heir whose rights would supersede those of any future children? But what matter now?—the count acknowledged her as Kate's mother and therefore presumably accepted that Conal was Kate's father, so the marriage would never go through.

Liam spooned up the last of his soup noisily, carried the empty bowl to the cupboard, and then squatted in the corner to caress the kitten who lay sleeping there. Destiny replaced the two flatirons on the hob and wandered over to the window to look out while she waited for them to heat.

It was a magnificent summer's day, the golden haze of sunlight lying mellow over the potato fields below, a perfect day for a wedding in any other circumstances, she thought. Downhill she could just see the cluster of cottages in the village, with their white walls ablaze in the sunlight. Of the old cottages, tumbled long ago in the time of the great hunger, there was no sign now.

Uphill between the trees she could just glimpse the stately gray walls of Ballymachree Hall, where her two daughters were, both of them probably as concerned as herself about their future. And here she was, halfway between villagers and gentry, where she had been these many years, belonging neither to the one nor to the other and distrusted by both. Sighing, she turned away from the window and crossed to the fire.

With a pad of cloth she lifted a flatiron and spat on it. Its hiss told her it was ready for use, and she glided it over the linen table-cover spread waiting. So engrossed was she in her task that she heard no warning sound until a shadow crossed the window. Someone was coming to the door, which stood ajar in the heat.

She knew it was he almost before her eyes told her, as if some emanation from his body preceded him and spoke to her, causing her to stiffen.

"Good day to you, Conal Carmichael," she said as his tall figure bent to enter the doorway. "I was expecting you to call."

As he straightened she saw that he was no longer wearing his fine coat and waistcoat of the morning, but only a fine white shirt and his breeches. His unruly hair had sprung free of its pomade and was leaping in wild black curls about his temples. His forehead was beaded with sweat, and he advanced upon her purposefully. Destiny put down the iron and retreated to the far side of the table.

"Destiny McPherson, I do not come to bandy words with you. I want this whole damn mess cleared up," he said abruptly. "Tell me that what you said this morning in the church was a pack of lies and I'll go easy on you. I'll forget the whole matter."

"That is what you would like, to forget it all, but it can't be put out of your mind that easy," she said calmly. "I bore you a daughter, and that was no lie. A fine, strong child, Conal, I bore you. No limping, deformed brat like your first wife." For the moment she had forgotten Liam's presence.

"Then why didn't you tell me?"

"And have you take her from me? No, by God, she was mine! Or you might have denied her then as you did today, and a fine fool I'd have been."

"Your child you wanted to keep, and yet you claim you let her go away? How much did you care for her, then?" Conal demanded.

"Let her go? I was forced to it by your cruelty, you villain! You starved us all till half the village died! I sent her away to give her a chance of life, and God saw to it that she prospered. Now she's back, I'll not see her fall into your cruel hands!"

Conal's eyes gleamed in anger. "But is Catherine my child, Destiny, or is it the other one, the dark-haired girl? She looks more like me. Are you saying it is Catherine only to vex me?"

"Aha! Now we come to it." Destiny smiled at him. "You would like to know that, wouldn't you?"

"And why should you not tell me?"

"Because you threaten both my girls. I think you have a fancy to wed the one and bed the other, but so long as you cannot tell which is your own child, you'll touch neither!"

The tone of triumph in Destiny's voice clearly angered

him, for she saw his hand tighten on the chair back, and he took a step toward her.

"Tell me, damn you!" he muttered, and then his tone changed. "Tell me, Destiny," he said more softly, "if only for what we once were to each other—and could be again, for you are a handsome woman and I am generous to those who please me."

His voice, purring like an ingratiating cat, irritated Destiny. "What we once were?" she repeated. "I was nothing to you but an incident to while away a stormy afternoon! And you, generous? I remember your generosity, Conal Carmichael. Women and children could starve in the hedges so long as you drew your rents! No, I want none of your generosity, only to see my girls safe from the likes of you!"

His face grew purple with rage, contorted to an ugly mask with furious frustration, and, coming around the table, he snatched up the flatiron that was lying on the hob, seizing Destiny's arm with his free hand.

"I've warned you before, Destiny McPherson, not to cross me or I'd teach you a lesson you'd never forget! Beating is too good for you. A scar on that lovely face of yours would serve to remind all my tenants that obedience to the master is their duty!"

He thrust the iron close to her face, and she felt its searing heat so close to her cheek that it sent waves of pain through her head. She shrieked.

"Oh, God! No!"

He laughed harshly, evidently enjoying his power.

"After this, no man will ever desire you again!"

Already her skin felt to be blistering under the intense heat, and Destiny felt faint.

"For the love of God, no!" she cried.

What happened next was never really clear to her. She was aware of a flurry of movement in the corner of the room, a thud, and then Conal's strangled moan before he let the iron fall and sagged drunkenly to the floor.

He lay in a crumpled heap, a trickle of blood seeping from his temple. Liam stood there a few yards away, his weight leaning upon his good leg while his clubfoot hovered off the ground. Beside Conal's head lay the cold flatiron, and by his foot the hot one was scorching a hole into the rug.

"Liam! What have you done!" Destiny cried, bending beside Conal's inert figure. At that moment Rosanna rushed in the open door.

"Mother! For God's sake! What happened?"

"I hit him with the iron. He was going to kill you," Liam said in a choked voice.

Rosanna knelt. "Is he dead?"

"No," said Destiny, "but he's unconscious."

McPherson walked in, and a frown of perplexity rutted his brow when he caught sight of Carmichael's supine figure. Destiny leaped up.

"The master slipped and hit his head on the iron," she said quickly. "For heaven's sake, get him home to bed and call the doctor."

"Slipped? How could he?"

"There's water on the flagstones. Wake up, man, the master needs help," she told him crisply.

McPherson pulled Carmichael to his feet and put his shoulder under his armpit. "Did you tell him what he wanted?" he asked.

"I did not."

"Then we're in for trouble, sure as fate, when he comes to. Damn you for a stupid woman, Destiny, for you'll be the ruination of us both," he muttered as he went out with his burden.

Rosanna patted the boy's head, and this time he did not shrink, Destiny noted. "Mother, McPherson was outside when you cried out," she said quietly.

"And he came running?"

"No, Mother. He turned away and went into the stable. I think he knew the master was threatening you, and turned a blind eye."

"Then he did no more than he promised," Destiny said.

"The beast! God, how I hate that man, Mother! I tell you, if ever he's found dead, you'll not have far to look for his killer, for I'll do it myself before I'm very much older, I swear to God I will!"

"Rosanna, hold your tongue. We'd best be getting the supper ready before he comes back."

But inwardly Destiny agreed with her daughter. McPherson was not only a bullying tyrant but a coward to boot. A man like him, one could only despise.

Twenty-one

Rosanna looked at her mother in deep concern. She was quiet, but her lip was trembling, and Rosanna knew she had had a hard time of it. Her blouse was torn where the master had evidently seized her, and her left cheek was angrily reddening.

"Did the bastard hit you, Mother?"

Destiny raised a hand to her cheek. "No. 'Tis a burn. He tried to burn my face and damn near succeeded. He would have the truth out of me, either by bribery or by threats, but I'll none of it. He'll learn nothing from me."

"Here, let me smooth butter on your face. 'Twill soothe the sting," Rosanna said, fetching the butter dish from the pantry. "He wants to know which of us is his child, Catherine or me, doesn't he? He sent for me to ask my birthday, but he still did not know."

"That's it, but I'll never tell him. That way he'll keep his hands off the both of you."

"He might," Rosanna agreed in a dubious tone, "but then again, he might choose to ignore you and marry Catherine."

"That he'll not, for there's not a priest in Ireland who would marry them and risk being guilty of the sin of incest," Destiny said with conviction. "Anyway, I doubt the count would permit it now."

"Then it seems for the moment you have the whip

hand, Mother, but Conal Carmichael will not let the matter lie there if he recovers. He'll kill you first."

"He will recover, won't he, Rosanna? He was not badly hurt?"

"And why should you care? We'll know when McPherson comes home. But tell me, Mother, for I must know, is that beast father to me or to Catherine?"

Destiny smiled gently. "You know I'd have no secrets from you, macushla, but this is one I must keep. While no one but I knows the truth, no one can tell. And I'd not have the master threatening you to get the truth. No, Rosanna, I'll not tell you. Nor Kate either if she asks. That way is safest for us all."

"Doesn't the count know?"

"He knows only that Kate is my child, but not who her father is. And the secret will go with me to my grave if I can keep you both out of that devil's reach."

Rosanna nodded. "I wish I could keep all men's hands off me that easy. There, now, how does your face feel, Mother?"

Destiny touched her cheek tentatively. "All the better for having the butter on. 'Twill soon heal, for it was not a real burn."

"That devil would have marked you for life. God, how I hate that man! And McPherson too, for the coward and bully he is! The world would be well rid of men like them."

Destiny smiled at her daughter. "All men are not vile, Rosanna. How's that young man of yours?"

Rosanna blushed and hurried to the pantry to replace the butter dish. "Oh, he's fine. Mother, Catherine says I can come home tonight, but would you mind if I go walking with Bob this evening first?"

"Again? You were up the glen with him last night."

"Oh, 'tis not what you're thinking, Mother. He's teaching me how to train the master's dog, that's all, great evil thing that it is."

"A big dog? A gray wolfhound?" Destiny asked. "I mind well he had a dog like that years ago, but this can't be the same."

"Sultan, his name is. And I can already make him come to heel and sit."

" 'Tis not the same. But go, by all means. McPherson is in an evil mood with me, and 'twill keep you away from his temper."

It was late before McPherson came home that evening. He glowered at Destiny, who sat alone in the kitchen.

"You must tell the master what he wants, Destiny, for he's in a terrible rage still," he said. Destiny sat up.

"He's recovered, then? God be praised, for that at least, for I would not have wanted his death on my conscience, wicked as he is."

"You said it was an accident," McPherson said sharply.

"So it was, but I'd have felt responsible if he'd come to harm in my house," Destiny replied coolly. "Now, take off your boots and go sit at table. I've a good roast ready in the oven for you."

McPherson thumped the kitchen table. "How can you talk of boots and roasts as if our whole lives weren't in danger, woman? Mr. Carmichael is still weak and abed, for the doctor says he has concussion and must rest for a day in bed, but he's furious still with you! He's told me plainly he'll know what he wants to know from you, or it's out of here and into the workhouse with us both! Would you have that happen, woman?"

"I've suffered worse than the workhouse in my life. I've endured hunger such as you'll never know. His threats won't frighten me," Destiny replied. "And he can do no more than evict us, for he can't punish a woman for holding her tongue."

"Oh, can't he, then? You don't know Conal Carmichael! And do you think I'm prepared to face poverty because of your stupidity, after all I've done for you and your ungrateful brat? Let me tell you, Destiny McPherson, that I am not! I'll beat the answer out of you first!"

Destiny watched in horror as he began to unbuckle the thick leather strap from about his waist, once slim but now thickening in middle age. She was accustomed to his roughness in the past, violence, even, on the occasions he knocked her about, but there was in his manner now a menacing, deadly serious air that showed he meant business. He would beat her unmercifully, she knew, for his whole life depended upon her giving in. His stubby hair bristled in a sandy halo about his purple face, and there was a cold, flinty look in those close-set eyes.

Mesmerized before that look, as a rabbit is by a snake's baleful stare, Destiny hovered motionless. With one hand he raised the belt while the other reached forward to seize her. In that second Destiny was galvanized into action, and she leaped to one side to elude his grasp. His fingers clutched her blouse, and as she wrenched to free herself, the thin material gave way, ripping apart with a hiss.

"No!" she cried. "Don't be crazy, husband! I'll have the law on you!"

He laughed hoarsely. "The master is the law hereabouts, and he'll thank me for this!"

The whip whistled and sang as it descended, and Destiny felt the sting of its bite in her shoulder. God help her, she cried inwardly, for McPherson would flay the skin off her and leave her a helpless, bleeding heap before he would stop.

She sank her teeth in the hand on her shoulder. McPherson, his right hand already raised for the second blow, cried at the sudden pain and let go. Destiny seized her chance and ran into the hallway and up the stairs. Fear lent her feet speed, and as she ran she could hear McPherson's heavy, pounding feet behind her.

Reaching her bedroom, she ran in and slammed the door behind her, shooting the bolt home and standing, heart banging in fear, as McPherson's footsteps approached. Finding the door locked, he thumped furiously on it.

"Open the door, blast you!" he replied.

"And have you kill me? That I'll not," Destiny replied, shrinking back toward the bed. He hammered and crashed on the door but could not breach its stout oaken panels. For several minutes he pounded and cursed vociferously, but Destiny would not open.

"Then, devil take you, you can stay in there till you starve, then you'll cry to be let out," he snarled. "You'll not get the better of me, woman."

Then for a long time there was silence. Destiny sat on

the edge of the bed and waited, trembling and afraid. No sound came from outside the door, and she could not tell whether he was still there, listening and watching, or whether he had crept downstairs. One thing was sure: she was not going to open the door to find out, lest he should pounce on her.

The shadows of the trees outside lengthened across the bedroom floor, and at last dusk began to fall. Destiny began to feel chilly in her torn blouse, and got up to fetch another from the press. A red weal glowed on the pale skin of her shoulder, and angry resentment began to replace her fear. If only some big bullying man could come along and teach McPherson a lesson, beating him as he had often beaten her!

Destiny sat pensive, debating what to do. If she escaped from the house, where could she run for safety? She would not be welcome at any of the villagers' cottages, nor could she go to the hall, lest she fall into Conal's hands again. The count might protect her if she could reach him, for there was no one else. And she could not be sure of his sympathy, although something in his manner had implied it. Surely he would stand by her, if only because he knew her to be Kate's mother.

Silence still pervaded the house, chill and ominous as a shroud. Of course, Tara had not come today, and mercifully Rosanna was to be out late, but what of Liam? She had seen and heard no sign of him all evening. Either McPherson was gone, or the boy was out; she would have heard McPherson's thwarted rage spent on the child otherwise.

As the night wore on, Destiny began to feel hungry. In her preoccupation with preventing the wedding, she had eaten neither breakfast nor lunch, and she had been locked in this room too early to prepare and eat supper. And she was tired, with the heavy feeling of stupor that overcomes one after long mental anguish when there seems no way out. She lay down on the bed and pulled the coverlet over her.

Once she sat upright, startled by a sound, which could have been a rustle outside her door. She sat motionless, straining her ears to listen, but she heard no further sound. It must have been only a mouse on its nocturnal foraging.

Soon after, overcome with exhaustion, she fell asleep. But it was no restful sleep of the contented. It was a strange, fitful sleep, filled with meaningless dreams. She awoke suddenly, trembling in a nightmare of ravens hovering over a corpse and of them swooping down, shrieking, to devour the snake that slid from the corpse's gaping mouth.

She lay still, shivering in the still night and trying desperately to replace the apparent reality of the sickening dream with true reality. It took some moments to recall that she was a woman alone, afraid of her husband's cruelty and of Carmichael's vengeance. Up among the elm trees near the hall she could hear an owl hooting its dismal call to the unheeding night. She slept again, restlessly, until the cock in the yard roused her with its dawn crowing.

Destiny sat up quickly and threw back the coverlet, just as a knock came at the door.

"Mother? Are you there?"

Destiny sighed with relief at the sound of Rosanna's voice and not her husband's. It was surprising he had not come back to demand his bed, but wherever he had slept, she was grateful for his absence. She unbolted the door cautiously.

"Is McPherson there?" she whispered. Rosanna shook her head, and Destiny stared at the girl's pale, tense face in alarm. "Come in, child. What's the matter alannah? Are you ill?"

Rosanna stayed standing by the door. "I'm all right, Mother," she said quietly, but her tense-lipped appearance belied her words. Her gown was awry and her hair as yet unbrushed, and it was not like her to appear thus, always proud of her appearance as she was. Destiny took her arm.

"What is it, macushla? I can tell something is wrong."

The girl's white face contorted in a vicious expression of hate. "McPherson! I hate that bastard! If ever that devil is found dead, I swear I'll be responsible, so I will!"

"Whisht now, Rosanna, and tell me what is wrong," Destiny urged. Rosanna seized her arm.

"Mother, you must do something quick. He says he knows your secret and is away up to the hall to tell."

Destiny grew pale. "He knows? How could he, for none but I could tell him."

"He says you talked in your sleep last night and he heard."

"But I didn't let him in! Oh, God! He must have been listening at the door! What a fool I was to sleep and let my tongue tell what my heart kept secret! Oh, God! How long has he been gone?"

"Not these ten minutes. Go after him, Mother, and stop him—or deny what he says, but for God's sake go!"

Destiny needed no further bidding. She ran swift as the wind down the stairs and out into the cool dawn air, out of the yard and up the hill toward the hall.

It was early still, she realized as she raced, panting, up the long drive, too early for the gentry yet to be up and about. McPherson would hardly have the nerve to disturb the master at this hour. He must be waiting somewhere, impatient for the chance to spill his news. She must take care not to let him see her.

Deeming it unwise to go to the servants' door lest he be waiting in the kitchen or the servants' hall, she hovered uncertainly near the house, near enough to see through the clipped yew that bordered a gravel walk and yet not be seen by anyone inside. She shivered, chilled by the morning dew on her bare arms. There was a small arbor along the walk, screened by bushes. She would wait in there until the house showed some sign of activity.

Count Nicolai Andreyev surveyed the food laid out on the sideboard for breakfast. Porridge, kippers, kedgeree, scrambled eggs—his stomach rebelled at the thought of them. He seated himself at the table and helped himself to a slice of toast.

The door suddenly burst open and his host strode in, a worried-looking housekeeper hard at his heels.

"Mr. Conal, sir, I must protest! The doctor said you were to stay in bed. You are not fit to be up and about yet, you with a bump the size of a duck egg on your head and all!"

"Hold your tongue, Mrs. Kidd, and fetch me coffee, do you hear?" Carmichael grumbled. The count stopped buttering his toast.

"Mr. Carmichael, are you recovered?"

"I'm well enough, Mrs. Kidd, stop glaring at me and fetch my coffee, will you? I'm not staying in my bed like some namby-pamby child, I tell you. Now, be off with you!"

"I'm glad you're feeling so much better," said the count, "for there is something I wish to tell you. I have decided to take Catherine and leave here. We shall return to London as soon as possible."

Carmichael stared. "Before we even find out the truth of this business? That doesn't make sense!"

"It may not to you, sir," the count replied smoothly, "but it does to me. I do not after all consider that you would make a suitable husband for Catherine, and she does not now wish to marry you. That is enough for me."

"Not suitable?" Carmichael repeated openmouthed. "How dare you, sir!"

"I thought you a man of charm and concern for others, but it seems I was mistaken. I must have assumed Mr. O'Keeffe's attributes applied also to his friends, but there I was sadly mistaken. Since coming here I have seen your bad temper and wild manners, and, frankly, I would fear for my daughter's welfare in your hands. So I am taking her home."

Carmichael sprang up from his seat. "Then the devil take you—and her! Go, Count, get out of my house as fast as you can, and take your mealymouthed brat with you!"

The count rose slowly. "Very good. I do not take your insult to Catherine seriously, for I recognize you are still ill and may not be responsible for your words. So if you will allow me to pass peaceably, I shall wake Catherine and warn her to prepare."

A cunning light sprang into Carmichael's black eyes. "But what if I am her true father, Count Nicolai, what then? You could not remove her without my consent!

That would interfere with your plans, I think, and perhaps soon we shall know."

"Nor could you marry her in that event, so what would you gain?" the count pointed out shrewdly.

Carmichael's cunning look turned to one of malice. "And her mother? You acknowledge the McPherson woman to be her mother—will you ask her consent?"

"You can be sure I shall do what is right," the count replied stiffly. "Now, please allow me to pass."

Without another word Carmichael stepped back, and the count walked with dignity from the room. Inwardly he felt too angry to go up to Catherine yet. He would walk on the terrace for a few minutes until the morning's air cooled his brain.

Destiny sat in the arbor, feeling more composed and warmer now that the sun had risen. Suddenly she was alarmed by the sound of footsteps crunching on the gravel.

Leaping to her feet, she then hesitated. To attempt flight would probably mean being seen, and if it was McPherson, she had no wish to feel his violent hands on her again. Better to remain still where she was in the hope that whoever it was might pass or take another direction.

Hearing the footsteps come closer and the sound of a distinctly masculine cough, she shrank back into a corner. With luck the profuse roses clambering over the arbor might screen her from sight.

The footfalls came closer, and then stopped so close to her that Destiny could hear a long-drawn sigh, and then the sigher approached the arbor and rounded it to the front. A tall, bearded man stared at her in surprise, and Destiny gasped in relief.

"Oh, Count Nicolai, I'm so glad it's you! You're the very man I wanted to see!"

Twenty-two

The count stared at her in undisguised surprise.

"Mistress McPherson! Why are you here so early in the morning?" he asked, and then his gaze traveled to her bare shoulder. "You are hurt, and your face is red. Has someone been beating you?"

"Ah, 'tis nothing, pay no attention to that," Destiny said eagerly. "What matters is the safety of my children. Count Nicolai, you must get Catherine away from here before it is too late. I fear for her safety at Conal Carmichael's hands if she stays here any longer!"

"It is strange you should say that, mistress, for I too wanted to see you."

"Listen," Destiny interrupted. "Has McPherson seen the master this morning?"

The count frowned. "I do not think so. But what has he to do with this?"

"You didn't see him in the hall?"

"Not unless he was belowstairs."

"He thinks he knows the truth about which is Conal's daughter, for he claims I babbled in my sleep. He may have the right answer or he could have the wrong one, for who knows what nonsense I may have spoken in a wild dream, but whatever he tells the master, Mr. Carmichael will believe it. No, don't stop me, Count, for her life could be at stake. If he believes Rosanna to be his child, he will insist on the wedding straightaway, and if he believes it is Kate, his anger will know no bounds. He will venge his spite on anyone—you, her, Rosanna even."

"And, most likely, you."

"That is of no consequence," Destiny said breathlessly. "What is important is that you take Kate to safety at once."

"Have no fear, Mistress McPherson, for I have already told Carmichael this morning that I am taking Catherine away and that whatever the truth, Catherine will not marry him. That is why I sought you."

"Me, sir? Why?"

"To secure your permission, as her mother."

Destiny smiled. "You have it, sir, and my blessing. Only, take her swiftly, before his wicked temper bursts out. And there is one more favor I would ask you, since I know you to be a kind and honorable gentleman."

"What is that?"

"That you take Rosanna too. She is a good and loyal girl, and she loves Kate dearly. I would not have them separated again if I can help it, and I know she will serve Kate faithfully. You'll have no cause to regret employing her, sir."

"I'll do that gladly, mistress, if you would be so kind as to do me a favor in return."

"I, sir? Do you a favor? Gladly, if I can." Destiny wondered what on earth she could do for a man so rich and powerful as he, but whatever he asked, she would do, for instinctively she knew here was one of those rare men one could respect and trust with one's life.

"Come with us, mistress, for I would happily take you and Rosanna too."

Destiny drew back. "Oh, no, sir, there is no need. I shall be happy in knowing that my daughters are safe with you."

"It is not a favor I do you, but you to me, if you will come, my dear lady," the count said in grave, gentle tones. "My Catherine has long lacked a mother's guiding, loving hand, and it is the one gift in the world I could not give her. I would redeem that omission now."

"But you are young still, sir. You may marry and give her that guide."

"Not I, for I told you the woman I loved is dead. But as I told you once, you are that woman reborn, I swear it, for I recognize in you, not only her face and form, but her steadfast courage, too. Come with us, I beg you, for you will make us all happy by coming."

Destiny reflected for a moment. She would have nothing to lose in leaving Ballymachree, only the wrath of both McPherson and the master once they discovered how she had cheated them. She gripped the count's hands impulsively.

"I'll accept your kind offer, sir, and may the blessings of God be showered on you! I'll take any position you offer, scullery maid or what you will, for I can clean and scrub as well as any woman. I'll earn my keep, sir, and bless you always for your kind heart."

A warm light kindled the count's grave eyes. "Good. Then that is settled. Come, let us walk farther from the house while we arrange what is to be done."

Destiny fell in step beside him, her heart suddenly freed of its burden of anxiety. God, but it was magnificent to have a man whose strength one could lean upon once again! Despite his quiet manner, the count was undoubtedly a man who would have his way and brook no opposition. He would not quail before Conal's furious rage.

"Those marks on your face and your shoulder," the count said as they walked uphill toward the wood. "Did McPherson do that to you?"

"The shoulder, yes. He whipped me, but my face was the master's doing."

"Carmichael? He struck you?" the count exclaimed.

"He threatened to burn me with the flatiron," Destiny admitted quietly. "But I don't think he meant it. He's a wild man, but I don't think he would really have marked me."

"Would he not? And he cruel enough to starve you all to death once! Oh, yes, I learned of that, belatedly. That's why I determined that he should have nothing of Catherine if he could be so cruel."

"Ah, yes, those were hard times indeed," Destiny said reflectively.

"And you showed your courage then, parting with one of your beloved children to save her. I shall not let you be parted from either of them again," the count said bitterly.

215

"Will you regret leaving your husband to come away to London?"

"That I will not. I never loved the man, and he knew it."

The count nodded in satisfaction. "Then let us go back to the hall and tell Carmichael what we intend. Your husband may have spoken to him by now, but that is of no account. I shall tell Catherine and Rosanna to prepare for the journey at once."

They were turning to walk back down toward the hall when a man's strong, clear voice singing came to them from beyond the trees.

> I know a valley fair,
> I know a cottage there,
> For in that valley's shade,
> I know a gentle maid
> Flower of the hazel glade,
>   Aileen Aroon.

Destiny screwed up her eyes against the sunlight. "Who is that? He sings an old Irish song, but his voice is a stranger's, I'm thinking."

The tall figure of a man appeared, a young man, ruddy-faced and pleasant, wearing a liveried uniform. He stopped in front of the count.

"Sir, my lady Catherine presents her respects and requests that you return to the hall. She is alarmed by Mr. Carmichael's mood."

"Then I come at once," the count replied. "Aren't you Mr. O'Keeffe's man?"

"I am, sir, Fellows by name."

Destiny looked at him more closely. So this was the young man who was keeping Rosanna company. He looked an honest, agreeable fellow, even if he was English.

"Is my husband at the hall yet?" she asked. The young man looked puzzled.

"Mr. McPherson, do you mean? No, mistress, I have not seen him there."

Destiny's heart felt a sense of relief, and she smiled at him.

"How comes it you know our old songs?" she asked as they walked. He smiled sheepishly.

"Your daughter taught me the song, in exchange for learning to train the dog, mistress. I can't remember all the words yet, but it has a fine air."

Suddenly the count stopped. "What's that," he demanded, pointing a finger upward.

Destiny followed the line of his arm. Above the copse of trees a swarm of birds flew thick and angry, circling and swooping into the trees. She shivered.

"Ravens, sir. They usually stay about the churchyard."

"Then why are they here, and so agitated too?" the count murmured. "Come, let's look, Mistress McPherson. Fellows, you go on and tell the lady Catherine I am coming."

The younger man strode off toward the hall, leaving Destiny to follow the count reluctantly. If there was one thing she loathed, it was ravens.

Count Nicolai was striding on ahead of her through the trees. As they neared the little clearing in the middle, he stopped suddenly.

"Oh, my God!"

Destiny felt alarm leap to her throat at his tone, and he turned suddenly upon her, taking her arm. "Come, quickly, away from here."

"What is it?" Destiny asked, knowing by some sixth sense that something terrible lay behind him. "For heaven's sake, tell me, sir! Let me see!"

For a second he hesitated, still gripping her arm, and then slowly he let go. "God forgive me, but you must know sooner or later. Prepare yourself, my friend, for a terrible shock. It is your husband, I fear."

He stepped back, and Destiny moved forward. A figure in a gray topcoat lay sprawled on the grass, the gray spattered with huge stains of crimson. And a sick feeling of revulsion filled her when she saw the handle of a grass hook protruding from his stomach, the blade sunk deep in the flesh. Ravens croaked angrily from overhead, but the flies carried on scurrying over the gaping flesh. The grass around was stained with patches of brown marring its lush green beauty.

Destiny reeled sideways, stunned and faint. The count caught and steadied her.

"Let me take you down to the hall and I'll send someone to fetch him. I'm afraid it's too late to help him. He's been dead for some time."

Destiny's stomach heaved. She could feel no sorrow for her husband's death, only revulsion at the manner of it. She stumbled rather than walked back through the trees toward the pathway. Then suddenly she stopped. A black pair of eyes glowed from the undergrowth. It was Liam.

"What is it?" the count asked.

"I felt faint. I can go on now," Destiny said weakly, unable to think clearly. McPherson was dead, and there, near his body, little Liam was hiding. Surely . . . Oh, no, it was too terrible to contemplate!

Once in the hall, Count Nicolai left Destiny to wait in the great vestibule while he sought Carmichael. Seated there on a monk's bench, tracing the pattern in the marble floor with her toe, Destiny could feel only one predominating sensation. McPherson was dead—and she was free.

Now there was nothing to keep her in Ballymachree. She could go away with her children and the count with a light heart. But her heart was far from light. The only life she had ever known was here in this lush green valley, the only people her own family and neighbors and the master. It would be hard to break the pattern of the known way of life to go and live in that strange country, England, even with those she loved most dearly in the world.

England. She shivered. The very word conjured up memories of poverty and squalor and sudden death. Poor Taff. He had been a warm friend, but for only too brief a spell.

But this time England would be different, she tried to convince herself, with a secure home in the count's household, no poverty or misery. So why should she regret leaving here? The thought that came to her, she tried to repel, but at last had to admit it. She was loath to leave the sight of Conal Carmichael. Beast though he was, the man still fascinated her, as he always had done. What a fool of a woman you are, Destiny McPherson, she told herself, to care about the likes of him! Hasn't he already done enough harm to your life? To the devil with him, and bad cess to him, and life for her would be the better without him!

A light footstep approached, and Destiny looked up to see Rosanna's alarmed face, as white as her starched cap.

"I was sent down to fetch you up to the drawing room," she told her mother, and then added, "Is it true what I overheard, Mother? Is McPherson really dead?"

Destiny rose to her feet. "These two eyes saw him lying in his own blood."

She could swear the look that leaped to her daughter's dark eyes was one of satisfaction. "Come, Mother, Catherine and the master and the count are waiting for you. And Mr. O'Keeffe is there too."

Destiny followed her upstairs and waited at the door while Rosanna entered and announced her. She heard Conal's deep voice say, "Bring her in, and then leave us," and Kate's clear voice followed swiftly.

"No, let Rosanna stay with me."

Destiny smiled to herself. Her daughter was of the same strong mind as Rosanna and herself, and she was glad of it. Rosanna beckoned her to follow, and Destiny entered the room.

Not a soul in the tableau before her moved, save for Rosanna, who quietly went to take her place behind Kate's chair and clasp her hands dutifully in front of her. Alongside Kate, the count stood impassively. Far beyond, in the window bay, she could see Philip O'Keeffe with his back toward the group, staring out over the garden. Conal stood by the fireplace, his back toward her and his forearm resting on the high mantelshelf. He was staring moodily into the fire grate. Destiny coughed.

"You sent for me, Mr. Carmichael?"

Conal turned about slowly, his dark gaze resting on her with curiosity.

"Mistress McPherson, what is this I hear about my bailiff?"

"The count and I found him in the copse not twenty minutes ago. He's dead." It was curious how she could say the words without emotion. Conal was quick to note it.

"And not by his own hand, I believe?"

"No sir. Someone had struck him with a grass hook."

Conal grunted. "Murdered. Then you understand that as lord of the manor it is my duty to find the villain who did it and bring him to justice. And I shall find him, I assure you, and hand him over to the magistrates in Cork."

"Yes, sir."

Still no one moved or spoke, and though the count's expression remained inscrutable, she could see both Kate and Rosanna looked pale and tense.

"Have you any idea who did it?" Conal asked quietly.

Destiny hesitated. Whatever her suspicions, she was not going to involve young Liam. "No, sir."

"Do you know where the grass hook might have come from?"

"It was Paddy Feeney's."

Conal's eyes showed interest. "How do you know that?"

"Not many people have one, sir, but Paddy has. He's had it these many years, to cut rushes up the glen for his basketmaking. He keeps it up there, wrapped in rags in an old hollow tree, to save carrying it up and down when he's loaded with rushes. Everyone knows that."

"So Paddy Feeney might be the killer?"

"No," Destiny said hotly. "He's the gentlest man alive. Anyone could have taken it from the tree."

"That's true, sir," Rosanna cut in quietly from the shadows at the edge of the room. "There's not a soul in Ballymachree but knows of the grass-cutter in the tree."

Conal turned sharply. "Hold your tongue, girl, and speak when you're spoken to. Now, Mistress McPherson, when did you last see your husband?"

Destiny lowered her head and answered in a whisper. "Last night, sir."

"What's that? Speak up, woman, don't be afraid."

She raised her chin haughtily. "I'm not afraid. I saw him last night, at suppertime."

"Not since? Did you not give him breakfast this morning?"

"No, sir."

"Did he not come to bed with you?" Conal demanded. The count intervened quietly.

"That is hardly necessary, Mr. Carmichael. Mistress McPherson has told us she had not seen her husband since last night. Surely it now remains to discover what time he has been seen since then."

Philip O'Keeffe's voice came from the window bay, quiet but firm. "He's right, Conal."

Conal spun around to face the two men. "But who might have been up in the copse either last night or early this morning? How are we to discover that, pray? It must have been someone who was lying in wait for him, someone with a grudge to bear. Now, who had a reason to hate my bailiff enough to kill him?"

"Who in Ballymachree did not?" Destiny exploded. "He was a man to be feared and hated, and Ballymachree folk have long memories. They'll not forget how gleefully he carried out your orders in the time of the hunger. Throwing them out to die in the hedges and the fields in the depth of winter! There's not a family who did not lose a mother or a child or two—and he watched it all and raised no hand to help! He gloried in watching them die, carrying out your cruel orders!"

Conal was staring at her, his black eyes glittering with fury and hate, his hands clenched, and his body half-crouched, as though he would leap on her. Kate gasped and Rosanna stared, transfixed. Conal advanced toward Destiny slowly, and she shrank back in fear at the depths of hatred in his eyes.

"And you, mistress? Did you not have reason to hate him? Hate him more than most? Were you not shackled to a man you despised?"

"I was, but I would not kill him!" Destiny cried, still backing away from that terrible look.

"No?" Conal said, and his tone was menacingly low. "Not even when you know he was about to betray your secret to me? Oh, yes, I know."

Destiny's heart leaped in alarm. Had McPherson managed to reach the hall and tell what she had muttered in her sleep after all? Conal was still muttering.

"Yes, I know, for Catherine in all innocence let slip to me Rosanna had told her McPherson was on his way to tell me. But he never came—because you waylaid him in the copse and silenced him!" With a great roar of triumph Conal leaped on her, seizing her arm.

The count stepped forward, wakened at last from his silent stance. "Let her go. You have no proof," he commanded fiercely. Philip came quickly across the room to join him.

"Conal," he said quietly, "don't be blinded by wishful thinking. Count Nicolai is right. Anyone could have had access to that grass hook, many people with just as strong a motive."

Conal reluctantly let go of her arm. "No," he said softly, his eyes gleaming with malice. "She did it, and I intend to hand her over to the magistrates for trial. Find as many other suspects as you will, Philip, but I know she did it to spite me, just as she always does. But she'll not get away with it this time. She'll hang for it, I swear!"

Twenty-three

Destiny could only gape in horror at Conal's vile, hate-filled accusation, but instantly the room was full of sound and movement. A babble of voices cried out in protest, and Kate's slender figure rose from the chair and sped across to challenge Conal.

"You will not touch my mother, sir! I forbid it, and I know the count will back me!"

"Indeed," said Count Nicolai with firm determination. "You shall not lay hands on this lady again. You have already threatened her with physical violence, and I shall not let that be repeated."

Destiny saw Conal's eyes search and find the rosy blemish on her cheek, and the way his expression changed instantly to one of good humor. He raised his hands deprecatingly.

"I have no intention of harming her, I assure you, Count, only of keeping her secure under lock and key until the magistrates can conduct their hearing. I would be failing in my duty as landlord of Ballymachree if I did not."

"You have no evidence that she was even near the copse," Philip pointed out. "You can hardly hand over a suspect with no evidence against her at all. Others may have been up there—you haven't inquired yet."

"I myself was there this morning," the count added in agreement, "and you do not accuse me. And I saw your man there, Philip."

"Fellows? Then send for him. Perhaps he can tell us something." Philip crossed to the bell rope and pulled it.

"I'll go for him, sir," Rosanna said quietly, and Destiny could see her daughter was still as white as a sheet. Kate nodded, and Rosanna left, returning within moments with Bob Fellows.

Philip spoke to his manservant. "Bob, did you see anyone up at the copse this morning."

"No, sir, only the count and Mistress McPherson. Oh, and a child."

"A child?" Conal repeated. Destiny's heart pounded in alarm. "What kind of child?"

"A boy, sir, about ten or so. Lame he was, limping as he ran."

Destiny saw the quick look of understanding in Conal's eyes. "Oh, him. The village-idiot child. No one else?"

"No, sir."

"Then you may go."

Destiny breathed a sigh as Fellows left. It was evident Conal did not attach any importance to Liam's presence. Rather the mention of the child had embarrassed him.

"If I may speak, sir?" It was Rosanna who spoke. All eyes pivoted toward her.

"Have you some evidence to give us?" Conal snapped.

"I have. My mother was still locked in her room when McPherson left home this morning. She did not come out until some time after he had gone, so she could not have caught up with him in the wood."

Her voice was low and clear, proud as a queen's, and Destiny's heart filled with pride of her. Conal glowered and turned to the count.

"Count Nicolai, I think you expressed your intention of leaving Ballymachree as quickly as you could. I do not wish to detain you here, but I fear urgent business with the magistrates will keep me occupied. I am sure Mr. O'Keeffe will escort you and your daughter safely to Cobh."

Destiny saw Kate's small face rise haughtily. "And when we leave, sir, we take Rosanna and my mother with us."

He smiled thinly. "Rosanna is free to go, but Mistress McPherson will have to wait until the justices have done with her. You may leave as soon as you wish."

"Not without my mother."

The count stepped forward. "That is correct. We shall stay until you release her, to see that justice is done. In the meantime, I trust you will afford us your hospitality a little longer, or I can find lodging elsewhere."

"Go or stay, as you please," Conal replied airily. "It matters little to me. I have my duties to attend to." He spun around unexpectedly on Rosanna. "Why was your mother locked in her room, girl?"

Rosanna shook her dark curls. "I don't know."

He rounded swiftly on Destiny. "Why did you lock yourself in? Did he beat you this morning?"

"No. Last night. He took his belt to me, and I ran from him. Locking myself in was the only way to escape his temper."

"He beat you with a strap, did he? So you hated him enough to kill him!"

"No, I didn't!"

"And you crept out of your room in the night to kill him, didn't you? We were wrong in supposing it happened this morning."

"No!" Rosanna cried. "I told you, I saw him go out this morning."

"You're in league with your mother to hide her crime. I know you and how you band together. You don't want to see your mother hanged for murder!"

"Conal . . ." Philip interjected, but Conal would not listen.

"No one saw him since last night, so it could be as I say, she killed him, and the girl alleges she saw him this morning so as to clear her mother. It's possible, isn't it, and even probable? The woman had a strong enough motive if he beat her with his leather belt for her arrogant ways, though she well deserved it."

"You're wrong!" Rosanna spat out angrily. "He treated her as badly as he treated everyone else—me, our maid Tara, the boy Liam—he bullied and threatened everyone in the village but you, and even you he had no respect for, but he feared you. But it was not my mother who killed him. I know."

"How do you know?"

"Because I told you she was locked in her room when I came home late last night. He was crouching on the floor outside her door. She never opened that door till after he left this morning."

"And that was when he heard her talk in her sleep?"

"Yes."

"How do you know that?"

Rosanna's proud look faltered, and she looked uncomfortably across at her mother. Destiny felt a premonition of fear.

"He told me so. He came to my room."

"Why should he tell you, and not just come straight to me?" Conal demanded.

"He . . . he promised not to tell if . . . if I obeyed him," she stammered, and then added viciously, "and I was fool enough to believe him!"

Philip O'Keeffe cut in quietly. "What are you trying to tell us, Rosanna? That your stepfather was thrusting his unwanted attentions on you?"

"Yes, sir."

Destiny's heart sank in despair. There was no end to

McPherson's villainies, but Rosanna was incriminating herself out of her own mouth.

Conal's eyes glistened. "Did he rape you, girl?"

Rosanna's reply was barely audible. "Yes." Destiny felt sick.

The count's tone was crisp. "So it would seem you have two suspects now, Carmichael, both with equally good motives for hating your bailiff and wishing him dead, but not a shred of evidence against either. Now what do you plan to do?"

Carmichael shrugged. "As I said, I shall hand the woman over for questioning. The girl is obviously making up a story to protect her mother. I'm not stupid. It's as the woman said, half the village could have had a reason for killing McPherson, but I know it was her. She's crazy—haven't you seen it for yourself? The way she stopped the wedding and all? She's out of her mind, and if the magistrates don't hang her, they'll send her to the lunatic asylum for sure. Either way, she'll not live to plague me again."

Philip advanced and laid a hand on Carmichael's shoulder. "Conal, the answer is clear. If you simply want Mistress McPherson out of the way, then let her go. She must leave her house to make way for a new bailiff, so let her go with the count and Catherine. You'll never see her again."

"No!" Conal roared. "I've listened to your advice too often in the past. Let Catherine leave and take her maid with her, but I want the woman! I must do my duty, can't you see? Now, get out of here, all of you but the woman."

He tugged the bell rope viciously. One by one the occupants of the room moved toward the door. The count turned to Destiny. "Do not fear, mistress. We shall be close by."

A maidservant entered as they left. Only Philip hovered in the doorway as Conal addressed her.

"Go tell two of the footmen to come here and take this woman to the cellars," he said, jerking a finger toward Destiny. "She is to be held in safe custody there and someone set to watch her. Go."

The maid bobbed a curtsy and withdrew. Philip frowned.

"Is that necessary, Conal? She will not run away."

"I'm taking no chances. Now, go."

As the footmen entered, Destiny saw that Philip O'Keeffe was still standing outside the door.

"Take her," said Conal, "and watch she does not escape."

"Have no fear, I shall not run away," Destiny retorted, her head held high. "My conscience is clear, which is more than some can say."

Conal smiled scornfully. "What are you implying, madam? That it was I who killed my own bailiff? You must be even crazier than I thought."

"No, for I had not thought of it, but come to think of it, I wouldn't put it past you. I was thinking rather of all your earlier crimes, the murder of those poor hungry tenants of yours and my husband and my sister, who died because of you."

"McPherson?"

"Jim Regan, the finest man in the county of Cork. I cursed you then, Conal Carmichael, and I renew that curse today. I pray God will hear me and strike you down for the evil, heartless man that you are!"

"Get her out of here before I take a whip to her!" Conal roared. The footmen each took hold of an arm and pulled Destiny to the door.

Philip O'Keeffe walked beside them along the corridor to the servants' stairs. "Have no fear, we shall watch over you and see justice is done," he told her. Destiny gave him a fleeting smile of gratitude before she was roughly bundled down the stairs.

Down the first flight of narrow, dimly lit stairs they reached the kitchen area, and from there another flight of steps, this time of stone and as gloomy as a tomb, led down to the cellars. Despite the heat of the day, it struck chill to the skin down here, and Destiny shivered. The flagged stone floors echoed to their footsteps as the footmen conducted her to one of the several heavy barred doors, opened it, and pushed her inside. Through the small grille in the door she could see the set, impassive features of the older footman as he slid the bolt home.

"I'll stand guard the first hour, and then you take over," he told the younger man. "Go tell Mrs. Kidd and the butler what's happening."

Destiny peered about her in the darkness. Far above her head was a small opening to the outside, closed and barred with metal rods. Her foot touched something hard. She bent to feel it. A sack, filled with something. Then her fingers discovered potatoes, several sacks of them heaped to one side of a small cellar, leaving a space only about six feet square in which to move. Resignedly she seated herself uncomfortably on a sack to await events.

It was cold down here, but at least it was day. Something tickled her foot. She bent to investigate, and found a large spider, which she brushed away. Thank heaven there were no rats!

How long would Conal leave her down here? she wondered. Long enough to cool her rebellious nature, he probably hoped, but he could not keep her long without evidence. McPherson. For the first time since she and the count found him, she began to think of her late husband. He had been a foul villain sure enough, but his was a terrible death. Destiny began to feel sorry for the man, to have to go to his Maker unloved and unmourned. Poor McPherson—he had never known love in all his life. What a tragic waste!

Voices outside made Destiny rise and go to the grille. The younger footman had returned.

"I'll sit for an hour, and then you relieve me," he was saying. The older man nodded and climbed the stairs. Destiny watched as the young man seated himself on a stool in the passage and began whistling to himself. She debated whether to engage him in conversation, to ask him what was going on upstairs, and decided against it. Better not to, though she sensed neither of the footmen enjoyed or approved of what they had been ordered to do.

She was about to return to her potato sack when a sound caught her ear, the rustle of a gown. To her surprise, she saw Kate's creamy silk gown gleaming in the half-light.

"I wish to speak with the lady," she said crisply to the footman, who leaped to his feet in surprise. "There is no need to unbar the door, so have no fear, I am not asking you to disobey your master."

"Ah, well," the footman stuttered, "I see no harm in that, my lady, but I'll not leave you alone, I'm afraid."

"Thank you, that will suffice."

Kate came close and held up her hands to the grille. Destiny gripped her fingertips through the bars.

"My lovely Kate! My girl!" she breathed.

"Mother, are you all right?" Kate's tone was full of anxious concern.

"I'm blessed by hearing you call me 'Mother,' macushla. Heaven is in my heart, and no one can rob me of that."

"Mother, we shall stay close by, and the count has sent Philip to Cork for a magistrate to come. Soon Conal will have to release you, since he has nothing against you. Only have patience, Mother, and soon you'll be free to go with us."

"My blessings on the count, for he is a good man and honest. I could have wished no better father upon you when I let you go."

"Mother," Kate's strained voice came through the grille, "tell me, please, who *was* my father? Was it Conal? I must know."

The tiny voice, reduced to a whisper, was filled with fearful anticipation.

"You know, girleen, I swore to tell that to no one."

"But, Mother, I must know!"

Destiny sighed, and in the cellar's darkness crossed herself. Dear God, guide me now, she prayed, or I ruin one daughter's happiness forever.

"If I tell you, Kate, will you swear never to speak of it to a living soul as long as you live? Will you swear to take the secret to your grave?"

"I will, oh, I will! Only tell me!"

The air was as still and silent as a church as Destiny

drew in her breath to answer. "Then know, it is your sister who is Conal's child, but she must never know."

She heard Kate's deep sigh and knew it was one of relief. "I swear it, Mother, Rosanna will never know from me. I shall never speak of it again. I'll go now, but I'll be back soon, as soon as the magistrate comes. Take heart, dear Mother, we shall soon all be together and away from here."

"God willing," Destiny replied.

She heard Kate murmur a few words to the footman, and then she was gone.

For the next half-hour there was silence except for an occasional scuffling sound among the sacks, which indicated mice, she hoped, and not rats. Then there came the sound of footsteps on the stairs and the bright voice of a girl; it was Rosanna.

"Hello, Jamie, I've brought sandwiches and ale for you and some bread and cheese for Mistress McPherson. Shall I set the tray down here or take it in to her?"

"No, I'll take it to her. Is it dinnertime already?"

"It is. Can I have a word with her, then? I promise I won't go near, only talk at the door. You know me, Jamie, I'm a girl to be trusted, aren't I? I didn't tell when I caught you in the drawing room that time, swigging the master's brandy."

Destiny watched her through the grille, her pretty face pert and teasing and her hands thrust on her hips in a provocative gesture. Tossing back her dark hair and laughing, she looked just like one of the gypsy girls at the Whitsun fair.

"Go on, then, just for a minute," he said with a begrudging smile. Rosanna's laughing smile changed to a look of deadly earnest as she came to the grille.

"Mother, are you all right? You'll be out soon, have no fear, for Bob told me his master has gone to Cork to fetch a magistrate to get you out. Then Catherine says we'll all be away together."

"You'll be leaving Bob," Destiny said.

"That I'll not, for Mr. Philip is to go with the count and Catherine to London. It's my guess he'll ask Catherine to marry him before long."

"Will he, now? Well, if he has the count's blessing, he'll have mine too."

"And I found Liam, Mother. He was crying, as miserable as sin, in the stable at home. He asked for you, so I brought him here. Poor boy! He's such a sad little soul."

"Where is he?" Destiny asked in alarm. "For heaven's sake, keep him out of Conal's sight."

"He's belowstairs with Mrs. Kidd. Mother, he's very upset. I think, from what little he told me, he found McPherson's body and it's frightened him. He might even have seen who did it."

"Then for God's sake make sure Conal doesn't find out, or he'll beat the child to death to find out what he knows!"

"Hoping to prove it's you, I've no doubt," Rosanna agreed. "Have no fear, I'll keep him out of that devil's reach."

The cold firmness in her voice suddenly receded, to be replaced by a tone of hesitant carefulness. "Mother, talking of the devil, there is something I must ask you."

Instantly Destiny knew what was on her daughter's mind. The same harrowing question that had troubled Kate. "Yes?"

"Mother, I can see Kate and me looking at each other at the time and wondering, hoping it's not ourself and yet not wanting to wish this terrible thing on the other. But I must know, or I'll never lie easy in my bed wondering if I've inherited his cruel, evil ways. For pity's sake, Mother, tell me! Am I that devil's daughter or not?"

The girl's fingers flew up to clutch her mother's through the bars. Destiny patted the fingertips gently.

"I'll tell you, mavourneen, only if you swear no torture will ever wrench the secret from you, that no one but you will ever know."

"I swear, in the name of all that's holy, Mother, I'll never tell!"

"Then lie easy, alannah. Your sister, Kate, is Conal's child."

She heard Rosanna's strangled moan and knew she was content. The footman heard the cry and came forward.

"Time's up, Rosanna. Go and tell Will it's time he relieved me, will you?"

Destiny saw Rosanna's quick smile of happiness before she mounted the stairs. Jamie unlocked the door and brought in the tray of bread and cheese and milk.

"Here's your food, mistress."

"Thank you."

But the tray lay unheeded on the floor while Destiny knelt and prayed: "Dear God, forgive the terrible lie I told, and remember only the good intention behind it."

Twenty-four

During the course of the long afternoon—at least, Destiny guessed it to be still afternoon, though with so little light falling from the grille high in the wall, it was hard to tell—she ate the bread and cheese so as to prevent the mice from being tempted out again.

From time to time she heard voices and saw her jailers changed from Jamie to Will and back again. After several changes she began to calculate. If they were relieving each other at hourly intervals, it must now be nearing six o'clock, and still no word from upstairs about her release.

Occasionally she could hear sounds from outside through the high grille, which must look out onto the stableyard, she concluded, for there were sounds of a cat mewing and buckets of water being drawn at the pump. Once a horse's hooves could be heard rattling on the gravel, and Destiny lifted her head expectantly. It could be Philip's horse if he had returned from Cork, but though she waited impatiently, still no summons came from upstairs.

The air, already cool down here, began to grow more chill, and Destiny grew uneasy. Let them not leave her here all night alone, she prayed. At any time it was chastening to be left alone and in the dark, but at night, when the rats would emerge to keep her company, it would be intolerable. Surely, even if the magistrate did not come to enforce her release, Conal would not be so malicious as to leave her all night without even a blanket? Surely he would at least send her some supper and some comforts?

As time dragged on, Destiny began to fear the worst. No sign or word from Rosanna or any of her allies seemed to indicate that Destiny would have to wait until the morning before she could taste the air of freedom again. Just as she was giving up hope, footsteps came clattering down the stone steps.

She looked out through the grille. It was Jamie, bending now to speak to Will, who was dozing on the stool.

"I'm to take Mistress McPherson upstairs, the master says. We can go back to our own duties."

"Thank the Lord for that," Will groaned, rising and stretching, "for I'm as stiff as a board. I've no fancy for the jailer's life, not after a day of this."

"Nor me." Jamie grinned, drawing back the bolt on the cellar door. "Come, mistress, the master wants to see you."

Destiny followed him out and up the steps, herself feeling stiff and awkward after so many hours of squatting on a sack. Up on the kitchen floor, where the candlelight dazzled her, she could see the faces of servants looking at her with curiosity as she passed, but Rosanna's was not among them.

Up the flight of wooden stairs she followed Jamie, through the baize-covered door into the great vestibule, where a dozen oil lamps glowed, casting a radiant sheen over the marble floor, and on up again, up the great balustraded staircase. The house was unusually quiet, and Destiny wondered if it was very late and everyone already abed.

Jamie led her past the drawing room and along a corridor until he reached a door, which he opened. Inside, in the middle of the room, stood a great tub full of steaming water. Destiny looked at it and then at Jamie.

"I thought I was to see the master?" she queried.

"You are, but the count insisted you were to be given the opportunity to clean up and change after all day in the cellar, and then have a good night's sleep here in the hall," Jamie told her. "So perhaps the master will send for you later, or possibly in the morning, as it's already so late."

"What time is it?"

"Nearly eleven. My lady Catherine has already retired. I understand she and the count are to travel tomorrow. I'll leave you now, mistress. One of the maids will see to you." Jamie smiled and left her.

Destiny went inside the room and closed the door, then sat down on the stool beside the tub, gazing into the rising steam. Tomorrow? Then it would seem that she had been cleared and they would all be free to go. The thought of lying in a warm bath was alluring, but she felt almost too tired to take off her clothes. Wearily she rose, turned the key in the door, and began to unfasten her bodice.

Another inner door suddenly opened, startling Destiny so that she gasped aloud. To her relief, it was Rosanna's darkly pretty face that hovered above the cloud of steam.

"Mother! Are you all right?"

"All the better for being out of that dark hole, macushla. Lord, I'm so tired."

"Here, let me help you while I tell you the news," Rosanna said, coming around the tub and helping Destiny to pull off her gown. "Get in, and I'll rub you down."

Destiny stepped in and lowered herself into the water's fragrant warmth. She closed her eyes in bliss. "What news, girl? Has Mr. O'Keeffe brought the justice?"

"Justice?" Rosanna laughed. "You know what they say, Mother, that when justice comes in, truth flies out by the back door, but it's not so in this case. Philip and the magistrate have not arrived yet, but the truth is out at last."

"What truth?" said Destiny dreamily. The soothing warm water made her want to sleep.

"Tara." Rosanna's tone was full of suppressed excitement, which Destiny could not understand. Tara? In the turmoil of the last few days she had almost forgotten the existence of her maid.

"I went down to Tara's cottage this evening, meaning to see her about minding Liam for me, since you said to keep him out of the master's way. I found her there crying her heart out, all alone and half-hysterical with fright."

"Tara? Frightened? Why?" Destiny could not follow Rosanna's drift at all. It seemed to have no bearing on their present problem.

"Mother, she confessed to me. It was she who killed McPherson!"

Destiny almost leaped from the bath in shocked horror. "Tara? For God's sake, girl, what are you saying? That girl couldn't throw a chicken's neck, let alone kill a man!"

"But she did, Mother, and she's been hiding in her cottage all day in terror. She told me, and seemed glad to be able to tell someone at last."

"What did you do?"

"I told her it was her duty to confess the truth and that in the circumstances the law would probably look kindly on her. So she came back here with me and told the count. He told the master, and Tara is now safely locked up. Not that she wants to run away."

"Not in the cellar, I hope?"

"No. In a servant's bedroom."

Destiny reached for a towel lying on a chair. "But why on earth did she do it, Rosanna? He was not a kind master to her, I know, but..."

"Because he caused her to lose her husband, the only chance she ever had," Rosanna said quietly. "You know the village custom—a man will take none but a virgin to wife."

"I know that well," Destiny replied in bemused tones, "but Tara was getting on, and plain as dough, bless her. She'd never had a man near her in her life. You can't mean..." Destiny's voice trailed away as memory brought back the vision of Tara's taut face, her abrupt decision to leave before her wedding, the cry in the night...

"Yes, Mother. McPherson raped her. He said he was sick of a cold, unwelcoming wife, and she had no chance to argue."

"My God," Destiny moaned. "Tara, and then you. The man was sick in the head. No wonder she wanted to kill him, her life ended and all, with her lover gone."

"And I'd have helped her strike the blow," Rosanna muttered, lifting a white silk robe from a chair and handing it to her mother.

"Poor Tara. No wonder she could not face me," Destiny said softly. "Will they let her off, do you think?"

"When they know the reason, I'm sure they will," Rosanna replied. "You and I can both testify in her defense."

"But the count and Kate are leaving in the morning, I hear?"

"Only to go to a hotel in Cork until this business is over," Rosanna reassured her. "Do you like your robe? Catherine sent it for you."

" 'Tis beautiful. Where's the boy now?"

"Liam? The count is taking care of him. Why are you so concerned about him, Mother?"

"Because he is Conal Carmichael's son by his first wife, disowned and hated by his father. Somehow, Rosanna, we must try to get Conal to recognize him and do his duty by the child."

Rosanna laughed dryly. " 'Twould be as easy to make the mountains of Mourne come down to Cork," she said. "But I find it hard to believe—the child a cripple and simple and all."

"He's not simple, just frightened. And I'm sure Conal could afford the money to have a surgeon see to his bad foot if he'd a mind to it," Destiny said.

"Or if not he, then Catherine would," Rosanna said thoughtfully. "After all, Liam is her half-brother, is he not?"

Destiny avoided answering. "But to recognize him would mean she could not inherit from Conal," she pointed out. "Liam has a prior claim."

"She won't inherit anyway if you keep your secret," Rosanna reminded her.

"To be sure. And would you give up your inheritance or cure his foot if he were your half-brother?"

"Without a doubt," Rosanna answered. "I would want none of the master's land or money, only a good man for a husband—and I think I've found him," she added softly. "Now I must go, Mother, for it grows late. A maid will take you to your room."

"Are you going to see your Bob?"

"In the morning, at dawn, not tonight. Good night, Mother."

Rosanna vanished through the inner door, taking Destiny's grubby gown with her. Destiny unlocked the door to the corridor and looked out. No one waited to conduct her to where she was to sleep. The whole house lay silent, and then the stillness was broken by a clock chiming downstairs. Midnight.

The last chime died away on the night air, and Destiny shivered. Kate's silk robe was a delicate delight to wear, but no comfort against the chilly air. A footstep sounded from the direction of the stairs, and Destiny turned expectantly toward it.

It was not a maidservant who appeared, but Conal Carmichael, dressed only in a fine white shirt and breeches and his hair tousled about his face. He looked fatigued and careworn. As he caught sight of Destiny, his dark brows arched in mild surprise.

"Mistress McPherson, not yet abed?"

She drew the thin robe tightly about her. "I did not know where I was to go."

"Have you eaten supper?"

She shook her head. "I am tired. 'Tis only sleep I want."

"Come. There are sandwiches and a bottle of wine ready in my room. We shall share them, you and I."

He was already leading the way. Destiny spoke to his back, noting once again the fine breadth of his shoulders. "I'd prefer to go to bed, sir."

He turned, and his expression was one of infinite weariness. "Let us eat first, Mistress McPherson, a farewell meal if you like, before we part company forever, this one favor I beg."

There was no tone of command in his voice, only utter weariness and sadness. Destiny felt a twinge of pity for the man, once so strong and commanding and now so abject and pathetic.

"Very well, but do not call me by that name anymore. Call me by the name I was proud to bear—Destiny Regan."

He grunted and turned away, leading her to a far room along the corridor. She followed him inside. An oil lamp glowed on a small table in the center of the room, on which a tray stood. In the far corner she could see the great four-poster bed with its counterpane folded back in readiness for its occupant. A fire glowed in the hearth.

"Close the door and come sit by the fire," Conal said quietly, but it was an invitation rather than a command. She closed the door and went to stand by the fire's warmth, while Conal opened the bottle of wine on the tray and poured it into a glass. Then he came over to Destiny and handed her the glass.

"God, I'm so tired. I think I'll just eat a sandwich."

"Have you no glass to drink? Here, then, have this, for I'm not thirsty," Destiny said.

He waved a hand as he bit deep into a sandwich. "Drink," he said, "I'll drink after."

Destiny sat down on the edge of a chair and sipped the golden liquid. It was delectable, honeylike in sweetness and warming the throat as it trickled down. How strange it was, she thought suddenly, to be sitting here in companionable closeness, with wine and firelight, with a man who had always roused fiery hate in her before. Not strictly true, she corrected herself. He had always aroused fire in her, but not always hate. There had been the times, the many times, she had desired him, but not now. All the proud, tempestuous fury in him was gone.

She became aware of his eyes upon her, but no longer filled with anger or desire. He was looking at her with a mildly curious and yet sad expression, and her pity for him deepened. He was looking older now, the gray in his temples exaggerated by the flickering firelight and the lines about his eyes deepened by the shadows.

"Tomorrow you shall go free, Destiny," he said, and his voice was hollow.

"Yes," she said. He made no mention of Tara's confession. Was she supposed to believe he was simply being charitable? She grew wary. She was too wise in his ways now to fall into a cunning trap.

"And your daughters, too—both of them. I make no claim upon either of them," he added.

"I am glad."

He sighed. "Will you thank me, Destiny Regan, that I make no claim on you or yours?"

"Why should I?" she said proudly. "I am innocent, and they are my children, not yours."

"One of them is mine," he corrected her, but his tone was still quiet and undemanding. "Will you not at least tell me which one? I promise not to make use of it, only satisfy my curiosity."

"I have sworn to take the secret to the grave," Destiny said firmly. "Why should I humor you now, knowing well I cannot trust your word?"

He sighed more deeply and took a swig of wine from the bottle. "No reason why you should, only to gratify me. I grow old, Destiny, and life seems barren. I have nothing left to live for. I should like to be able to think of my child once in a while when I sit by the fire and wait for death."

Destiny felt confused, and took another gulp of wine. This was not the Conal Carmichael she knew, and it was hard to know how to respond. Then his words reminded her of something she had overlooked.

"Think of your child while you sit by the fire? You can do more, Conal. You can look to his future, for you have that child—your son, Liam. Recognize him and care for him as you should. Educate him and have his foot cured. Then you can have a future to look forward to."

Conal moaned and turned away. "Liam," she heard him mutter. "He was sent to me as a punishment. What greater cross can a man bear than a crippled, lunatic child?"

"He's not mad—far from it. He's quick and intelligent, and loyal too. He needs love, that's all."

"Don't we all?" Conal's voice in the shadows was no more than a whisper, pathetic as a child who has lost its mother. Destiny felt the pity swell inside her. This was the root of Conal Carmichael's unhappy life. He lacked love, had always lacked it, and now he could see that his life ahead would be barren. For two pins she could have rushed across the room and flung her arms about him.

Instead she sat there, stiff and clutching the glass tight. What right had he to expect consolation in his depression, after all the misery he had needlessly caused? He should taste a little suffering for a change.

"Acknowledge the boy, and you'll be glad one day," she said quietly. He made no reply, nor did he move from the shadows. Destiny tore her gaze away from him, unwilling to be tormented by the sight of his abject figure. She looked instead at the great, inviting bed and longed to lie down and sleep.

Rising from her chair, she put the glass down on the table. "Thanks for the wine. I'd best be going to bed now. Think on what I said, Conal, for I think it will bring you happiness to care for another and watch him grow to manhood."

Conal turned slowly and fixed his great black eyes upon her. "You think he could be cured?"

"I'm sure of it. And educated, for he is bright."

He took a step closer to her and stopped, not three feet from her, and she could see the wistful look of pleading in his eyes.

"I'll barter with you, Destiny Regan. Give me this night and I'll acknowledge Liam."

Startled by the earnest intensity in his eyes, Destiny stepped back and felt the fringe of the counterpane under her heel. "What do you mean, Conal?" she stammered, hardly able to believe what she guessed.

His voice was hoarse. "You understand me well, Destiny. A night with you, with your arms about me, that's what I need. I'm so alone, Destiny. I need your love, if only for this night. Please, tonight, for tomorrow you will be gone."

"And in return you'll own Liam as your son?"

"I will. Oh, Destiny!" He raised his arms and stepped toward her. Destiny slipped to one side.

"Then write it down. I'll not believe you until you write down that Liam is your son and give me the paper."

His laugh was humorless. "You don't believe me, do you? You never trusted me."

"You never gave me cause. Write it down." Destiny's voice was firm, but inside she was trembling. Much as she longed to cradle him in her arms, she was not going to be cheated by him again.

For a moment he looked at her, his face taut and haggard. Then, with a grunt, he walked to a mahogany secretaire by the window and took out paper and a quill. Dipping the quill in the inkstand, he wrote in quick, scratchy bursts. When he had done, he brought the sheet of paper to her.

"What does it say?" Destiny asked.

"It says, 'I, Conal Carmichael, hereby acknowledge Liam Dooley to be my son, born of my wife, Christine Carmichael, in London on May 7, 1853, and acknowledge that he is my sole heir.' Does that satisfy you, Destiny?"

"It does. Thank you."

He laid the paper on the mantelshelf and turned to her. "Thank me as you have agreed, and in the morning you shall have the paper."

With a smile Destiny held out her arms to him. "Gladly, Conal."

With a sound that was somewhere between a cry and a moan, he rushed toward her and took her in his arms, lifting her and carrying her to the bed. There he laid her down gently and lay beside her, his head on her bosom. Destiny folded her arms about him and stroked his hair tenderly.

The tension around his eyes began to ease, and he closed his eyes. She traced a fingertip along the line of his cheek and mouth and began to croon softly.

> When, like the rising day,
> Love sends his early ray,
> What makes his dawning glow

>Changeless through joy or woe?
>Only the constant know,
>   Aileen Aroon.

It was, she realized, the song young Bob Fellows had been singing up by the copse just before the ravens had given warning of death and he found McPherson. The ravens. Her eye sought out the mark on Conal's neck. Yes, there it was, a tiny black blemish just below his ear, shaped just like a sitting bird. And only she knew that his daughter carried the same mark.

The song ended, she lay still. Conal's eyes were closed, and she did not know whether he was sleeping. He stirred restlessly and reached up an arm. It fell across her breast, and his eyes opened.

"You are soft and warm, Destiny, and so comforting."

She smiled tenderly. He could be a child speaking to his mother. That was what he sought—the tender reassurance of maternal love such as he had not savored since he was a baby. Poor Conal! She cradled him closer, and saw his tranquil look change to one of eagerness.

"You were mine once, long ago in the cave, and you did not barter then," he whispered. "Be mine now as you were then, without reservation. Forget all that has been in between, and let us be as we were then, young and free."

"There is a difference, Conal. Then you took me by force and against my will. This time it is my will."

He lifted his head to gaze into her eyes. "You do not hate me, then, as you said you did? You cursed me even."

"No. I do not hate you."

"Then tell me you love me," he whispered. His hands slid the silken robe from her shoulders and moved persuasively inside. Destiny felt the warmth in her mounting to excitement. "Tell me," he pleaded. His touch grew more urgent.

"Mo ghra thu is máter loim."

Twenty-five

Early rays of dawning sunlight filtered through the gap in the drawn curtains, casting a long slant of light across the floor and onto the tumbled bed. Destiny stirred and yawned. Then, remembering where she was, she looked down at Conal. He looked like a peaceful child, his eyes closed and his face relaxed in contentment. One arm lay sprawled on the pillow above his black curls. She smiled as she recalled the night, so full of ardor and yet tenderness.

She was content. At least if she and Conal Carmichael were never to meet again, she could sometimes think of him in London and not feel the old bitterness. The night had done that, at least. She would think of him kindly now, knowing how gentle he could be, and the memory of the heartless, selfish Conal would be softened by the memory.

Moving cautiously so as not to disturb him, she slid out of bed and pulled on the silk robe that lay on the floor. She would let herself out quietly and let him sleep on. As she tiptoed across the parquet floor, she suddenly remembered. The paper.

Crossing softly to the fireplace, Destiny reached up to the mantelshelf and lifted the folded paper. As she did so, it crackled, and she darted an anxious gaze toward the bed. Conal stirred and sat up.

"Destiny?" he said, throwing his legs out of bed and pulling on his trousers. "What are you doing?"

"I didn't want to disturb you, you sleeping so peaceful and all," she said, standing there uncertainly and clutching the paper. He just sat there looking at her, and then he held out his hand.

"Give that to me, Destiny."

She held it tighter. "No, you promised me, Conal. It was a bargain, remember? I honored my part, and now I want to take this to the count. He'll see it's all done right."

"Give it to me." His voice was hard now, cold and demanding, as in the old days. Destiny felt a flicker of fear. She should have anticipated this. She might have guessed he would not change so easily. He was as scheming as ever.

"Won't you let me have it after all?"

He laughed, and the hardness in his laugh made her shiver. "What kind of fool do you take me for, woman? Do you think I'd want my friends in London to know I have a cretin cripple for a son? I'd be the laughingstock of all London society. Give me that!"

"I will not!" Tears, not of self-pity but of rage at her own stupidity, sprang to Destiny's eyes. What a fool she had been to let herself be taken in by his pretense! Aye, that was the cruel part. He had claimed to be helpless and lonely, desperate for love, and she had been gullible enough to believe him.

He strode across the room to her, his hand outstretched. "I shall not ask you again. Give me that paper!"

"No!" she screamed. "You promised!"

Conal raised his hand, either to snatch or to strike, but Destiny darted toward the door before he could do either. In a leap he was upon her, grappling with her arms, his eyes gleaming.

"Give it to me, woman, or I'll kill you!" he snarled, and his expression was venomous. Destiny recoiled in horror, but he would not let her go. She held the paper above her head, her arm extended behind her, and he fought to reach it. She kicked and bit at him, but his face remained a determined, maniacal mask of fury.

"I'll kill you, you bitch!" His hands fastened on her throat, squeezing and crushing till Destiny was gasping for breath. "You bitch! You foul slut!" he roared.

Destiny felt her tongue choking in her throat, and a pink haze reddened to crimson before her eyes. Dear God! Help me, or I am dead!

There was a sudden pounding in her ears, like the sound of someone banging on a heavy door, but she realized it was her own blood pounding and that the end was near. In seconds Conal Carmichael would have killed her and won his way yet again. Dimly she saw movement behind his shoulder, and struggled feebly to cling on to life.

"Holy Mother of God!" A vision of Rosanna appeared behind Conal, and alongside her Philip O'Keeffe and the great gray wolfhound. Vaguely words came to Destiny's ears. "Sultan! Seize him, boy, get him!"

Suddenly Conal's hold on her throat was relaxed as a great mass of fur leaped between them and sent Destiny reeling to the floor. She lay there, stunned and only half-conscious, hearing a deafening sound of snarling and shrieking. As the fog in her brain cleared, she looked up to see a dog hurling itself again and again at Conal's body. As she dragged herself up to a sitting position, the great hound sank its teeth into Conal's throat.

He reeled over backward, stumbled, and fell, screaming and tearing at the brute, but the dog would not release its hold. Standing over Conal's prostrate figure, it kept on snarling. Conal's eyes were wide in terror.

"Call him off!" Destiny gasped, unable to get the words out of her twisted throat. "For God's sake, stop him!"

Blood, already seeping down the front of Conal's chest, began to spurt from his throat. The figures at the door stood mesmerized. As Destiny stumbled in an attempt to rise and help him, she realized it was too late. Conal's throat was ripped open and his windpipe broken and hanging bloodily. Philip leaped on the dog and dragged it off, then thrust it outside the door.

"Christ have mercy on us!" Rosanna whispered, her eyes wide in horror. "What have I done?"

Philip bent over Conal. "Fetch a surgeon, quick, Rosanna." The girl fled. Philip spoke to Destiny. "Hold his head. I'll fetch water and cloths to try to stem the bleeding, but I think it's too late."

Destiny lifted Conal's head and laid it in her lap. His

eyes were open still, wide, as if he could not understand. The count and Kate came running.

"Oh, my God!" said the count. "Catherine, this is not for your eyes."

"I'll stay with my mother," the girl said quietly. Destiny heard her but did not look up. Conal's eyes flickered and came to rest on her. She tried to smile reassuringly, but inside there was only blind fear and a terrible agony.

Philip came back, and with him, Rosanna. Philip knelt beside Destiny.

"He cannot breathe. He cannot last long."

He picked up the piece of paper that had fallen to the floor, and read it. Then he looked at Destiny.

"Is this true?"

She nodded. Philip passed it to the count, who read it, then folded it and put it in his pocket. Rosanna was staring at Conal.

"The curse, Mother. It came true."

Destiny took her eyes from Conal at last and looked at her daughter. "Curse?" she repeated vacantly. Nothing made sense anymore.

"I remember now," Rosanna whispered. "You used to say you cursed him, hoping that one day he would stew in his own blood."

Destiny trembled and felt sick. Dear God! Did you listen to my curse all that time ago? And I forgot to deny it later.

" 'Tis all my fault," she muttered. "I cursed him!"

There was a rattling sound in Conal's throat, and his lips moved. Destiny bent her face close to his. "What is it, Conal, what are you saying?"

There was a faint, rattling sound, and then his eyes closed. Destiny put her lips to his forehead and wept. Catherine put a hand on her mother's shoulder.

"He's gone, Mother. Come away now, there's no more you can do."

"No, leave me be," Destiny cried.

"Catherine is right," Count Nicolai said gently. "Come, Rosanna and Catherine will take care of you."

Destiny rose slowly to her feet and left the room. The front of the beautiful white silk gown was sodden with a huge crimson stain. Conal's blood, she thought; the curse I laid on him has brought his blood onto me. Dully her bemused brain registered the thought that no act of contrition or penance would ever be great enough to atone for this terrible, mortal sin.

"I killed him," she moaned. The count and her daughters walked close behind her.

"No," said the count firmly. "He was about to kill you. You have Rosanna's presence of mind to thank that you're still alive." At the head of the stairs he stopped.

"It was a blessing I had just come in with Sultan when I heard you scream," Rosanna said. "And it serves that devil right, attacking you like that."

"Don't talk like that," Destiny chided her. "We should pray that his soul may find peace, for he never did in this life."

"Strangely, though," said the count reflectively, "he seemed oddly at peace at the end. What did he say to you?"

Destiny hung her head and made no answer. Conal's final words were the one crumb of comfort she had to cling to, the words that indicated that all was forgiven.

"Yes, what did he say, Mother?" It was Kate's clear young voice. Destiny shook her head gently.

"I heard," said Rosanna. "I was next to you."

"And what did he say?" her sister prompted.

"He spoke in the Irish, and he told her he loved her. He has a strange way of showing it, though."

"Love takes strange forms at times," Count Nicolai said gravely. "Now, take your mother and find her some clothes."

Some weeks later a carriage drew away from Ballymachree along the road toward Cork. Destiny leaned her head against the glass of the carriage window and looked out over the potato fields, only dimly aware of the conversation between Philip and Kate and Count Nicolai. The younger couple sat opposite, deep in conversation, but the count alongside Destiny spoke only now and again.

"I knew they'd find Tara not guilty," Kate was saying.

"And now she's been offered a position in a household in Cork, she'll be fine."

"Rosanna is happy about that," Philip remarked.

"Rosanna has eyes and mind for no one but your manservant now." Kate laughed.

"Just as I have for you," he replied.

"And what will you do with young Liam? He's happy enough traveling with Rosanna, but what's to happen when he gets to England?"

"I shall confirm his birth and title to the Carmichael land, but that presents little difficulty, and then we'll arrange for a surgeon I know at one of our hospitals to have a look at his foot. After that, schooling and all that a young gentleman should have."

"Most of all he needs love," Kate said, and inwardly Destiny agreed. Here she was leaving behind Ballymachree and all she had ever known and loved. She looked up the hill toward Jim's grave in the common pit, and then down to the church, where she could still see the elms where Conal lay in the churchyard tomb. He, proud and rich though he was, needed love like the rest of us. Count Nicolai seemed to read her thoughts.

"Remember the living need love and comfort too," he said softly. "Liam, your daughters . . . and I. And most of all, you, my dear."

He laid a hand gently over hers, and left it there while the carriage clattered along the Cork road. Destiny felt no more wistful longing, only a gentle, powerful sense of peace and tranquility.

ABOUT THE AUTHOR

ERICA LINDLEY was born in Bedfordshire, England, but brought up and educated in Yorkshire, and considers herself—"but for an accident of birth"—a Yorkshire woman. Married to an education officer, she has four lively children and began writing as an antidote to domestic routine. She now devotes her working time mainly to researching and writing historical novels, but she still manages to take an active interest in community affairs and social welfare.

More Bestsellers from SIGNET

☐ THE RETURN by Evelyn Anthony. (#E8843—$2.50)†
☐ CLANDARA by Evelyn Anthony. (#J8064—$1.95)
☐ THE FRENCH BRIDE by Evelyn Anthony. (#J7683—$1.95)
☐ THE PERSIAN PRICE by Evelyn Anthony. (#J7254—$1.95)†
☐ THE POELLENBERG INHERITANCE by Evelyn Anthony.
(#E7838—$1.75)†
☐ BELOVED CAPTIVE by Catherine Dillon. (#E8921—$2.25)*
☐ WHITE FIRES BURNING by Catherine Dillon.
(#J8281—$1.95)
☐ REAP THE BITTER WINDS by June Lund Shiplett.
(#E8884—$2.25)*
☐ THE RAGING WINDS OF HEAVEN by June Lund Shiplett.
(#E8981—$2.25)
☐ TIMES OF TRIUMPH by Charlotte Vale Allen.
(#E8955—$2.50)*
☐ MOMENTS OF MEANING by Charlotte Vale Allen.
(#J8817—$1.95)*
☐ GIFTS OF LOVE by Charlotte Vale Allen. (#J8388—$1.95)
☐ SO WONDROUS FREE by Maryhelen Clague.
(#E9047—$2.25)*
☐ SWEETWATER SAGA by Roxanne Dent. (#E8850—$2.25)*
☐ THE DOCTORS ON EDEN PLACE by Elizabeth Seifert.
(#E8852—$1.75)*

* Price slightly higher in Canada
† Not available in Canada

Buy them at your local bookstore or use this convenient coupon for ordering.

THE NEW AMERICAN LIBRARY, INC.,
P.O. Box 999, Bergenfield, New Jersey 07621

Please send me the SIGNET BOOKS I have checked above. I am enclosing
$_____ (please add 50¢ to this order to cover postage and handling).
Send check or money order—no cash or C.O.D.'s. Prices and numbers are
subject to change without notice.

Name _____

Address _____

City_____ State_____ Zip Code_____
This offer is subject to withdrawal without notice.
Allow 4-6 weeks for delivery.

SIGNET Books You'll Enjoy

☐ **WARWYCK'S WOMAN** by Rosalind Laker. (#E8813—$2.25)*
☐ **GLYNDA** by Susannah Leigh. (#E8548—$2.50)*
☐ **WINTER FIRE** by Susannah Leigh. (#E8680—$2.50)
☐ **WATCH FOR THE MORNING** by Elisabeth Macdonald.
(#E8550—$2.25)*
☐ **THE CRAZY LOVERS** by Joyce Elbert. (#E8917—$2.75)*
☐ **THE CRAZY LADIES** by Joyce Elbert. (#E8923—$2.75)
☐ **THE WORLD FROM ROUGH STONES** by Malcolm Macdonald.
(#E8601—$2.50)
☐ **THE RICH ARE WITH YOU ALWAYS** by Malcolm Macdonald.
(#E7682—$2.25)
☐ **SONS OF FORTUNE** by Malcolm Macdonald.
(#E8595—$2.75)*
☐ **LORD OF RAVENSLEY** by Constance Heaven.
(#E8460—$2.25)†
☐ **THE PLACE OF STONES** by Constance Heaven.
(#W7046—$1.50)†
☐ **HARVEST OF DESIRE** by Rochelle Larkin. (#E8771—$2.25)
☐ **MISTRESS OF DESIRE** by Rochelle Larkin. (#E7964—$2.25)*
☐ **TORCHES OF DESIRE** by Rochelle Larkin. (#E8511—$2.25)*
☐ **ALL THE RIVERS RUN** by Nancy Cato. (#E8693—$2.95)

* Price slightly higher in Canada
† Not available in Canada

Buy them at your local
bookstore or use coupon
on next page for ordering.

Recommended Reading from SIGNET

- ☐ ASPEN INCIDENT by Tom Murphy. (#J8889—$1.95)
- ☐ LILY CIGAR by Tom Murphy. (#E8810—$2.75)*
- ☐ BALLET! by Tom Murphy. (#E8112—$2.25)*
- ☐ WINGS by Robert J. Serling. (#E8811—$2.75)*
- ☐ EYE OF THE NEEDLE by Ken Follett. (#E8746—$2.95)
- ☐ SAVAGE RANSOM by David Lippincott. (#E8749—$2.25)*
- ☐ THE BLOOD OF OCTOBER by David Lippincott. (#J7785—$1.95)
- ☐ FOOLS DIE by Mario Puzo. (#E8881—$3.50)
- ☐ THE GODFATHER by Mario Puzo. (#E8970—$2.75)
- ☐ PHOENIX by Amos Aricha and Eli Landau. (#E8692—$2.50)*
- ☐ THIS HOUSE IS BURNING by Mona Williams. (#E8695—$2.25)*
- ☐ THE MESSENGER by Mona Williams. (#J8012—$1.95)
- ☐ TWINS by Bari Wood and Jack Geasland. (#E9094—$2.75)
- ☐ THE KILLING GIFT by Bari Wood. (#J7350—$1.95)
- ☐ THE REBELLION OF YALE MARRATT by Robert H. Rimmer. (#E8851—$2.50)*

* Price slightly higher in Canada

Buy them at your local bookstore or use this convenient coupon for ordering.

THE NEW AMERICAN LIBRARY, INC.,
P.O. Box 999, Bergenfield, New Jersey 07621

Please send me the SIGNET BOOKS I have checked above. I am enclosing
$_____ (please add 50¢ to this order to cover postage and handling).
Send check or money order—no cash or C.O.D.'s. Prices and numbers are
subject to change without notice.

Name _____

Address _____

City_____ State_____ Zip Code_____

Allow 4-6 weeks for delivery.
This offer is subject to withdrawal without notice.